The Red Queen's Daughter

By Jacqueline Kolosov

DISNEP • HYPERION BOOKS/*New York*

For Bill

And for Sophia,
daughter I have waited for

Text copyright © 2007 by Jacqueline Kolosov
All rights reserved.
Published by Disney • Hyperion Books, an imprint of Disney Book Group.
No part of this book may be reproduced or transmitted in any form
or by any means, electronic or mechanical, including photocopying, recording, or by any
information storage and retrieval system, without written permission from the publisher.
For information address Disney • Hyperion Books, 114 Fifth Avenue,
New York, New York 10011-5690.
Printed in the United States of America

First Disney • Hyperion paperback edition, 2009
1 3 5 7 9 10 8 6 4 2
Library of Congress Cataloging-in-Publication Data on file.
ISBN: 978-1-4231-0798-9

Visit www.hyperionteens.com

Then shall a Royal Virgin reign . . .

—MERLIN

*Love is but a frailty of mind when 'tis not
to ambition joined.*

—SIR THOMAS SEYMOUR

The Tudors

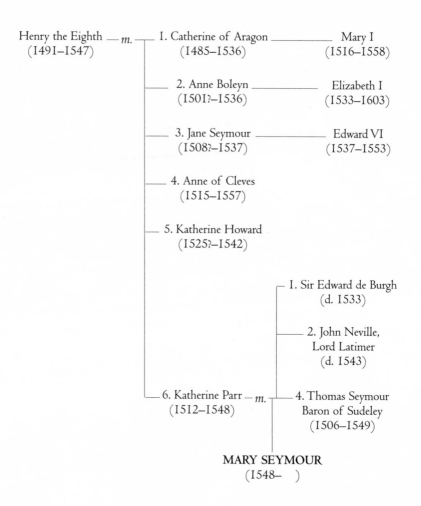

Henry the Eighth — *m.* — 1. Catherine of Aragon ——————— Mary I
(1491–1547)   (1485–1536)   (1516–1558)

———— 2. Anne Boleyn ——————— Elizabeth I
(1501?–1536)   (1533–1603)

———— 3. Jane Seymour ——————— Edward VI
(1508?–1537)   (1537–1553)

———— 4. Anne of Cleves
(1515–1557)

———— 5. Katherine Howard
(1525?–1542)

┌— 1. Sir Edward de Burgh
(d. 1533)

——— 2. John Neville,
Lord Latimer
(d. 1543)

———— 6. Katherine Parr — *m.* —— 4. Thomas Seymour
(1512–1548)   Baron of Sudeley
(1506–1549)

MARY SEYMOUR
(1548–   )

The Seymours

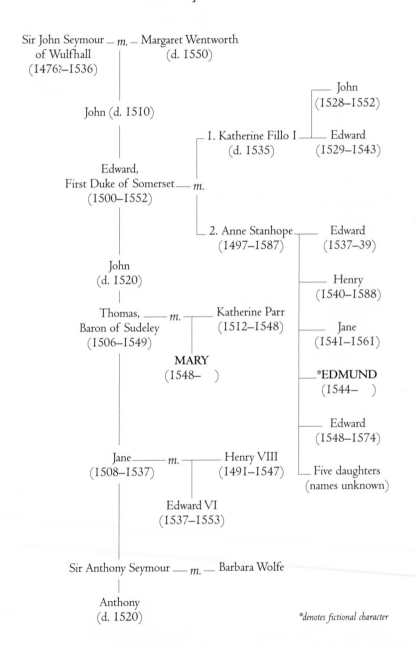

Sir John Seymour — *m.* — Margaret Wentworth
of Wulfhall   (d. 1550)
(1476?–1536)

John (d. 1510)

Edward,
First Duke of Somerset — *m.*
(1500–1552)

     1. Katherine Fillo I
       (d. 1535)

       John
     (1528–1552)

       Edward
     (1529–1543)

2. Anne Stanhope
   (1497–1587)

     Edward
   (1537–39)

     Henry
   (1540–1588)

John
(d. 1520)

Thomas, — *m.* — Katherine Parr
Baron of Sudeley   (1512–1548)
(1506–1549)

MARY
(1548–)

     Jane
   (1541–1561)

*EDMUND
(1544–)

     Edward
   (1548–1574)

Jane — *m.* — Henry VIII
(1508–1537)   (1491–1547)

Edward VI
(1537–1553)

   Five daughters
   (names unknown)

Sir Anthony Seymour — *m.* — Barbara Wolfe

Anthony
(d. 1520)

*denotes fictional character

PROLOGUE

DECEMBER 17, 1557: THE BITTER COLD day before they buried the duchess. Even after so many years, I can still see my nine-year-old self standing among the shadows in the great hall at Grimsthorpe, where the duchess's body had been laid out for a final viewing. With her white hands folded over her small belly and her golden tresses arranged around her porcelain face, my late mother's best friend looked as if she were sleeping, not dead; I almost expected her to wake from her nap and ask me to stitch some clothes for her lover, or mend a bit of finery on one of her own gowns.

What will become of me now? Since my guardian's death three days earlier, this single question had reverberated through my mind. Although the duchess had spent very little time with me during the last few months, I could not ignore the fact that she had been the only one to claim me from the gloomy nursery at Sudeley Castle. I may have been the daughter of the late Queen Katherine Parr, who had died six days after giving birth to me, but I was also the child of Thomas Seymour, the treasonous courtier executed on Tower Hill when I was eight months old. After his execution, the crown seized all of my mother's remaining properties and her wealth, and I—her sole heir, a child who had once slept on satin sheets in a bed of canopied velvet—suddenly found myself penniless and alone.

Not even the duchess, who had fallen dangerously in love with the handsome Master of the Horse who cared for her thoroughbreds, could explain why my mother had trysted with Thomas Seymour in the moonlit gardens of Chelsea Manor after Henry VIII's death. Not even the duchess—who lost her life in a riding accident after she crashed into a tree because she was staring deep into that same Master of the Horse's eyes—could explain why my well-born, well-educated mother gave up her properties, her jewels, and most of all her stainless reputation, in order to marry my father.

I knew my father had married my mother to better his own fortunes. How could I have concluded anything less when I had stood visiting his grave, a chill drizzle dampening my skin and hair, just months before? As I held tightly to the duchess's hand, I listened to her read to me the words—my father's own words—carved into the headstone: *Love is but a frailty of mind when 'tis not to ambition joined.*

After we returned home, the epitaph continued to

linger in my memory. "Why were these words written on my father's grave?" I asked, once the duchess and I had sat down to a dinner of roast quail and potatoes.

The duchess focused her sorrowful, cornflower blue eyes on me and said, "Because your father lived by these words, Mary. He never acted without first considering how an event would benefit him."

"Even when he asked my mother to marry him?"

"Even then." The duchess wiped the tears from her eyes, for she inevitably fell to weeping whenever she spoke of my mother. "What you are too young to understand is that your father was not just courting a woman when he asked your mother to be his wife. He was courting Henry the Eighth's widow. Provided that he did not lose his head, your father knew that in marrying your mother he would rise in power and in influence, not to mention in wealth."

"So my mother was nothing more than a prize?"

"No, Mary, your father's intentions were more complicated than that. And yet, I'm afraid I cannot call them honorable."

"Why?" I said.

"Such stories are not fit for a child."

"Please tell me," I said, and I grabbed hold of her hand, hoping to impress upon her why I now so desperately needed to know what my parents' lives together had been like.

For a few moments the duchess hesitated, but then something within her overruled her misgivings, and she said, "Because, after Henry the Eighth's death, your father tried to marry the king's youngest daughter."

"The Princess Elizabeth?" A strange tingling coursed through me as I spoke her name.

The duchess nodded.

"You mean my mother was not his first choice?"

"I'm afraid not, child." She tried to draw me close, but I pulled away.

"The princess refused my father, didn't she?" I said, suddenly understanding why a sorrowful sort of rage always simmered in the duchess's voice when some visitor mentioned Thomas Seymour's name, for the duchess herself almost never spoke of him.

"Yes."

"So he began courting my mother?"

"He did."

"Did my mother know this?" I said, forcing myself to hold the duchess's gaze.

"Not until much later," she said softly. "Once the Princess Elizabeth came to live with them, your mother knew your father had designs on Elizabeth. But by that time, your mother was pregnant with you. By that time, it was too late."

Following this discovery, I lost my appetite and ceased

playing out of doors. It was not long before all color vanished from my cheeks. A few days later I appeared in the duchess's room wearing a dress I had outgrown the summer before, a dress that once more fit perfectly. Only then did she bring forth from a secret compartment of her wardrobe a packet of my mother's letters, which someone had tied together with a silk ribbon.

"In telling you about your father, I'm afraid I may have said too much," the duchess said, once we found ourselves sitting side by side on her great bed. "Although I cannot lie—your parents' marriage came to no good—you must always remember that your mother loved your father with the best part of herself. Do you understand, Mary?"

When I shook my head, the duchess sighed, then opened one of the letters, and read aloud to me my mother's words: " 'My lord, I can require nothing more than I have: your heart and your good will during this life. . . .'

"Your father's heart," the duchess said again, as if through repetition she could impress upon me the meaning of these words. "That is what your mother wanted. That is why she married Thomas Seymour. Having been married to three old men before she met your father, she was hungry for love, Mary. For love, she sacrificed everything, which is why I now find you in my care."

That December afternoon, as I stood in the great hall, one last time holding the duchess's now cold hand, newly aware that yet another woman had lost all to love, I had no doubt that it was my mother's love for my father that had cost her, not just influence, wealth, and admiration. Love had cost my mother her very life.

CHAPTER ONE

It was after the duchess's funeral that I met the woman who would become my new guardian. Our meeting took place during that crepuscular hour when the sky turns a deepest blue before fading into black. So silently did she move that neither Jack, my beloved wolfhound, nor I heard her enter my small bedroom in one of the manor's draftiest rooms, where we lay curled beneath two thick wool blankets beside a scantily laid hearth, trying to stay warm.

When the newcomer placed her hand on the small of my back, I rolled over to face her. I felt I knew her instantly. Breathing in the fragrance of her skin, so like the cool dark of a forest in spring, I said, "You've come for me, haven't you?"

"Yes. I am Lady Strange." Her violet eyes glinted in the firelight, and the sapphire at the base of her throat seemed to radiate an energy that filled me with calm. "You are to live with me from now on. I will raise and protect you as my own daughter."

A sort of trembling, like the dancing of new leaves, overtook me.

"You may not know it," Lady Strange said, "but you were born when Mars, symbol of power and potency, was in Scorpio, the most secret of all the water signs."

"What does that mean?"

"It means, my dear girl, you have a destiny."

This word was new to me. Nevertheless, I liked the sound of it. I knew that *destiny* must mean something marvelous.

After I packed my single trunk and said good-bye to the duchess's French seamstress, Antoinette, the single other person who had taken the trouble to look after me (especially since I had proven myself proficient with a needle at the age of five), Lady Strange and I traveled by carriage away from Grimsthorpe, accompanied by Jack.

I sat between my new guardian and my old friend,

warmed and comforted by blankets of the finest purple wool. As the mantle of night enveloped our carriage, and the chill rain battered the roof of the carriage, Lady Strange leaned close and told me stories about my mother. But instead of dissolving into tears, like the duchess, when Lady Strange spoke her eyes remained dry and clear.

"You knew her, then?" I asked.

"I was privileged to meet your mother a few times," Lady Strange said. "Each time, I came away believing that she was a brave, intelligent woman. You see, Mary, during an era in which people believed that educating a woman would only teach her to write love letters, your mother proved herself capable of both learning and virtue." She placed her hand on top of my own. "Given how much she did for the female sex, I could not help but admire your mother a great deal."

Immediately I was reminded of the love letter my mother had written to my father, a letter that now seemed more the exception in my mother's life than the rule.

"Did the duchess never show you the books your mother wrote?" Lady Strange asked after a while.

I shook my head.

"That is a great shame." Then, as if she could see my

disappointment through the darkness, she added, "But you are still so young. We have plenty of time."

"What sort of books did my mother write?" I asked, drawing closer to her, soothed and attracted by her cool, gentle tone.

"Spiritual books of prayer and meditation," Lady Strange said. "Your mother's words comforted many people during difficult times. And with her words, she proved to the scholars at Oxford and Cambridge that a woman could be a man's equal if she was given the chance to develop her mind."

I leaned back in the carriage and stared into the night, marveling at how little I knew about my mother's life. But this time I did not feel discouraged or ill at ease. No, I sensed Lady Strange would help me light the way.

In short, I trusted her.

The hours passed, until at last we arrived at an old house built of the most beautiful cream-colored stone. An ancient wood surrounded the house. According to Lady Strange, somewhere deep within that wood lay a bottomless lake.

"Tomorrow we will explore my country," Lady Strange told me as we stepped out of the carriage and Jack bounded off in the direction of the woods, "but not a minute before."

At the sound of these words, Jack paused, and even the trees seemed to draw closer to listen.

I knew then that my own destiny—whatever that word meant—would somehow connect me with the mysterious power my new guardian possessed.

The next morning I awoke in a downy bed beneath a lace-edged quilt of silver satin in a room the color of sunflowers. For a moment I was afraid I was dreaming and would open my eyes only to find myself in my drafty room at Grimsthorpe once more. But then I remembered what Lady Strange had told me about my mother: *She proved that a woman could be a man's equal if she was given the chance to develop her mind*, and I knew I was not dreaming.

"Can you believe our good fortune, Jack?" I whispered, noticing how cozy my old friend looked as he lay beside the fire that had burned gently all through the night.

In reply, Jack thumped his long tail and yawned.

Lying in my soft, warm bed, I thought further about my conversation with Lady Strange, remembering those first words she spoke to me: *My dear girl, you have a destiny.* Although manners should have prevented me from pressing her, as soon as she stepped into the room with a breakfast of buttery, raisin-filled scones and tea, I climbed out of bed and asked her what this marvelous thing she called *destiny* involved.

Only after laying a new log on the fire, and smoothing out the single crease in her dress did she say, "You are to be a white magician."

"What is a *white magician*?" I asked, drawing closer.

"A white magician is an agent of God on earth," Lady Strange said, choosing each word with care. "A person singled out to use knowledge and enchantment to improve the lives of the people entrusted to her care."

Although I liked the sound of the words *knowledge* and *God*, for they seemed to create immediate links to my mother, *enchantment* was a word I had never heard before.

"*Enchantment* may have a foreign sound," Lady Strange said, running her long, smooth fingers through my hair, "and yet it is a delicious word, is it not?" When I did not reply, she said, "Enchantment, my dear Mary, simply means the white magician relies on the help of good spirits and spells, coupled with all she knows about the natural world, to effect a change for the better."

"Such a person must be very important, indeed," I said. And despite all that Lady Strange had told me the night before, as I stared at the reflection of my small, pale face in the glass on the wall, I found it nearly impossible to picture myself in such a role.

"She is," Lady Strange said, and poured us each a second cup of tea as Jack lapped up his portion from a bowl. "Does such a role interest you, Mary?"

"Yes," I heard myself reply.

"Very good," she said, and this time she smiled. "Now, if you're to be a proper white magician, then you and I have much work to do. Are you prepared to work hard, Mary?"

"Do you expect me to stitch and sew?" I asked.

"Heavens, no." Lady Strange raised her hand to her lips. "Whatever gave you such an idea?"

"Well, this is the kind of work I did for the duchess. It is all I know how to do," I said fearfully, so strongly did I dread losing my new friend's favor.

Lady Strange stood and walked over to the window. "How can it be that you have already forgotten what I told you about your mother, Mary?" she said, fixing me with her strong, intelligent eye.

"I haven't forgotten," I said.

"Good. Now then, listen closely. I want you to learn to read and write. I want you to be able to speak Italian and Latin, to understand history and literature, to look closely at all that exists around us, from the birds of the air to the plants that fill our gardens and woods. Quite simply"— she stretched out her arms and the curtains fluttered behind her—"I want to train your mind."

"No embroidery?"

Lady Strange shook her head. "It's clear we'll need to set to immediate work dispelling the duchess's influence. You may have spent nine years in her care, yet you are first and foremost your mother's daughter. And I have told you that she was learned as well as good, have I not?"

"Yes," I said.

"Then there is the example of the Princess Elizabeth."

I trembled a little, for at the sound of this name, I found myself reminded of what the duchess had told me about the Princess Elizabeth and my father's attempts to marry and then to seduce her. And yet, when Lady Strange spoke Elizabeth's name, that same wondrous tingling overtook me. In place of shame, I now felt possibility.

"Is the Princess Elizabeth a fine scholar?" I asked.

"One of the very greatest." Lady Strange's eyes darkened to violet pools. "In fact, the two of you have a good deal in common."

"Such as what?" I asked.

"Patience," Lady Strange said, then opened the curtains

so that sunlight further brightened the golden room. "Like you, the princess lost her mother when she was very young. She lost her father's affections as well, for Henry the Eighth rarely came to see her, and for a time had her declared illegitimate."

"Why?"

"The truth is, Mary, the king was in love with Jane Seymour, his third queen. He felt sure that Jane, unlike Elizabeth's mother, Anne Boleyn, would give him a male heir."

"And Elizabeth stood in that future heir's way?"

"She did. You see, my dear," Lady Strange said, her tone of voice prompting me to sit up a little straighter, "you are cleverer than you think."

"Tell me more about Princess Elizabeth's life," I said, aware of the quickening of my heart.

"The most important lesson is that although the princess was often neglected and at times even harshly abused, she sought refuge in the capacities of her own mind, a habit your mother encouraged during her years as Elizabeth's stepmother. Once I even heard the revered scholar Roger Ascham say Princess Elizabeth's mind would soon surpass his own."

"But I'm no princess," I protested.

Lady Strange stroked my reddish-gold hair. "Maybe not, but you are the daughter of a queen."

At the sound of these words, my whole being seemed to lighten.

"Now then, I put the question to you a second time. Are you prepared to work hard, Mary? Are you prepared to put body and mind into the task of learning?"

"Yes," I said clearly.

"Very good." She motioned to the wardrobe. "It's time for you to get dressed. Then I want you to follow me."

"But where are we going?" I asked, walking over to the wardrobe, where I was amazed to find an array of perfectly suitable clothing in just my size.

"Into the woods, of course." Lady Strange sifted through the wardrobe's contents until she found a warm flannel gown for me to wear. "Be mindful of information, Mary. Did I not tell you that we would explore my territory today?"

"Yes," I replied.

"Well then, next time be sure to connect the two statements," she said kindly.

After I dressed, I followed Lady Strange downstairs. In the hallway, a pair of sturdy leather walking shoes awaited me, as well as a purple woolen cloak exactly like my new guardian's.

Once we were bundled up, we stepped outside into the bracing air of late December. Jack followed a pace or two behind, for not even my adventurous, long-legged hound wanted to risk losing his way in this new place. There was a strong breeze that morning, and as we neared the shelter of the wood, the wind seemed to forget its direction among the thick canopy of trees.

How long we walked, I'm not sure, for minutes and hours surrendered all meaning in a close space that allowed so little light. Yet despite the way the wind burned my cheeks, Lady Strange's company created a peacefulness and confidence in me that I had never known before.

At last we reached a huge tree, its grooved trunk the size of a small cottage.

Lady Strange turned to face me. Beneath her cloak, I felt sure I could see her sapphire necklace shining like a third eye. "Here you will find the proof of your calling," she said.

When she pointed to the tree, I stared and stared, but still I did not understand.

"Wait and see. No," Lady Strange said, motioning to the heavens just visible through the filigreed branches of the highest trees, "wait and *believe*."

From the pockets of her cloak she retrieved six polished, honey-colored stones. Two of these she placed in my gloved hands. I held them up to my face and saw embedded in each a tiny object. The first held a leaf, the second, some sort of insect.

"These stones come from the Baltic Sea on the far reaches of Russia's empire. Do you know what they are made of?"

I shook my head, still entranced by the dramatic color and the wonders inside.

"Petrified tree sap," Lady Strange said. "Hence the leaf and the bee. Legend has it that amber, for this is the stone's name, comes from the tears of the sisters of Phaëthon, who was struck down by a lightning bolt from Zeus."

"But that's only a legend, right?" I said, shivering a little, not because of the cold, but because I did not like the ideas of tears living on in the form of stones, as though such a thing preserved sorrow forever.

"Yes and no," Lady Strange said. "Proper study of the elements reveals that the true origin of this stone is petrification over time and under the proper conditions. That said, the legend takes its starting point in our beliefs. It's therefore possible that both the scientific explanation and the story are true."

"How can two things be true at once, especially two things that are so very different?"

A steady fire seemed to burn behind Lady Strange's eyes. "In time you might just discover how. In fact, I might say that this will be a great challenge in your life's work. As a white magician, you will often face contradiction." Noticing my furrowed brow, she continued, "For example, a person who has done great wrong may simultaneously prove capable of good."

A shadowy image of my father's face rose before me, only to flicker and fade away.

"For now, let's go back to your task," Lady Strange said, as if she had seen the direction in which my thoughts were heading. Once more, she pointed to the amber stones. "I want you to set the stones around the base of this tree trunk. Be sure to place each stone an equal distance apart."

One by one, I placed each of the six amber stones around the base of the tree. As Lady Strange passed each stone to me, I took note of the other things preserved inside. In addition to the leaf and the bee, there was a tiny twig, a very small insect like a flea, and a pattern that reminded me of a spider's web. The sixth stone was absolutely clear. Somehow, I sensed that this clarity signified the transparency of truth. A single look from Lady Strange confirmed my intuition.

Once I had arranged the stones, Lady Strange placed her hands on my shoulders and pressed my body against her own. As soon as I felt her heart beat, the bark of the tree shifted into a most extraordinary pattern. Instead of deep vertical lines, I saw actual words.

"Can you read, Mary?" Lady Strange whispered.

Despite my guardian's faith in me, shame filled my heart. "Only a very little."

"Well then." She touched my hair. "Read what you can."

With Jack beside me, I studied the letters for a long time. Eventually, I made out a few of the characters written there. "*Queen . . . school . . . white.*"

Lady Strange bent down and kissed me. "Very good. Later today you and I will begin studies, and soon you will be able to read the entire message in one breath."

"Now listen to the message, which I committed to memory a very long time ago." Looking deep into my eyes, Lady Strange read, "*'Fetch the red queen's daughter from the house of shadows. Bring her to your own home beside the dark wood. School her well in the white magician's wisdom so that she may go forth into the world and fulfill her calling when the virgin queen ascends the throne.'*"

I touched my reddish-gold hair. "I'm the red queen's daughter," I said, exaltation and terror rising within me. "Aren't I?"

"Yes," Lady Strange said, kissing me a second time. "And you have a calling, another word for destiny."

"And you're to be my teacher," I said, connecting what she had told me earlier with the present moment.

"That's right." She smiled.

"But who's the virgin queen?" I asked.

Lady Strange pressed a finger to my lips. "In time," she said. "All in good time."

CHAPTER TWO

THAT WINTER, WHILE SQUIRRELS NESTED IN the hollows of oak trees, and each and every bear drowsed in some warm den or cave, we drew ourselves closer to the hearth and prepared me for my destiny. This meant we studied.

We began with a primer filled with the letters of the alphabet, and within a matter of days I found that I could read and write words using every letter. Among my favorites were words like *alchemical, brilliant,* and *cryptic.* But I favored humbler words, too, words like *dog, pickle,* and *sunset.* The words led to sentences, and from sentences I progressed to paragraphs. Before the last snowfall, I actually sat down and read my mother's book of prayers and meditations from first page to last. As I read the words of dedication: *Collected out of holy works by the most virtuous and gracious Katherine, Queen of England,* my rib cage seemed to open, and I felt my whole being fill with pride.

Come April, the crocuses, daffodils, and violets had returned to adorn the ground, and the rosy-bellied robins, reddish-brown chaffinches, persistent linnets, and thimble-size wrens began to sing in the trees, and we took our work out of doors.

"Legend has it that pansies were once in danger of vanishing from the earth," Lady Strange said one blissful morning after we stepped outside to examine the fanciful lion's-headed blossoms in her garden.

"Why?"

"Because the pansy was so fragrant that people plucked it almost to extinction. In despair, the pansy prayed it might lose its odor and no longer be sought."

"Did the pansy get its wish?" I asked, momentarily distracted by Jack, who had just torn off after a white rabbit.

"To answer that question, sniff the blossom and find out."

I pressed my nose deep into the flower and inhaled. "Scentless."

Not only did Lady Strange show me how to find enchantment in the things of daily life, she also schooled me in early magic. One of the first spells I learned helped me to improve my powers of hearing.

When Lady Strange presented me with the ingredients—a spoonful of molasses, a slice of very fine bread baked with honey, and some blackberries—I gazed at her, puzzled. "You expected some less homely ingredients, I see," she said cheerfully. "Still, you mustn't dismiss these things so quickly. For your hearing to improve, you must understand what each ingredient contributes. Only after you have determined this can you bring them together. Then you must eat the mixture in three swift bites while picturing an owlet."

"A baby owl?"

"Precisely. The owlet's role, too, you must understand."

"Molasses is the slowest-moving sweetener I know," I considered, "not to mention the darkest."

"Very good, Mary. What might the significance of this be?"

"To hear well, one must not move too quickly," I said. "One must pay attention, especially when one is in unfamiliar surroundings."

"Precisely," she said, then pointed to the bread.

"Fine bread suggests hearing is among the most refined of the senses."

"Again, a very good answer," Lady Strange said. "But do

not forget honey's role. What might honey contribute to such fine bread?"

I closed my eyes and pictured the bees that worked industriously at their hives. "Persistence," I suggested. "Persistence coupled with attention."

Lady Strange stroked my hair. "Very good. Now for the blackberries."

"This is the most difficult of the ingredients," I told Lady Strange. "I cannot imagine what a tart, blue-black berry has to do with hearing."

"Think further," Lady Strange instructed.

"All I can think of is how much animals like them."

Lady Strange's eyes brightened, and she leaned closer. "What kind of animals?"

"Birds, deer, bear. But they are all so different."

"Yes," Lady Strange said significantly, "they are."

And then I understood. "All of these creatures depend upon their hearing for survival."

"Just as you shall," Lady Strange said. "You will need to cultivate your powers of attention, never neglecting the value of what you hear." She pointed to the molasses, the bread, and the berries. "Now combine them, and once you know what the owlet signifies, eat this delicious treat in three swift bites."

I secretly hoped Lady Strange would tell me the owlet's role. Now I began to understand that my own desire figured into the answer. All owls possessed excellent hearing. Yet an owlet was not yet mature, which meant an owlet did not fully understand the power of its gifts. Quite sure I understood, I raised the bread to my lips, then ate it all in three bites, picturing the small, powerful bird.

"Well?" Lady Strange said. "What do you notice?"

We were standing in the garden, a place I thought I understood intimately. Now, for the first time, I could hear the blades of grass tickling each other in the breeze. "I believe I can even hear the birds in the trees cleaning their feathers."

"Yes," Lady Strange said. "I believe you can. Meaning?"

"I practiced the spell correctly."

Along with early spells such as this one, Lady Strange continued to instruct me to look at the natural world closely with each of my five senses. As a white magician, my powers of observation would be my primary tools in unearthing any suspicious, as well as any praiseworthy, situation or behavior.

"By learning to listen to and to look closely at all that lies around you," Lady Strange explained, "you will be able to draw conclusions and make judgments based on what you observe. Although human beings will be your primary subjects, it is nature that will provide you with the most fertile training ground."

I learned to articulate subtle differences between the oak tree and the elm, the night sparrow and the wren. Rooks, finches, larks, moles, badgers, foxes, stones, heather, heal-all, crabgrass, watercress, water, bumblebees, honeybees, butterflies, moths, even the tiniest mayfly— nothing escaped my attention.

Starlings nested in hollow trees as did the screech owl. The whip-poor-will, the night bird with the beautiful song, nested along the ground. So many differences. So many similarities. And yet they were all birds, which meant they could fly. Like insects and bats. Like leaves when the wind lifts them into the air . . .

Everything was connected.

To strengthen my character, an essential action, given that I would eventually find myself surrounded by ambitious, even manipulative, people, Lady Strange encouraged me to connect the virtues of the material world with the developing parts of myself. Chief among the virtuous materials I studied were stones. As the Italian physician Camillus Leonardus wrote in his *Mirror of Stones*, "Whatever can be thought of as beneficial to mankind may be confirmed by the virtue of stones." Ceaseless study of these and other elements helped me to distinguish the crucial differences between particular virtues, such as beneficence (smoky quartz) and generosity (peridot), cheerfulness (amethyst) and courtesy (citrine topaz).

Lady Strange put it best when she said, "As in alchemy, so in life. The alchemist continually seeks the process whereby to purge the baser metals of all impurities and so turn iron, copper, mercury, and tin into silver or gold. So the white magician is always seeking a way of perfecting her own state."

On August 30, 1558, my tenth birthday, Jack and Lady Strange and I sat on a blanket among the fragrant roses and the beds of chamomile and lavender that thrived in her abundant garden. After feasting on a white, almond-flavored cake as light as a fairy's wings, accompanied by glass after glass of delicious pink lemonade, Lady Strange brought forth from the deep pockets of her dress a small but perfect opal on a silver chain. "This precious gem is to be a symbol and silent helpmate in the work ahead."

"It's beautiful," I said, noticing the way the many colors suspended within the opal shimmered in the light.

"Pray, tell me why it's significant that your stone shall be the opal," Lady Strange said as she clasped the necklace around my throat.

Recalling *The Book of Virtues*, a slim but potent book by the great alchemist Pierre de Boniface, I said, "The opal's strength is that it encompasses four main colors and, therefore, four main virtues."

"Very good," Lady Strange said. "Continue."

"Because the opal contains the redness of rubies, the wearer of the opal should make herself praiseworthy. So too, she should possess the clear vision that is the chief virtue of the emerald. The purple of the amethyst should make her cheerful. As for the fourth color . . ." I bit my lip. "I'm afraid I cannot seem to remember."

"The fourth color is blue like the bluest sapphire," Lady Strange prompted.

"But how can that be? The sapphire is the most powerful of all the gemstones."

"So you must understand the magnitude of your task," Lady Strange said. "Now tell me, what does the sapphire contribute to your portrait?"

I focused on the sapphire Lady Strange never removed from her neck. "Great responsibility."

"Yes. So you see, with this tenth birthday gift of the

opal, you understand the very noble qualities you must possess."

Blessed with such a stone, I felt both awed and virtuous. *I had a destiny.*

Still, there remained one key question. "Who is the virgin queen? Please, tell me the name of the one I will serve."

"Very well, the time has come. Think, Mary, of the opal, which contains within it the properties of the ruby, the emerald, the amethyst, and the sapphire. But think, too, of the opal as possessing the milky whiteness of a pearl of great price. And pearls, as we both know, are both the creation of an oyster and the tears of heaven."

"Yes," I added, feeling a strong current deep within me, "and pearls are supposed to render their wearer pure and noble."

"Very good. So when the time comes, you will serve a virgin queen who will favor the milky pearl above every other jewel."

"But who is she?" I asked, almost believing that the indigo and red-throated songbirds, too, hung on Lady Strange's words, so silent did the air suddenly become.

"Who is Henry the Eighth's least likely heir to the throne?" Lady Strange asked, answering my question with one of her own.

"The Princess Elizabeth?"—*That same tingling*—"But how can that be when her half sister is queen?"

"Have I not told you that all things are possible?" Lady Strange's cheeks instantly became as rosy as the finch's crown.

"You have."

"Well, then." Lady Strange stood, and I followed her to the far end of the garden, where a hundred varieties of roses thrived. "Very soon there will come a great change. Then it will be Princess Elizabeth's turn to rule."

"But won't Elizabeth marry, like her sister?" I asked, reminded of the way Queen Mary's hopeless passion for her husband had made her painfully eager to do his will. "And then won't Elizabeth's strength be siphoned by her husband?"

Lady Strange picked a white rose and plucked a single petal from its frilly blossom. "Don't tell me you've forgotten the words inscribed on the tree, Mary."

The current grew stronger, and suddenly it was as if I again stood deep in that wood: *School her well in the white magician's wisdom so that she may go forth into the world and fulfill her calling when the virgin queen ascends the throne.*

Lady Strange's eyes held my own, and I felt almost as if the sapphire at her throat were making a connection with the opal. I touched my stone.

"So you understand," Lady Strange said. "Unlike her half sister, when Elizabeth inherits the throne, she will not take a husband. She will be England's first ruling female monarch. At least she will begin that way. It will be up to you to ensure that the virgin queen overturns the terrible precedent of her father's court. Henry the Eighth unleashed chaos into the world. He surrounded himself with soft-spined people who would not contradict his will. The brave, the outspoken, he banished or put to death. Now his daughter Elizabeth has been sent to order that chaos."

The virgin queen, I thought, suddenly sure my father had not succeeded in seducing Elizabeth, though he may have tried. Otherwise, the prophecy on the tree could not proclaim her chaste.

Lady Strange reached out to touch my reddish-gold hair. "Elizabeth has been sent to order the chaos," she said again. "But she cannot do it alone."

With these words, the familiar fiery warmth I had come to associate with Elizabeth burned more strongly.

CHAPTER THREE

THAT SAME YEAR, JUST BEFORE THE COLD AND rainy winds of early December turned to ice and snow, events happened just as Lady Strange had foretold. On the fifth day of that month, Queen Mary died of a combination of high fever and grave disappointment, and the Princess Elizabeth was publicly announced her half sister's successor. Throughout England, messengers proclaimed the news from the steps of churches, from within the marketplaces, and all along the cities' and villages' bridges and roads.

On January 15, 1559, the frosty morning of Elizabeth's coronation day, Lady Strange and I woke in that chilly, amorphous hour before dawn when anything seems possible and the world does not feel entirely real. Outside, a blanket of fresh snow covered the ground, its whiteness symbolic of the promise ahead; its chill, suggestive of the danger. After bathing in a blend of rosewater and chamomile, we dressed by candlelight in our finest silks and smoothed our hair with perfume. Onto our fingers we placed gold rings, and in tribute to our future virgin queen, around our throats we wound strands of the finest milky-white pearls.

Then, after breakfasting on milk and toast with sweet strawberry jam from the summer's garden, our coachman helped us into the carriage. Our destination was Westminster Abbey, where generations of England's kings and queens had been crowned.

"You are a faithful, trusting girl, Mary," Lady Strange said, raising my chin and examining my features as if seeing me for the first time. "You will make an exquisite white magician. Today I have something further to contribute to your education."

As on the other occasions when she shared with me something very serious, my guardian's violet eyes seemed to glow. Yet now, for the first time, her youthful face seemed much older, as if an ancient woman were staring out from behind her eyes.

"My people were part of the great courts of England long, long before the Tudors established their reign," Lady Strange began. "In the days of the Plantagenets, when Eleanor of Aquitaine traveled to the Holy Land late in the twelfth century, one of my ancestors, the Lady Miranda, traveled with her. It was Lady Miranda who brought back the sapphire I now wear."

"Given that the sapphire is the gemstone of responsibility, the Lady Miranda must have been a very wise woman."

"She was indeed," Lady Strange said, pleased by my ability to understand. "What I have not told you is the source of this particular sapphire. Like every object in nature, the sapphire has a legend attached to it."

I pressed close to her and breathed in that familiar forest-green scent.

"According to the most ancient philosophers, the sapphire was the gemstone that adorned the gates of the Garden of Eden. When man was cast out of Paradise, the gates exploded, and the sapphires were scattered to all parts of the globe."

I reached out and touched the sapphire. It was always warm, but at that moment it seemed to burn, and I quickly pulled my hand away.

"The Lady Miranda bequeathed the sapphire to my sister, Maude, who became renowned for her acts of charity. With the help of Eleanor's son Richard the Lionheart, Maude founded a hospital for sufferers of leprosy." Lady Strange's fingers closed around the sapphire. "My sister lived up to the virtue of the stone."

"Your sister." I drew back. "But that can't be. Don't you mean your great-great-grandmother, or someone like that?"

"No," she said, the forest scent intensifying. "I spoke correctly."

"But how can that possibly be?"

"Must you really ask that question?" An enigmatic smile played about Lady Strange's lips.

Then I knew. *Magic.*

Lady Strange raised my hand to her lips and kissed it. "Bright girl. Until Henry the Eighth's time, my family was always present at court. My people did not belong to the governing class, however. We were scholars, advisers—"

"White magicians?"

The same enigmatic smile. "Every once in a while. Of course, in this capacity we had to practice our craft in secret, especially after Henry the Eighth came to the throne, for he was violently suspicious of those who carried an aura of mystery about them.

"Can you tell me, Mary, what happened to my people in such a situation?" she said, a vengeful look momentarily penetrating her eye.

Despite the dryness of my throat, I managed to say, "They were banished."

"The lucky ones, yes." Lady Strange's skin turned to ice. "My uncle, my sister, my father, and I were the only ones left by this time, and the king hated my sister because she was beautiful, determined in her work, and indifferent to his advances."

My heart throbbed. "What did he expect of her?"

"He wanted my sister to give him a bastard son."

For a moment I thought it was the whiteness of the landscape beyond our carriage that made me dizzy, but then I realized that my spinning vision stemmed from the awful significance of Lady Strange's words.

"Did the king kill your sister?" I asked at last.

"Yes."

A sharp blade scraped my insides. "And your uncle?"

"Banished."

It required all of my strength to ask the next question. "And your father?"

Lady Strange's face turned as pale as an ermine in winter. "My father died of a broken heart. You've heard of such a thing as a figure of speech, but in my father's case, the words became truth. My father was a good man, and he loved us dearly. He could not survive his daughter's death."

By now, both Lady Strange's heart and my own were beating with such force I felt as if the streets beyond the carriage were shaking. (I still do not know. Perhaps they were.)

"My father's last words to me were as follows." Lady Strange closed her eyes and said, "'Remember where you come from, and never cease to love your country. When the time is ripe, you will avenge these crimes, not with any violence, but with the white magic that is your birthright. Listen and look for the signs, and all will be well. But most of all, always remember who you are.'"

My guardian opened her eyes, and they immediately met my own. "'All will be well,' my father said to me. Do you know why he could speak so confidently about the future, Mary?"

I stared at Lady Strange, and for a moment or two I was deathly afraid I would not be able to give her the correct answer. Until I realized my guardian was gazing at me with love.

And suddenly the words were there. "Because he knew about me. He knew you would find me."

For the first time in our year together, Lady Strange began to cry. Yet her tears were like nothing I had ever seen. They were infused with a golden light. So entranced was I by their shining beauty that I did not think to wipe them away. I looked more closely, realizing the gold was not just present in her tears. Rather, gold seemed to surround her.

"So you see it," Lady Strange said.

"Yes—"

"Tell me, my dear Mary, what it is you see."

"All around you . . . I see a glow, a golden glow."

Lady Strange beamed like the rising sun. "That glow is an aura, Mary. Through the symbolism of color, you will be able to discern a great deal about a person through his or her aura alone."

I leaned back in the carriage and looked at the world through new eyes, for all around myself, too, I saw an aura, but mine was of silver. As I was later to learn, my mother's aura had also been silver.

"Look!" Lady Strange pointed to an intricate network of high-steepled, many-windowed buildings in the distance. "We are almost there."

High above my head the strong towers seemed to pierce

the heavens. When the sun broke free of the clouds, Westminster Abbey shone forth, a blaze of stained glass against a stone facade. Gazing at the Abbey, I understood for the first time why the great cathedrals of Europe were built as monuments to God's power and man's central place in His plan.

After we stepped down from the carriage, we made our way on foot over to the entrance. Remarkably, despite the throngs of people, as soon as Lady Strange approached, the crowd made room for us to pass.

Inside, the abbey smelled of exotic incense, and unlike the blustery outdoors, was overwhelmingly warm. Holding tightly to Lady Strange's hand, I walked beside her as a guard led us into the nave, where the nobles sat.

Illuminated by thousands of torches and candles, the stained glass windows formed a jewellike tapestry of color. Even the weak winter rays forced their way into the stone interior, as if the earth and the elements wanted to welcome and bless the young queen's reign.

Very few children were among the nobles gathered here, and from the stares I received, I understood my presence was neither welcome nor was it understood. The hard gazes of the nobility told me a ten-year-old girl was too young to be of value to the politic court.

Only when Lady Strange introduced me as "the late Queen Dowager Katherine Parr's daughter" did a number of those pinched faces open.

One very old woman arrayed in dove-gray silk even took my hands between her own and pressed them to her heart. "I remember your mother," she said, her fresh green aura affirming that she spoke the truth.

"Tell me what you remember," I heard myself say. "Please."

"Gladly," the old woman said, as light came into her pale blue eyes. "I saw her last at Cambridge some two years before the king's death. It was springtime, and the lilacs were in full bloom. On that day, Cambridge's finest minds appointed your mother as the university's patroness. I still remember Roger Ascham's famous speech." With perfect clarity, she continued, "'Speak to us often, erudite Queen,' Mr. Ascham said, 'For we rejoice vehemently in your happiness because you are learning more amid the occupations of your dignity than many of us do in all our leisure and quiet.'"

"Roger Ascham spoke these words?" I said, reminded of the great scholar's praise of Elizabeth—the belief that her mind would soon surpass his own.

"He did, my dear," the old woman said, then raised my fingertips to her lips. "Your mother was an honor to our sex. Remember that."

"I will," I promised.

The old woman's words confirmed what the expressions on the other nobles' faces suggested. Though more than a decade had passed since her death, and despite her scandalous marriage to my father, the people of England continued to remember and honor my mother.

That day, not only did I learn in what high esteem the people of England still held my mother, but I began to trust more deeply in my gifts, for the auras swiftly provided me with a wealth of knowledge about the thousands of people gathered there. Because Lady Strange had schooled me in the symbolism of color, I could now intuit much about the characters of the people gathered there without speaking to them. Although there was a dangerous preponderance of ambitious red and sycophantic shades of bronze, I also found plenty of trustworthy chartreuse and intelligent sunflower yellow.

The auras of the courtiers and grand ladies intrigued me, as did the dazzle of their many jewels. Recalling Boniface's book, I wondered how many of these men and women actually lived up to the virtues of their gems. How many were truly praiseworthy like the ruby, clear-sighted like the emerald, purposeful like the tiger's eye, or genuinely gracious like the garnet?

As if she had read my thoughts, Lady Strange said, "The study of how closely or how far a person strays from his or her stone's virtue will be an essential part of your life's work as a white magician, as will be your ability to puzzle through the significance of each aura."

Shortly thereafter, accompanied by great pageantry and a gala of trumpets, Elizabeth glided through the doorway of Westminster Hall, dressed in coronation robes of gold cloth trimmed with ermine, her costume embroidered with jewels, her person surrounded by a luminous purple aura that attested to her regality.

Elizabeth's hair, of rich reddish gold, curled about the pale oval of her face. I knew from my studies that the color of her hair, her hazel eyes, and the generous width of her brow marked her as a Tudor. But her nose and her fine bowed lips brought to mind a copy I'd seen of the sole sur-viving portrait of her mother, Anne Boleyn.

For a long time I studied my future queen, marking not

only her intelligent beauty, but the extraordinary affinity between the two of us. I, too, possessed auburn hair, and like Elizabeth, the paleness of my skin was set off by eyes slightly more gold than hazel. In their own way, the traces of red and gold in our coloring seemed a connection between us: England's first reigning Protestant queen and me, the magician destined to strengthen her reign. And then there was the fact that red and gold linked us both to my mother, Elizabeth's stepmother.

Over the course of the next hour, the solemn ceremony transformed a young woman, just twenty-five years old, into an all-powerful sovereign. Gold, the purest of all the metals, allied Elizabeth with the sun, the source of light, power, life itself. The fur of the rare ermine stood for purity. Diamonds and rubies bedecked her coronation robes, but for the most part, Elizabeth's jewel of choice was the milk-white pearl. Thousands of them endowed her person with radiance. Gazing at her, I felt secure in the knowledge that she radiated the purity and nobility of her pearls.

After the service ended, *Queen* Elizabeth stepped forth. In her hands, she held a golden orb representing the cosmos and a scepter that stood for her authority. Most important, she now wore a crown, the ultimate symbol of her divine right to rule. In the center of her crown shone a great sapphire very much like the jewel that glinted just above my guardian's collarbone.

Understanding the connection I was making, Lady Strange said, "Yes, the sapphire in the young queen's crown also finds its origin in Eden's shattered gates."

I leaned close and whispered, "What would happen were your sapphire to come together with the queen's?"

A truly frightening grin passed over Lady Strange's face. "Whosoever possessed both gemstones would have to understand the great responsibility of her or his position, for taken together the two sapphires would make that person doubly powerful."

Before leaving Westminster Abbey, all of the nobility passed before the young queen to express their joy in her rule and to profess their loyalty. Great lords knelt to kiss her bejeweled hand. Grand ladies—duchesses and marchionesses dressed in velvet gowns adorned with furs—wept.

When it came my turn to kneel, I bowed my head, and my body trembled so fiercely I thought I would faint. Only by thinking of all that Lady Strange and I had spoken of that morning was I finally able to compose myself.

Because he knew about me. He knew you would find me.

Still, when it came time for me to speak to my queen, my lips failed to form words; so that it was Lady Strange who said, "Your Most Royal Majesty, may I present your loyal servant, Lady Mary Seymour, the late Katherine Parr's daughter."

"Look up."

I did, and the radiance of my queen nearly blinded me.

"My most loyal Lady Mary," she said, her voice gentle. "It is a great joy to find the noble Katherine Parr's daughter here among us. When you are older, I will ask you to come to court and visit me. Perhaps, one day, you will even join my inner circle as one of my honored ladies-in-waiting."

My heart leapt at such an invitation, for it was in keeping with everything Lady Strange had said. Once more dropping my gaze, I bowed even lower and said clearly, "Such a position would be my greatest honor."

CHAPTER FOUR

VERY SOON AFTER ELIZABETH'S CORONATION, worry lines began to mar Lady Strange's youthful features, the light dimmed in her violet eyes, and she began to pace her rooms deep into the furthest reaches of the night. At times she became so agitated her teacup trembled in her hands. Jack, too, noticed, for he often whimpered when he followed her up the stairs each night, and sometimes he lay down at the foot of her bed, as if on the lookout for the one who had done this to her. "Dear Jack," Lady Strange said. "There is no intruder. It is just that the time is out of joint, and so my body is manifesting the signs."

Eventually, Lady Strange less cryptically revealed the reason for her anxiety: problems at Elizabeth's court. First, the queen's councilors were urging her to marry and produce an heir. They listened not when she said, "I am married already to the realm of England."

Over the last year I had familiarized myself intimately with the history of England. I therefore knew enough about the prevailing belief that a woman's first duty was to marry and bear children to recognize the difficult position in which Elizabeth's unmarried, childless state placed her. There were rumors that the queen's councilors had questioned her chamber women and laundresses to see if she menstruated regularly, for they could not conceive of a woman who did not want to fulfill her biological destiny.

Even worse than these internal pressures were the threats from abroad. "The French king has declared Elizabeth a bastard," Lady Strange explained. "He is attempting to set his Scottish daughter-in-law, Mary Stuart, the granddaughter of Henry the Eighth's sister Margaret on the throne."

"Shouldn't we intervene?" I asked. After all, I was the white magician destined to ensure the health and goodness of Elizabeth's reign. How could I stand by idly as she struggled with forces at home and abroad?

"Didn't you tell me that a large part of the chaos Henry the Eighth hurled into the world involved lineage?" I pressed, for we both knew the Catholic Church did not recognize the Protestant Elizabeth as Henry's legitimate heir, which was why the French king could try to force another Catholic Mary onto England's throne, a woman the French king could manipulate.

"Your thinking is clear-sighted, and your intentions honorable," Lady Strange said. "Still, I'm afraid it's far too early for you to go to court, my dear." The furrows in her forehead deepened. "You and I still have a great deal of work to do. No," she considered, "Elizabeth will have to rely on her own strengths until you come of age. For now, you and I will repair to the Canary Islands so that I can recover my health."

And so, when the first crocuses broke forth from the thawing English soil, and the first chaffinches returned to the newly budding trees, we packed just two trunks apiece. (Lady Strange was very specific about a white magician not becoming too wedded to her possessions.)

After bidding farewell to the house that had been my first home, we traveled to the coast. Just outside of Dover, we boarded an enormous ship destined for the small village of Armonía on one of the Canary Islands.

We arrived after a month-long crossing. Unlike the English house beside the dark wood, in Armonía we lived high atop a hill that overlooked the turquoise water. Our house was of whitewashed stone with a red tile roof. Cypress trees shaded the house from the sun, and there was a cobbled path that led all the way from the house to the sea. As if by magic, upon our arrival we found a garden burgeoning with tomatoes, peas, lettuces, and a plethora of herbs all ready for our use. Here, too, there were apricot and pear trees and a dozen bushes bearing a wealth of sweet berries.

In this balmy place where the air never chilled one's skin, and where the earth held the nourishing scents of fruit and sun, I applied myself to my studies. Seated at a desk beside a window overlooking the jewel-toned sea, I learned enough to read with real understanding the occult philosophers: Ficino, Ptolemye, Paracelsus, Agrippa, and even the contemporary Englishman, Robert Recorde, who had mysteriously disappeared from England just before Lady Strange made the decision for us to come to Armonía.

From each of these thinkers, I gained new insights into how necessary it was for the white magician to remain absolutely committed to using her talents toward ensuring the well-being of others, and not to enrich herself or her power for its own sake. Although each of these thinkers differed on certain points, they all believed the greatest danger a magician could face came not from the outside world, but from within. "The wit is wronged and led awry, if mind be married to the ground," Ptolemye wrote. Translation: under absolutely no circumstances should the white magician allow herself to be corrupted by pride, selfishness, or desire—the baser passions.

During our years in the Canary Islands, not only did I plow through books, reading occult philosophy as well as masterpieces of literature and political thought, but I continued to look closely at the natural world. I familiarized myself with a host of plants and flowers, including the exotic bird of paradise, which was not a bird at all, but rather a thick-stalked plant with an orange and purple flower that resembled the body of a bird in flight.

In many cases, the things of the natural world were connected with stories that revealed clues to their properties. Among these was the heliotrope flower, a plant whose name signifies its desire to turn (*trope*) toward the sun (*helio*). "Why do we not add this flower to the ones in our garden?" I asked Lady Strange. "Do we not need the sun's energy also?"

"The story behind the flower will explain why. According to the ancients, the heliotrope sprang up in the place where a maiden died for lack of the love from the sun god Apollo." Lady Strange cocked an eyebrow and said, "Somehow, despite its beauty, I cannot endure having such a flower around."

Reminded of the ways in which the heliotrope's history only confirmed my belief in the dangers of women falling in love—dangers confirmed by the disastrous experiences of Queen Mary, the duchess, and especially my mother—I vehemently agreed.

After a few weeks in Armonía, the worry lines that disfigured Lady Strange's face dwindled and then vanished; light returned to her eyes, and litheness to her movements. Although she did not reveal to me the secret of her cure, I suspected it had everything to do with the balmy climate and a golden-fleshed fruit with thorny spines that she ate with her fingers every morning and afternoon before she lay down for a nap.

As her health improved, we began to take long walks beside the water. There, she spoke to me of the other world, that of the spirits. "They are always here all around us. Yet it takes a very practiced and very pure eye to be able to see them."

"I may be able to believe in such a realm, and yet I'm afraid I cannot picture it," I told Lady Strange. "Nor can I understand how they can be right here." I gestured to the air. "Around us."

"In time, you will understand that reality extends beyond the world as we know it. Think, Mary, of the examples of our own day. Some event happens, and it entirely changes the way we perceive the world."

"Please," I said, for my head was spinning with images of spirits nesting in trees, along clotheslines, and in the eaves of houses. "Give me a straightforward example."

She considered a moment. "Up until the last century's end, we did not know certain lands existed. Then the Italian navigator, Christopher Columbus, appealed to the clear-sighted Queen Isabella, who, as you know, favored the prophetic emerald. With Isabella's support, Columbus set sail and found himself in a new land. The land had always existed. Yet his arrival there changed our understanding of the very nature of the world.

"And then there is the example of your mother's court during her years as Henry the Eighth's queen. You now know enough about her life to understand what a powerful precedent she set as a woman of accomplishment and learning."

"I do," I said, reminded of the fact that even Henry VIII, who was nothing less than tyrannical in his quest to keep women in a subservient place, recognized my mother's gifts. The proof lay in the trust the king had in her ability to supervise the education of not just his daughters, but the education of Prince Edward, his son and heir. Thanks to my mother's example, more women were being educated than ever before.

"So you understand, Mary?" Lady Strange said.

"I think so, for you are telling me that this is how it will be with the spirits. Just as my mother's intelligence confirmed a latent truth about women, so I will discover the spirits' presence although they are already here?"

"Yes. You will find them at the proper time, or," and here an echo trailed after her words, "they will find you—"

"And then?" I asked.

Lady Strange seized hold of my hand. "It won't be long until the relationship feels as natural, and as necessary, as our own."

A world of spirits remained abstract, and yet it was easier for me to believe in spirits in a place surrounded by azure water, where almost every plant imaginable (and some plants I had never dreamed of) grew to terrific heights and produced the most gorgeous, not to mention the most fragrant, blossoms.

"It's time for us to translate some more of your learning into action," Lady Strange said on one of our long walks some two months after our arrival. "Let us begin with the spell I asked you to commit to memory last night. I told you its purpose. Surely," she said, gazing at me expectantly, "you are a little curious to see how it will work."

"Of course," I replied. "Still, I find it remarkable to believe that if I recite the words of the spell, I will actually be able to compel a bird or crab or even a fish to speak to me."

"But why?" Lady Strange said, as we stood beside the ocean, our feet warmed by the white sand. "After all, I have told you about so many, many spells. This one"—she winked—"is very good for beginners. Of course, you must get every word right. Otherwise, the spell might backfire."

As a pair of seagulls soared above us, she said, "Are you confident that you know the spell? Have you practiced it just as I asked?"

"Yes," I said, and crossed my fingers. Although I had practiced speaking the words, I had recited it only one dozen times instead of two, for I had wanted to go for a swim.

Lady Strange shielded her violet eyes from the sun. "Now then, let me hear the words while the seagulls are still within the range of your voice."

"Cinnamon comes from a sapling cut only when it's flush," I began, eyes closed, trying to picture the words as I spoke them. "But the golden grains of paradise are born from a glossy-leaved plant that bears fragrant, lavender blossoms when the sea is at high tide. Caraway, like mustard, is a seed. In order to increase one's store, the careful planter must scatter the seeds in the . . ."

"Why do you hesitate?" Lady Strange said. "You're doing very well."

Despite the way she was smiling at me, I knew I wasn't doing very well, for I had forgotten the rest of the incantation. Gazing into Jack's compassionate eyes, how I wished my loyal friend could have provided me with the answers. *If only you could speak*, I found myself thinking.

After a few minutes had passed with me just standing there, Lady Strange said, "Now you will have to repeat the entire incantation again." She gazed up at the seagulls that were moving farther and farther away. "Of course, it's not likely they will stay and speak with you now."

"What about Jack?" I asked.

"Jack?"

"Yes." I stroked his rough brow. "Isn't it possible to cast a spell that would make him speak to me?"

"Mary," my guardian said sternly, "I cannot possibly encourage that sort of spell. You and Jack have a special language, one not governed by words. To tamper with the understanding you have established over the years would not be a good thing."

"But—"

"No, Mary." She placed a firm hand on Jack's brow. "In this matter, you must trust me."

Looking into Jack's reassuring eyes, I knew she was right. I would never forget the years at Grimsthorpe Manor, when he slept beside me in my chilly bed, or the days he walked at my side, never outrunning me or leaving me behind. And yet a part of me still longed to hear Jack tell me all he knew, for I wondered what he would say if he were given the chance.

A few minutes later, a hermit crab crossed our path, and Lady Strange said, "Try it again."

"Cinnamon comes from a sapling cut only when it's flush," I began a second time. "But the golden grains of paradise are born from a glossy-leaved plant that bears fragrant, lavender blossoms when the sea is at high tide. Caraway, like mustard, is a seed. In order to increase one's store, the careful planter must scatter the seeds in the . . ." This time when I stumbled, I decided to insert a word of my own. "In order to increase one's store," I repeated, opening my eyes and fixing them on the first thing I saw, "the careful planter must scatter the seeds in the deep blue sea."

"Mary, no!" Lady Strange said, jumping forward as if to cover my mouth with her hand.

I looked down at the hermit crab only to realize that he was no longer a crab at all. Instead, he seemed to be half crab and half fish, for where his claws should have been, he now sprouted fins. Helpless, I watched the poor creature flail about on the sand that should have been his home.

"The careful planter must make obeisance to the spirits and correct herself," Lady Strange said, taking hold of the crab. "The seeds of the caraway must only be scattered to a mild, northern wind, and the creatures of the sea must return to water, while the sand dwellers remain in their native terrain."

As Lady Strange spoke, the hermit crab's fins returned to claws.

She laid him on the sand, where he seemed to stare at me with absolute fury, then scuttled away at a fast pace, as if in fear of his life.

"Mary," she scolded. "If you do not know a spell, then under no circumstances should you pursue it. Have I not told you that every action has its consequence?"

"Yes," I said, grateful I had not improvised the words of the spell on a creature I loved as much as Jack.

CHAPTER FIVE

By december of 1562, my guardian had fully recovered her health and was as beautiful and alive as she had been when we first met. Shortly after Easter we began to talk of voyaging back to England, even undertaking preliminary preparations, only to learn that a plague had overtaken London, claiming three thousand souls a week, and wreaking further havoc in the countryside.

For our own safety we waited to return until the following autumn, when the pestilence had ended. We established residence at Lady Strange's childhood home of Moonsway, a pink, three-story fairy tale of a house with a mature garden, not too far from my mother's former, beloved house of Chelsea Manor on the outskirts of London. The days flowed happily there, for we were close enough to the city to keep the present lively, yet far enough away to remain free of its fatigue and congestion, its illness and crime.

We did not journey to court, but every once in a while Lady Strange entertained visitors. On these festive days we dressed in our finest clothes; Bess, our new housemaid, prepared salt cod and pickled eggs, nut pudding, gingerbread with fresh cream, and other delicacies. Sometimes we danced at these parties, and sometimes we sang. On such occasions, Moonsway shone with the glow of tall beeswax candles and buzzed with intelligent, at times riddling conversations I worked hard to understand.

Days stretched on into weeks, and weeks became months. The somber landscape of winter was soon brightened by the green buds of spring. Come summer, the garden burst into life with roses, gillyflowers, marigolds, lavender, and all manner of herbs. Throughout this time, I not only helped Lady Strange to entertain guests but I continued my studies, setting aside at least two hours of each day to reading and writing, a precedent I knew my queen followed also.

Until one August morning I awoke with a stomach tied

up in sharp knots that forced all the breath up into my chest, where it seemed to get trapped between my rib cage and my heart.

Unused to such inner tumult, I dressed, then sought out Lady Strange, who I found breakfasting in the quiet comfort of her bedroom. Dressed in a gold-threaded dressing gown, she sat on a divan, her small, slippered feet resting on purple cushions. Behind her, sunlight lilted through the crescent moon–shaped windows.

No sooner had Lady Strange poured my morning cup of tea when she said, "Something is troubling you."

My eyes met hers. "I'm afraid I don't feel well."

Lady Strange cocked an eyebrow. "Bellyache?"

I nodded.

"A chilled, unsettled sensation in the region around the heart?"

Again I nodded.

"Difficulty breathing?"

Again the nod.

"And your hands?" She leaned closer. "Is there discoloration around the knuckles?"

"Yes," I said, alarmed by the blue tinge of my skin, and suddenly concerned that I may have contracted some terrible, untreatable illness.

"This is good news," she said, allowing her violet eyes to rest on my own.

I swallowed hard. "It is?"

"Yes." Her eyes darkened, and the sapphire at her neck seemed to emit extra heat. "I thought it would be at least another year, perhaps two, before you were ready to make her acquaintance, but the signs are all here."

"Signs?" I asked. "Whose acquaintance? I don't understand."

Lady Strange sipped her tea, nibbled at another hot scone. "Cordelia's."

"But who is Cordelia?"

Lady Strange's face glowed. "Your good spirit." She slipped her arm around my trembling shoulders. "In all of our training, I've emphasized that your life would connect with lives from that other world."

"Yes," I replied, remembering those rather abstract words spoken during our final year in the Canary Islands.

Lady Strange stroked my cheek with her long, elegant fingers. "Then what's troubling you?"

"I thought I'd feel more prepared."

"Darling girl, everyone feels that way about the great events of their lives."

Nestling closer to my guardian, I asked, "What must I do?"

"You must perform an essential ritual, precisely and with reverence. Specifically, on this day you must drink plenty of clear fluids sweetened only with a little honey. The water will help purge any poisons from your system."

"Water?"

"That's right. You are to drink water and tea only, no milk, nothing that comes from an animal whatsoever. Your diet must consist solely of fruits, vegetables, and grains. Is that understood, Mary?" she asked, her tone grave, for she possessed firsthand knowledge of my penchant for sweets, which I consumed whenever I could, in public or on the sly.

"Perfectly," I replied.

"Very good. In addition, I will ask you to wash—by your own hand—your finest undergarments of white muslin."

"But why?" I said, none too eager to take up the time-consuming task of washing white muslin.

"So the spirits will understand you are willing to purify yourself and work hard on your own. You'll also need to go to market—no asking Bess for help—and buy these items." Lady Strange reached for her writing tablet, then wrote down a list of herbs with well-known healing and purifying properties: lavender, for tranquility; thyme, for patience; marjoram, for wisdom. "And heal-all to reinforce the cure," she concluded.

I groaned. "So many of them?"

"Yes. Once you return home with the herbs, you'll need to grind them up, then bathe in the compost so that your skin can absorb as many of the essential properties as possible."

One thing was clear: these ritualized actions were going to be an all-day affair.

Because of my prescribed diet, supper consisted solely of a salad of cucumbers, radishes, carrots, and lettuce. There were also figs, almonds, and a great loaf of bread.

"Cook has told me a dozen times today, but are you sure that this is what your ladyship requested for supper?" Bess asked when she brought this unusual meal into the pale green dining room.

"Yes," Lady Strange replied, lifting the bowl from Bess's outstretched hands. Plucking a single radish from the dish, she raised the vegetable to her lips, then popped it into her mouth. "Delicious," she pronounced.

Bess's mouth formed a great big O. Then she quickly hurried from the room.

Once Jack discovered Lady Strange and I were dining on vegetables, he, too, abandoned the dining room for the kitchen, where a leftover leg of mutton awaited.

Over our unusual meal, Lady Strange explained, in hushed tones, the next step in contacting Cordelia.

"You will not be there to guide me through the process?" I asked.

Lady Strange shook her head and bit into a carrot. "No. You will have to undertake this initiation on your own."

Before I lay down to sleep, I set a velvet pouch on the table in the little sitting area that adjoined my own silver bedroom. Around the pouch, I placed a grouping of white stones and a single white rose, potent symbols of honesty and fidelity, respectively.

At precisely ten minutes before two o'clock in the morning, I rose from my bed and lit the long, white candle Lady Strange had given me. Careful not to wake Jack, I tiptoed into the sitting area.

There, as Lady Strange said, I found the contents of

the pouch spilled onto the table by a hand other than my own. Only now did I see the pouch's contents: a thimbleful of gold dust and a translucent crystal ball balanced upon a volcanic rock cut into the perfect shape of an equilateral triangle, that ultimate symbol of balance. Gold is alchemy's highest metal. Crystal suggests wisdom and prophecy; volcanic rock is metamorphic and so signifies transformation.

Each one of my senses intensified, and my body quivered as I set the candle down, then placed the white rose behind my ear.

Once you are wearing the white rose, place a fingerful of gold dust on each cheek and in the center of your forehead. Only then will you be ready to lift the crystal in both hands and take it over to the window. . . .

The crystal felt strangely heavier than it had in the pouch, although this could have been my imagination and fatigue, for it was the thick of night.

Repeat the proper incantation nine times as you stand before the window, your eyes half closed, your gaze directed both at the moon and at the crystal in your hands.

"Wise spirit of the other realm, come to me now, for I approach you with the purity of mountain water, and with all of the solemnity of winter. Wise spirit, I beg of thee, come."

I spoke the incantation nine times, and each time, the crystal grew warmer so that my hands seemed to be gradually catching fire. The crystal became so hot that when I looked down, it was glowing.

I dropped to my knees, almost losing my grip on the object in my hands.

And that's when I saw her.

Within the crystal, very faintly at first, then a bit more clearly, the face of a young woman appeared. Her thick, black hair fell loosely down the length of her back, reaching almost to her knees. She wore a garland of white roses interlaced with yellow lilies, and she held a lily in her outstretched hand, the floral symbol of purity and innocence.

When the spirit reaches out to you, be sure to accept her gift gratefully, whatever that gift might be.

Amazement rippled through my fingertips as the flower passed through the crystal into my own hands.

"Thank you," I said, my voice filled with reverence. "Are you Cordelia?"

The spirit nodded but still did not speak.

"I am honored to meet you. I am Mary Seymour, Katherine Parr's daughter."

"And in three hours you will be sixteen years old." Cordelia's voice flowed like clear spring water.

I nodded as the completeness of her understanding washed over and through me.

Cordelia seemed to draw closer, so that I had the sensation of being in the same room with her; but when I looked again, I realized that I was still talking to the figure in the crystal.

Only then did I notice the burn marks around Cordelia's neck, blue-black marks that seemed to have been made by a rope. Her mantle of hair hid the marks well, but eventually the marks and their meaning came to light. Her slender, damaged throat manifested all the signs of hanging.

Cordelia registered my shock, but she did not directly address it. Instead she continued to speak in her temperate but persistent way. "Although you are not the daughter of a king, you are the daughter of a queen, one of England's finest women, esteemed highly and rightly so. Your mother's mark is clearly upon you."

"I am Sir Thomas Seymour's daughter also," I said, shame crimsoning my cheeks, because I needed to declare this relationship, not just to the people among whom I lived, but to the spirit world as well.

Cordelia frowned. "You must not feel responsible for your father's wrongdoings. None of us can help the parents or families into which we are born. My father, too, made many mistakes. And my sisters were among the most evil creatures ever born."

"Will you tell me about your father?" I asked.

"He was a good man, but he made many bad decisions. Worst of all, he allowed himself to be guided by flattery and untruths. When he finally recognized his mistakes"— she touched her burned throat—"it was too late."

"Couldn't you have helped him?" I asked.

"At that time I did not have the courage to stay and help him confront his errors." Her voice became low. "That is why it is my duty to help you face your destiny."

Cordelia's eyes met mine, but I remained silent, wondering how her story would connect with my own. "As you already know, it is your sacred and secret duty to make sure Queen Elizabeth's reign remains a healthy and profitable one. In a short time, you will journey to court to help protect her from the plots of scheming courtiers and the machinations of foreign powers eager to undo her hardwon authority. At times, you will have the opportunity to advise her."

"Yes," I replied, well aware of the importance of my own good judgment in ensuring the good judgment of my queen.

"Very good. Tonight our communion will be brief," Cordelia continued. "But we will speak to each other regularly, at least once each month when the moon is the shape of a perfect crescent, and your own monthly cycle has ended."

Listen for the instructions.

"Tomorrow, you will find a slender white dog on your doorstep. Under no circumstances are you to allow the dog to be banished."

"But our maidservant Bess will be furious," I explained. "We had trouble enough convincing her to allow my hound, Jack, to enter the household."

An almost girlish lightness softened Cordelia's features. "How does Bess feel about Jack now?"

"She tells me he's a lot of trouble and mess, and yet I know that she is fond of him."

"Well then, have a little faith here, too. As you will discover, people, animals, all creatures and elements of the world are not as they initially seem. Nor do they always speak the truth. Or perhaps you have already discovered this?"

"I may have," I replied, reminded of the auras I now saw around people.

"Tell me," Cordelia said.

"I see a gold aura around Lady Strange."

"Lady Strange manifests the aura of a magnificent and very old, very pure soul."

"And Bess emanates a burnished shade, like the coat of a fawn."

Cordelia did not laugh, but her features lightened a little. "Despite her quandary with dogs, your Bess is a good woman, someone you can trust. This is important to know. The fact that you see colors tells me you are gifted, more gifted than I knew."

Her face drew even nearer the glass, and I saw the burn marks more vividly. Yes, there was no doubt: she had been hung.

"Trust your gifts, Mary. They are the tools you will need to use in dangerous work ahead."

No matter how I had been preparing myself for this moment, I shivered and recoiled from the glass.

"It is natural to be afraid," Cordelia continued. "Your fear will be a teacher. Listen to it, but do not let your fears govern you."

I swallowed hard, then forced myself to reply, "I won't."

"Very good. Now our first meeting has ended. Remember, look for the white dog. And beware of the man who boasts of being the lionheart. A true lionheart will never proclaim his nature," she said, her face becoming very pale.

Cordelia's image began to fade.

"Wait," I cried. "I'm not sure I understand."

Still the vision continued to grow fainter.

"I'm sorry." Cordelia raised her hand to her lips and blessed me with a kiss. "I must go now. No more time—" The last words she spoke were "Happy Birthday," whispered so that I could just make them out.

Once again I found myself alone, the only proof that she had really been there, the yellow lily I held in my hand.

CHAPTER SIX

O<small>N AUGUST 30, THE MORNING OF MY BIRTH-</small>day, I awoke to Bess screaming from downstairs, "Beelzebub's apprentice in a white coat!"

The white dog!

I threw on my robe, then rushed down the stairs, Jack beside me.

Sure enough, there in the yawning entryway stood Bess, trying to shoo an immense white dog from the front step. In her left hand she held a broom. She poked the dog with its handle, all the while stomping her feet.

The dog, however, would not budge.

"I'm sorry to make so much commotion on your birthday, Lady Mary, but this nuisance has been sitting on the step since seven o'clock. I don't know why he's come to our house, for he doesn't belong to this neighborhood."

Bess had barely gotten the words out when the dog fixed his startling, light blue eyes on me, bounded past her, and leapt—full force—into the house, landing squarely at my feet, where he "bowed," if a dog can indeed be said to bow.

Meanwhile, Jack's own droopy ears perked up, and he lumbered over to me, too. Unlike the graceful stranger, Jack landed on my feet.

"Well, I never . . ." Bess said. "A huge dog comes jumping at you on your sixteenth birthday, and your fool of a hound squishes your toes. What a way to begin this first year of womanhood."

"It certainly beats being kissed by a prince," I replied.

Bess just shook her head. Despite the fact that her own husband had run off with at least half a dozen dairymaids and fathered twice as many illegitimate children, all of whom poor Bess worked hard to support, she could not understand my own deep aversion to love and marriage. "The love of a man is worth all the trouble in the world," she was fond of chanting.

What she failed to understand was that a dog's loyalty was worth ten times that of any man.

Now the extraordinary dog held out his paw, as if he were a gentleman giving me his hand.

Close inspection of that paw revealed a tattoo shaped like a triangle—like the base of the crystal ball. Was the allusion to the metamorphic rock a sign of a spirit's transformation into a dog?

Bess protested, but I insisted on bringing the dog into the walled garden until Lady Strange should pronounce it (and here I quote Bess) "permissable to have yet another hairy beast in the household of two such elegant ladies."

With the great dog following a step or two behind, and Jack sticking close to my heels, I entered the section of the garden where Lady Strange now cultivated an astonishing variety of roses with names like Crimson Pillar, Falstaff, Pegasus, Discovery, Crystalline, and Gemini.

Almost immediately, Lady Strange stepped into the garden, Bess trailing behind her.

When my guardian joined me on a bench not far from the roses, the dog climbed to his feet and once again, he seemed to bow.

"This is the most peculiar dog I have ever seen. Even the queer blue of his eyes is all wrong. A dog's eyes are always brown," Bess insisted, a deep flush suffusing her cheeks. "Truly, m'lady, I cannot help but think such an arrival is a bad omen on the young Lady Mary's sixteenth birthday."

"I beg to differ with you, Bess," Lady Strange said. "This dog's eyes attest to his special nature."

Bess just stared back at my guardian, clearly unconvinced.

Once she had gone, muttering all sorts of complaints under her breath against dogs, Lady Strange wrapped her arms around me. "Happy Birthday, Mary. My own dreams told me you had been successful." She turned to the dog, who continued to regard us calmly. "Am I right in believing this dog has come in concordance with Cordelia's wishes?"

"You are," I said. Then, without even thinking about it, I added, "His name is Perseus."

As if in affirmation, the dog bowed and laid a long paw in my lap.

Lady Strange stroked Perseus's head. "Remarkable that you should have been sent a dog named for the brave man who slew the gorgon and turned the giant Atlas into a mountain."

"Yes," I said, understanding that Perseus's strength meant I would face dangers that would require the help of a dog whose namesake was a gorgon-slayer.

I must not be afraid.

With the noble Perseus stretched out at our feet, and Jack close beside him, I proceeded to tell Lady Strange all that had passed between Cordelia and myself. When I reached the part about the burn marks around her neck, I said, "She was hung, wasn't she?"

"Yes."

"Are you familiar with her history?" I asked shakily.

"Not the particulars. What I know is this: from the time your care passed into my hands, I knew Cordelia would be your spirit. There is an affinity between you."

Again, the burn marks flashed before me.

"What is this affinity?" I asked, Cordelia's pronouncement that I live as fearlessly as possible echoing through me.

"That is for you to discover." Lady Strange stroked Perseus's shaggy head. "This magnificent dog will help you to find that affinity. He is of the Russian breed that a shrewd Englishman brought into the country from Muscovy, not more than a decade ago."

"He's a wolfhound, then?"

"The specific name is Borzoi. Clearly, Perseus has all of the noble properties of that loyal breed. We will have to see if he is also wolf*like*."

72

A week passed, then two.

Each morning, I awoke with the feeling that something must happen soon. I sensed Perseus awaited some change also, for each night before I blew out the candle, he inspected each and every corner of the room, even going so far as to peer behind the white linen curtains, and within the four sections of the wardrobe Lady Strange had used as a girl. Only after the inspection was complete would he lie down on the divan not far from the foot of my bed.

It was on the morning of September 12, just five days after Queen Elizabeth's thirty-first birthday, that a special messenger delivered a letter embossed with the queen's own seal. Clad from head to toe in blue velvet, he stood in the parlor with his elaborately plumed cap on the table beside him. After calling out my name, the messenger, whose black hair was as well-curled as the trio of white ostrich-feather plumes on his cap, handed me the letter.

I looked to Lady Strange, and was just about to ask her to read it, when the messenger said, "Her Highness specifically requested that no one but you read the letter."

With my heart pounding with such rigor I had trouble

hearing my own words, I read aloud the queen's invitation to come to Whitehall Palace.

Immediately.

"Mercy," Bess cried, wiping her face in her apron.

"Merciful news, Bess," Lady Strange said, laying a cool hand on my shoulder.

My stomach lurched, for at last I had received my summons. The messenger was to take me to Whitehall this day for an overnight stay.

Of course, Perseus would come with me. Unfortunately, my beloved Jack would have to stay behind. I could not possibly bring two huge dogs with me to Queen Elizabeth's palace. Besides, I did not know how Jack—who hid from spiders—would fare, were he to be confronted with danger.

Back in my room, I knelt on the floor beside Jack, unsure of how to say good-bye to him. He alone had slept beside me in my narrow bed at the duchess's drafty house. He alone had followed me down its dim passageways, his clicking toenails reassuring me that I was not completely an orphan.

Somehow, in all my years of training, I had never considered that the time would come when he and I would have to part. "I'm not abandoning you, old friend," I said as I stroked his rough fur and gazed into his calm eyes. "Once the visit is over, I'll return," I said, imprinting his good dog scent onto my memory. "Then you and I will spend hours bounding across the lawn and exploring the hillside."

I did not add, "and our life will go on as it always has," for I could not possibly know what the future would bring.

As if he understood my reluctance to go, Jack licked my hand and laid his head along my shoulder.

Minutes later, Lady Strange entered. I closed my eyes and breathed in her fortifying, forest scent so that I could recall it—and her—once we were apart. Afterwards I stood and listened as she reminded me of court etiquette, then urged me to help her pack my things. "Remember to always kneel in the queen's presence and do not lift your gaze until she gives you permission."

Although we had been over many of these things before, the proper fork, the proper spoon, what not to wear to a ball, as well as various hierarchical forms of address—all these freed me from contemplating my imminent separation from Jack, and from my gardian, not to mention all that awaited me at the queen's palace.

In the midst of these goings-on, Lady Strange produced a small leather box, which she handed to me. "Open it," she said.

Inside I found a shining amethyst, a perfect circle, mounted on a gold pin. I lifted the amethyst out of the box and cradled its cool weight in my palm. "It's exquisite."

"Yes. And what is the chief virtue of the amethyst?"

"Cheerfulness."

"Very good." Lady Strange's eyes glowed. "What else is the amethyst valued for?"

I closed my eyes and thought hard. Though not as rare as sapphires, amethysts were extremely hard to find in England. "I'm sorry," I said at last. "The rarer virtue escapes me."

"Really, Mary, I find this difficult to believe, especially given your own skepticism regarding romantic love."

Clutching the brooch to my breast, I said, "It protects the wearer against such intoxication."

"Precisely." Lady Strange pressed the tips of her fingers together. "This particular amethyst belonged to your mother. I have been saving it for you since you came into my care."

My lips trembled, and I clutched the brooch more tightly. *My mother.* "But why didn't the amethyst protect my mother against my father?" I stammered. "And how did this brooch manage to escape the seizure of her belongings?"

Lady Strange flashed me a cryptic smile and said, "The amethyst is a powerful amulet against intoxication in love. Yet no gem can ensure invulnerability. The behavior of Henry the Eighth, who favored diamonds, and of Queen Mary, who favored rubies, should be proof enough of that."

"As always, you're right," I said, reminded of the teaching that the wearer of diamonds was supposed to be chaste, devoted, and brave. One who favored rubies should merit praise, as did the ruby's first wearer, a young woman who saved a stork from certain death. After rescuing and healing the creature, the woman set it free, only to have the bird return with the gift of a ruby as clear as its own red eye.

"As for the second part of your question—how the brooch escaped confiscation—after your father's arrest the duchess somehow made sure to protect the gem. On the day I came to claim you, I found it among her things."

"Shall I pin it on at once?" I asked. Both my hands shook, for until that moment I had never seen any of my mother's jewelry. The gift seemed a direct link to the woman I should have known intimately.

"It's not safe to wear the brooch while you travel," Lady

Strange said. "But be sure to pin it on securely when you dine with the queen in the evening."

"I will."

"And remember, do not let the amethyst fall into someone else's hands. It's a perfect specimen and therefore quite powerful. In fact, it's possible the amethyst could be used against you."

"I won't," I promised, kissing Lady Strange, then concealing the box within the inner compartment of my traveling bag.

Having finished packing, we returned downstairs where Perseus, the messenger, and the coachman waited. Descending the staircase, I seemed to move in slow motion, aware of every footstep, every smell, every sound. I took note of my guardian's elegant posture as she glided down the staircase just a few steps ahead of me: her head held high, her carriage erect. I memorized the piney smell of the hall and the way the sun slanted through the tall windows. Even the little spider's web in the corner above (which we never disturbed despite Bess's protests) became doubly precious. No matter if the trip were only for two days, the wheels of destiny had been set in motion. My old life was ending, and a new life was about to begin.

Jack had followed me to the foot of the stairs, closely

observing every sign of my departure. "I'll be back soon, old friend," I whispered, then pressed my lips to his warm, furry brow.

When it came time for me to say good-bye to Lady Strange, I found that I could not do it. Quite literally, my mouth would not form the words.

My guardian slipped her arms around my shoulders and enfolded me in a close embrace. "Remember that I love you, and remember who you are," she said, reminding me with this statement, of the final words spoken by her father all those many years ago.

CHAPTER SEVEN

FROM LADY STRANGE I HAD GLEANED SOME knowledge of Whitehall, the queen's favorite palace, which she had inherited along with at least sixty others upon her accession to the throne. Unfortunately many of her palaces had been allowed to fall into ruin by previous rulers and now proved too costly to restore. Others she leased or lent to men who could afford to maintain them. Still others held bad associations, and though she kept them up, she stayed away.

Whitehall was different.

More than any other palace, Whitehall was connected with Elizabeth's parents' courtship. During the final unhappy years of his marriage to Catherine of Aragon, Henry VIII wooed Anne Boleyn in Whitehall's many gardens and later in its many splendid bedrooms.

"All this has been done to please the Lady," one of Henry VIII's councilors wrote of Whitehall's establishment in Anne Boleyn's honor. "The Lady Anne likes it best at Whitehall," the same councilor wrote. "Despite its great size, at Whitehall there is no room for the queen."

During the honeymoon period of their relationship, Henry VIII married the already pregnant Anne in the palace's most private chapel. It is quite likely that Queen Elizabeth had been conceived in one of its many lavish bedrooms.

Yet the palace was no architectural gem. In fact, one foreigner who saw it actually called the place "a shambles." Nevertheless, the queen loved Whitehall. The athletic Elizabeth loved the outdoors, and Whitehall contained a tilting arena for tournaments, great stables, and three tennis courts. There were also man-made pools filled with exotic fish, not to mention phenomenal gardens that bloomed all through the year; and orchards devoted to the apple, the peach, and the pear. Beyond extended forests in which the fearless young queen liked to hunt.

Whitehall was situated some twenty furloughs from Moonsway. Although the distance was not great, England's roads remained extremely poor, and so we traveled slowly, traversing meadows, farms, and orchards. In the fields, corn and wheat ripened. In the orchards, peaches and plums grew heavy on the branch.

As we passed, one of the women working in the fields approached the carriage, and the driver immediately stopped for her.

When he did, the woman pressed a basket of the most fragrant peaches into my hands. "For the journey," she said.

"Let me at least pay you for them," I said, drinking in their sweet scent and noticing that they were so fresh the fuzzy bloom still crested the fruit.

The woman shook her head, then gazed deep into my eyes as if she knew where I was going and why. "Fare you well, miss," she said at last. "The peaches are a gift."

"Thank you," I replied, comforted by the early dawn shade of her aura. Dawn: the sign of a new day. Yet another sign that my own calling had begun.

When we crossed the River Thames, a group of small boys sat fishing beside a pool. No sooner had they spotted the carriage emblazoned with the royal seal than they rushed to the road to glimpse the face within.

"Is it the queen passing?" one of the children cried.

I held out my hand and waved. After all, what harm could there be in letting them believe they had glimpsed the queen? When they grew older, they might look back on this moment with a fondness that extended to their queen and therefore blessed her reign.

As the coach progressed through England's countryside, the still, green landscape seemed to unfold around me like my own future. The meadows just beginning to bloom with heather and chamomile became the training I would soon put into use. The wide, open sky became the limitless expanses of my own mind. And the occasional river or pond recollected the life-giving nature of white magic. As I watched the rooks dip and rise in the crisp air, my body seemed to soar.

At last, after more than five hours of traveling, we arrived at Whitehall. Although Lady Strange had told me that Whitehall was the largest palace in all of Europe, now that I had come face-to-face with the massive network of buildings and stables extending deep into the twenty-three acres of surrounding land, the palace proved greater than even I imagined.

"How many rooms lie within?" I asked the driver.

"At least two thousand, m'lady," came the gruff but polite reply.

I had studied the queen's palaces, but now my learning seemed abstract, and it frightened me more than a little to think of myself navigating the long corridors with their endless rooms and secrets. Who knew what I would face here?

Lady Strange's words floated back to me. *Remember who you are.*

At the main entrance, a fleet of well-dressed servants, each one clad in a different shade of velvet, was already waiting. I stepped out of the carriage, and the servants bowed, one by one by one.

"I have orders to take you to the queen directly," one of the servants said.

I followed him up the stairs and into the palace, trying hard to keep up with his rapid pace. Study of Elizabeth's habits told me that in each of her palaces the queen laid out her personal apartments in exactly the same way, for Elizabeth was fond of order and regularity.

The queen's apartments were like a series of Chinese boxes, each room more private than the next. There was the great hall, then the guard chamber, presence chamber, and privy chamber. Beyond this last room lay the queen's own personal bed, sitting, and dining rooms.

"To which chamber are you taking me?" I asked the servant.

"To the privy chamber, m'lady."

My heart beat fast. To be admitted to the privy chamber was very rare. I understood that I was being honored indeed.

The deeper into the palace we traveled, the more lavish the setting became. Here, Whitehall's walls shone with gold and silver. There were exquisite oriel windows, wondrous murals, and the most beautiful tapestries garnished with mother-of-pearl and precious stones. Even the draperies were of the most exquisite Indian painted silk. When I looked up, I found myself dazzled by the ornate ceilings showing flowers and leaves carved from mahogany. All around me, orange tiger lilies and white narcissus bloomed in high crystal vases or silver pitchers, so that as I passed from one room to the next, I inhaled their ambrosial fragrances.

We progressed through one room with a beautiful virginals, and I paused to touch the instrument's delicate strings, reminded of my mother who, Lady Strange had told me, had delighted in music all her life. Once my mother, too, walked through these corridors. Yet she did not navigate these rooms as a visitor. No. She stepped through the palace as queen, mistress of all she surveyed.

I carried myself a little taller after that.

From time to time, we encountered groups of the queen's councilors engaged in heated debate about commerce and the cost of new ships, topics with which I had little familiarity. Reassuringly, there was also a small group busy discussing the power of reading the stars, a topic I knew well.

While the councilors roamed the palace rooms deep in politic conversation, well-born women swished through the halls, their long silk or satin skirts in a rainbow of colors sashaying after them. They, too, spoke of the day's events. Yet their conversation seemed more subdued; and from what I overheard, it was peppered with gossip of a more private and delicate nature.

Over and over again, a single phrase lilted through me. *This was once my mother's world.*

At last we reached the privy chamber, and my eyes lit on the famous portrait of Henry VIII and his descendents by the painter Hans Holbein. The immense painting stretched the length of a palace wall.

After the birth of his only son, Edward, Henry VIII had the portrait commissioned. The only figures portrayed here are the king, his parents, and his third wife, Jane Seymour, who died just after giving birth to the little prince Henry so craved. The portrait made clear the fact that in Henry's diseased court, a woman was only valued for her ability to produce a male heir, which was why Jane Seymour—who was already long dead by the time Holbein painted it—was the only woman, other than Henry's mother, pictured. As for Mary and Elizabeth, princesses in their own right, neither of the king's daughters figures anywhere on the huge canvas.

I gazed at the portrait of the king and his dead queen heaped with jewels (Henry even wore a bejeweled dagger with a mother-of-pearl handle at his waist), forcefully reminded of the violent abuses of Henry's reign. Not only had he violated the virtues of the gems, but he was selfish and audacious enough to flaunt the portrait before his daughters, a constant reminder of the inferiority of their sex.

It rather amazed me to think that Elizabeth had kept the portrait, for it emphasized her father's perverse certainty that she would be written out of the lineage of England's rulers. How unhappy her childhood must have been, despite the presence of my mother in her life. How heartsick and how desperate she must have felt at times, knowing her father had convicted her mother of adultery, then sentenced her to death.

As Lady Strange had told me long ago, the real reason for Anne Boleyn's death was that she had not borne Henry a son. After Elizabeth's birth she miscarried two times, her losses most certainly brought on by overwhelming fear and pressure. During the days that preceded Anne Boleyn's execution, her terrifying, hysterical laughter reverberated up from the Tower dungeon.

"I need a male heir to ensure the Tudor lineage," Henry fumed. "What good are daughters except as magnets for wooing wealthy foreign powers?"

And yet Henry was wrong.

In the end, this daughter, England's solitary queen, did inherit England's rule.

"Although I may not be a lioness, I am a lion's cub and inherit many of his qualities," Queen Elizabeth was fond of saying.

I remembered the words on the trunk of that ancient tree: *School her well in the white magician's wisdom so that she may go forth into the world and fulfill her calling when the virgin queen ascends the throne.*

Lost in thoughts about the painting, the tree, and all that these things signified, I had only just recovered myself when another elegantly dressed footman stepped forward.

"Good day, m'lady," he said, bowing.

"Good day."

Spying Perseus, he said, "I will have to obtain the queen's permission for your dog to come inside."

Butterflies swooped through my belly. *She must allow Perseus to accompany me into her presence.*

"Well?" I asked nervously, once the footman returned.

"You may both come in."

Perseus's presence beside me bolstered my strength, and I stepped inside, keeping my gaze lowered as I approached the queen, who sat on a high chair upholstered in garnet velvet at the far end of the room. Although the distance between us amounted to only thirty feet, it seemed to take forever for me to reach her, but at last there I was, bowing deeply, then waiting for her to give me some sign.

"Look up, Mary," she said, her voice as sonorous as a well-tuned violin.

I did. The queen graced me with a slight bow of the head. In her reddish-gold hair, which she now wore in an elaborately coiffed arrangement, shone large white pearls. The queen's gown was of pale yellow satin, and her feet were clad in cloth-of-silver slippers. Around her neck she wore several more strands of pearls.

Although still lovely, the queen had aged a good deal since the last time I had seen her. I could not expect anything less from a woman who was the sole ruler of England, a country that had recently been divided along religious lines; a country striving to be at the forefront of exploration, trade, and the arts. Nevertheless, I was reassured by the radiant purple aura enfolding her. As I had hoped and believed, her fair-mindedness as a ruler had not changed. She heeded the virtues of her preferred gem.

"I trust you are happily returned to England," she continued.

Elizabeth extended her hand, and I kissed it, all the while admiring the long, tapered fingers for which she was so well-known.

Her gaze traveled to Perseus. "Who is the distinguished companion at your side?"

"My dog, Perseus, Your Majesty."

"A fair-eyed dog named for the slayer of gorgons." The queen's expression momentarily turned more playful, and she ran her fingers along the length of her longest rope of pearls. "I approve of such a name."

I smiled. The queen returned my smile.

In a less formal voice, she said, "You are probably wondering why I brought you here."

"I am, Your Majesty," I replied, being sure to speak clearly.

"You are now sixteen," she said, and her eyes glinted with some feeling I could not quite register. "You have reached the peak of young womanhood. It is time that I begin to play a part in your future."

I startled a little at the queen's precise knowledge of my age. Despite her necessary ignorance of my identity as a white magician, was it possible that in some way she knew that it was in her best interest to search for me now? After all, Elizabeth was now thirty-one, the same age as my mother when she married Henry VIII and took her place as Elizabeth's stepmother.

"I have been mindful of your birthday since the day you were born," the queen continued. "I would be a hard-hearted woman indeed, were I not to remember a child whose middle name is my own. Your mother loved me like her own daughter at a time when I was both motherless and unfavored.

"Why, one of the first actions she undertook as queen was to write to me and invite me to visit her at court. It's hard to express how much that invitation meant at a time when I had not been welcomed into my father's presence for more than a year. How could I possibly help but think favorably of Katherine Parr's only child."

"Thank you," I said, bowing deeply. "Such kindness goes straight to my heart. My guardian, Lady Strange, has told me of your closeness."

"Ah yes, Lady Strange." The queen's pallor intensified. "There was some trouble with her family here at court when I was but a small child."

Afraid the queen would eventually recollect the monstrous history of my guardian's family, and simultaneously famished for knowledge about her relationship to my mother, I took a great liberty—I interrupted. "Unfortunately, Lady Strange did not know my mother very well, which is why I would be so grateful and honored if Your Majesty would tell me more about her."

The queen's face lost its abstracted look, and her features gentled. "Truthfully, Mary, I would like nothing better, for just as your mother loved me like a daughter, so I obeyed and loved her almost as if she were the one who had given me life." A slight crease slipped across the queen's brow, and my own eyes fell on the bejeweled *AB* pinned to her bodice: Anne Boleyn.

"Surely, you know I lost my own mother just before my third birthday," Elizabeth said gently.

"Yes," I replied, returned to the knowledge that motherlessness was something my queen and I had in common.

"Until Katherine Parr entered my life, I was lonely and all too often exiled from the favors of my father," Elizabeth continued, speaking so rhythmically it felt as if she were tilting time's hourglass upside down in her mind. "How I rejoiced when your mother told the bishop marriage to my father was her wish. I rejoiced, for in your mother I knew at once I had found, not only a benevolent stepmother, but a friend.

"Not once did your mother ever prove herself anything but virtuous and full of good intentions. I was ten years old when she invited me to court. On the day of my arrival, she complimented me on my skill at languages, then took upon herself the duty of supervising my education."

Two perfect tears pearled at the corners of Elizabeth's eyes, then slipped down her cheeks, and I understood why pearls were associated with the tears of the heavens, and why one who wears pearls must try very hard to be pure and noble and full of understanding; for at that moment Elizabeth gazed at me with such empathy and compassion I knew she, too, recognized the similarity between her story and my own.

Even if Elizabeth and my father had once been attracted to each other, I had absolutely no doubt now that he alone had been to blame. My queen had been an isolated girl desperate for a father's love. My father had tried to take advantage of that loneliness at both Elizabeth's and my mother's expense.

"How proud your mother would have been were she alive to see you now," Elizabeth continued. "You are as lovely and as intelligent-looking as she was. In your case, as in hers, I cannot believe reality belies appearances."

"Thank you." Again I bowed deeply, for Queen Elizabeth was paying me a profound compliment.

"The honor, in this case, is mine, Mary, for you are the very print of your mother, whom I consider to be one of the few gifts of my early life, as well as a model for just authority." Elizabeth paused, the significance of all that she said sinking deep into me. "My own model of queen-ship began with your mother's example."

Reminded of the woman who had given me the peaches on my way to Whitehall—*A gift from one who will never forget your mother's kindness*—it was now my turn to pearl tears.

The queen stood and came toward me, moving so gracefully I barely detected her footsteps. She touched my arm. "I hoped my words would give you pleasure."

"They do give me pleasure, Your Majesty," I explained,

as Elizabeth herself wiped the tears from my eyes. "I am only a little weary from traveling, and this is my first time away from my guardian. I am more sensitive, I suppose, and then to hear you speak of my mother with such warmth . . ."

"I understand," she said gently. "Still, I would like this visit to be a joyous occasion."

"As would I," I said, curtseying.

She placed a hand upon my shoulder. "Here is my idea. Shortly, I will have to attend to some matters of the state. I will therefore call my ladies-in-waiting, and you will take your evening meal with them. Afterward you will have a good, long rest. In the morning, once you feel renewed, I will show you some things that I have kept over the years, all of them invested with your mother's presence. I will share my dearest memories of your mother with you. Does this please you?"

"Very much, Your Majesty."

Elizabeth signaled to the footman, and three ladies stepped silently but swiftly into the room, the only sound, the rustle of their heavy gowns.

Unlike the queen, these women were clad in simply cut gowns of black, white, and pale green. They wore almost no jewelry, with the exception of a slender strand of pearls or a gold cross on a long velvet cord. Each of the women bowed. They introduced themselves as Lady Mary Hastings, Lady Frances Howard, and Lady Alice Cavendish.

"These are the youngest of my ladies-in-waiting," the queen told me. "I am therefore certain you will find you have plenty in common with them. I say *youngest*"—here her gaze held my own—"but I do not mean least mature, for in one of these ladies I have a budding and brilliant scholar. Lady Alice Cavendish is as levelheaded as my most revered and aged councilor."

Lady Alice Cavendish, whose alert green eyes and high forehead seemed proof of her intelligence, beamed at such praise, her spectacles fogging a little.

"Lady Mary Hastings is a woman most experienced in matrimony," the queen said, and here her hazel gold eyes darkened a little. "Dear Lady Frances Howard, a very close kinswoman, is as innocent as a rose that has not yet opened."

Despite the high compliment, the swan-necked, golden-haired Lady Frances lowered her eyes and sniffled. Meanwhile, Lady Mary Hastings preened at the queen's words even though they were not entirely praiseworthy, especially coming from a virgin queen.

"Ladies," the queen said, her voice and her manner becoming very grand, "I present Lady Mary Seymour, daughter of my father's last wife, the queen dowager Katherine Parr."

With graceful bearing, each woman inclined her head in my direction and said what an honor it was to meet me.

Of the three, I found myself most drawn to Lady Alice Cavendish because her aura radiated an amber glow. (Amber is close to fawn, trustworthy and upright Bess's color.)

Lady Mary Hastings's aura was slightly orange, however, and this gave me pause, for possessors of the orange tend to be self-important, and although energetic, they tend to tax other people's energy. Yet orange is a harmless enough color. In Lady Mary Hastings, who plucked her eyebrows into a painfully fashionable, thin line, and clearly used cosmetics to whiten her olive complexion, I sensed artificiality and a superfluous attention to surfaces.

Only the milky-skinned Frances Howard's faintly rose aura was tinted by a melancholy blue darker than her blue-gray eyes. This concerned me, for such a combination suggested a person of a romantic nature who was also very sad.

"For the remainder of today, I entrust Mary's care to

you," the queen continued. "See that she has a nourishing meal, and be sure her room has the finest sheets on the bed and the most comfortable pillows. Her mother was among the people dearest to me, and it is my wish that she be treated with the highest honor."

"Yes, Your Majesty," the ladies replied in unison.

Once more, Elizabeth gave me her hand to kiss. Then, with a swish of her elegant gown, she retreated from the room, each one of us bowing deeply as she passed.

CHAPTER EIGHT

W ITH PERSEUS AT MY SIDE, I FOLLOWED THE
queen's ladies-in-waiting to the Hyacinth Room, so
named because of its deep blue furnishings and floors.
Here, even the ceiling had been painted the sultry blue
of that flower, and a trio of servants outfitted in
hyacinth uniforms brought an assortment of savory
and sweet dishes for our evening meal.

Given the high expectations placed on a lady-in-
waiting, I knew I would not see the real expressions of
these women in Elizabeth's presence, where the ladies
had to speak charmingly and with great wit.
Emissaries as well as companions, they were the
smaller planets around her shining sun.

I understood the delicate and necessarily politic

position of a lady-in-waiting, for my own maternal grand-mother had been lady-in-waiting to Henry VIII's first wife, Catherine of Aragon. My mother had been named for the tempestuous monarch's first queen, a Spanish princess who had sailed the ocean to become the royal bride of Henry VIII's older brother, Arthur. It was Arthur's death that brought his younger brother, then a mere "Prince Harry," to the throne. Had it not been for the loss of Arthur, supposedly a man noble in spirit, who knows how differently history might have unfolded.

In the Hyacinth Room, Mary Hastings loosened her stomacher. Alice Cavendish cleaned her spectacles, then removed a small book from the cord around her waist, opened it, and began to read. These were not the manners I expected from the queen's ladies, even in private.

Yet the person whose behavior struck me the most forcefully was Frances Howard of the rose-blue aura. Before the meal was served, Frances began to weep, her tears dropping, one by one, onto her plate. It was clear that this was nothing unusual, for neither Mary Hastings nor Alice Cavendish took any notice of her situation.

Being so new, I did not know what to say, so I just sat stiffly in my chair and tried to avoid staring.

If Frances proved herself to be silent and miserable, the

buxom, slope-shouldered Lady Mary Hastings was her antipode. In between bites, this chatterbox rambled on about her family's properties, the horses she'd had a distant but very important relative bring over from Spain, and her husbands.

"I wed my first husband, Lord Vernon, when I was fifteen. My parents thought me a bit young to marry, but Lord Vernon was an excellent match, for he served the queen when she first came to power. Overwork killed him," she continued, nibbling a cooked carrot as she spoke. "I promised myself that I would not allow my parents to marry me off a second time to a member of the queen's cabinet. My second husband, Lord Hastings, whom I married the day after I turned eighteen, served on no councils. A man of leisure, he spent his days hunting and riding. Still, even with a non-politic husband I fared no better," she went on, spearing an asparagus. "Within a fortnight of our marriage, Lord Hastings died in his sleep—the doctor's diagnosis: extreme and somewhat unaccountable fatigue. Last month marked my nineteenth birthday. Who would have thought I'd already be twice widowed?"

In the middle of this unsavory monologue, Frances Howard burst into sobs.

I turned to comfort her, but Alice looked up from her book and motioned for me to leave Frances alone. From across the table Alice mouthed the word "Later."

I confess that I was eager to escape from Mary Hastings's tiresome travail. Yet I was equally eager to understand the source of Frances's misery. So as soon as the servants poured our final glass of wine, and each of us emptied it, I followed Alice to her rooms.

"Although, at sixteen, Frances is the youngest of the queen's ladies, poor Frances is also the one who happens to be in the deepest of trouble," Alice told me. "Unfortunately, I see no remedy."

"What could possibly be so oppressive?" I asked, thinking of the queen's nonpareil praise.

Alice's gaze narrowed. "I am certain Frances is at least two months gone with child."

A cold shudder coursed through me. "Has she confided in you?"

"Certainly not. Such a thing—well, it would be impossible to speak of. My father's fourth wife gave birth to three children while I was still at home. I am an expert at recognizing pregnancy's telltale signs: crying spells, flushed cheeks, morning sickness, not to mention strange appetites." Alice's expression was completely in earnest when she pressed my arm and said, "I have seen Frances eat a whole plate of herrings at one sitting."

"If Frances is pregnant," I said, "then she is at great risk, is she not?"

Alice's face grew very grave. "The greatest. The birth of this child will bring her only misfortune, given how strict the queen is about each lady's conduct. No kissing, no love letters, no romantic entanglements of any kind while on duty, unless of course the queen has given her explicit permission. The queen expects those of us who are not already widowed, like Mary Hastings, to rejoice in our virginity, as she rejoices in her own. Even women experienced in the intimacies of marriage are expected to be discreet and absolutely chaste, although with Mary Hastings, Her Majesty has gotten more than even she bargained for. I fear that Mary Hastings might wind up in the Tower before she's through."

"You see," Alice continued, speaking more softly now, "despite the queen's desires that we conduct ourselves like angelic virgins, nearly every lady-in-waiting is here to make a brilliant marriage."

"Is that your purpose for being here?" I asked.

Alice frowned. "Not an easy question to answer. Last May when I turned seventeen, my parents paid the queen three thousand pounds to gain me admittance to her inner circle. They'd like me to wed before my next birthday. The trouble is, finding me a suitor will not be so easy. I'm no rosy-cheeked beauty and my dowry is nothing to speak of." She grinned, as if each of these things was a blessing in disguise. "Besides, I am so nearsighted I can barely see a foot in front of me without my glasses."

Drawn to Alice's openness, not to mention her warm amber aura, I leaned closer. "Why are you here then?"

"For the education. Never in my life will I have such an opportunity. As you must know, for I have been educated just enough to appreciate that you are Katherine Parr's daughter, Her Majesty is a paragon of the new Humanist learning, and she expects her ladies-in-waiting to be knowledgeable as well. The Queen can read and speak Latin, French, Greek, Spanish, Italian, and Welsh. These days, even when she is immersed in matters of state, she devotes two hours every day to her studies."

"So you have learned a great deal since you've come to court?"

"Oh, yes." Alice's voice warmed with enthusiasm. "While at court I've read philosophy, literature, and history. I've even begun to study a little of the sciences. When I have finished with the natural sciences and the study of the oceans, I will turn to astronomy and possibly"—she grinned mischievously—"to the more occult." The green in Alice's eyes intensified. "My greatest fear is that some minor nobleman will take a liking to me and propose. Then I'm done for."

"I see." I realized how far we had strayed from our original conversation. Simultaneously, I understood what a great deal Alice and I had in common. Even if Alice wasn't trained in white magic, she was predisposed toward looking at the world through the same lens as I.

Alice blushed. "I'm sorry. I haven't finished telling you about Frances Howard, have I?"

I shook my head.

Alice crimsoned. Then, without saying another word, she went to the door and checked the hall. "The palace is all ears, and you never know where you might find a spy pressed against a keyhole."

Perseus seemed to stiffen at the word *spy*.

Assured that no one was listening, Alice returned to my side. "I suspect the man who seduced Frances to be your late father's own nephew, Edmund Seymour, the late Duke of Somerset's son."

I took great care not to show any emotion. Though his name registered, I knew very little about Edmund

Seymour, son of the late Lord Protector under the boy king Edward, and a courtier who had risen greatly during Elizabeth's reign.

"Why do you suspect him?" I asked.

Alice fiddled with the strand of pearls at her throat, and I noticed a single bead of coral embroidered into the chain. "Because I know him to be dangerous and ambitious."

"Isn't that a commonplace here at court?"

"Yes, of course. There is always too much gossiping, backbiting, and vying for position. Still, my dear Mary, there are degrees. Edmund Seymour is one of the shrewdest, and this trebles his threat. There have been many times when I caught the great Seymour watching Frances."

I moved very close. "Is it possible that he's in love with her?"

Alice scowled. "I do not believe such a man capable of love. In truth, I suspect him of much more sinister motives."

"Please," I said, eager to understand. "Tell me what you suspect."

Alice narrowed her eyes. "It's a diseased picture I will show you, Mary."

Reminded of my calling, I took a deep breath and said, "I'm prepared for it."

"Well then, I think he's trying to ruin Frances so she won't be able to make a successful marriage," Alice said, her voice as hard and cold as ice.

"But why?"

"Because the queen likes Frances," Alice said sharply. "It is therefore fair to assume that she will help Frances marry a man who will rise at court. That man will be Edmund Seymour's competition. At least, a man like Seymour would see the relationship in such a way. By preventing Frances from making a legitimate marriage, he is destroying the competition before it even arrives on the scene."

"What if he gets caught?"

Alice coughed a little, then said, "Edmund Seymour is not a man to allow himself to be ensnared."

Beside me Perseus's body tensed.

"What is Frances going to do?" I asked.

"What can she possibly do? In the presence of the queen she manages to play at cheerfulness, though it's clear to anyone who looks closely her smiles are all make-believe. As you saw for yourself, when she's among the other ladies-in-waiting, poor Frances weeps. I'm afraid it's just a matter of time until the queen discovers the truth and doles out the punishment."

"And if she confesses?"

"She might have the queen's forgiveness, but she'll still be ruined," Alice explained. "Surely you know that a deflowered virgin, especially a pregnant one, is absolutely worthless in the politic game of marriage."

CHAPTER NINE

FOLLOWING THIS GRIM CONVERSATION, ALICE escorted me to a purple-and-cream-colored bedroom not far from her own. The room had high ceilings and long windows overlooking yet another spectacular garden abloom with English roses. Below, the winding walkways were lined with tall shrubberies and decorated with pink pebbles. "Welcome to the Heliotrope Room," Alice said, then gestured for me to step inside.

With its tranquil colors and clean white furniture, the room was inviting. Yet the name troubled me more than a little, for I still recalled that story about the maiden who fainted dead away at the loss of Apollo. "Do you know why this room is named for the heliotrope flower?" I asked.

"Unofficially, this is said to be the room where Henry the Eighth first made love to Anne Boleyn."

I gripped the bedpost and tried not to visualize the hefty king with his second queen, who would die violently just four years later. So too, I tried not to think of why on earth I would be asked to sleep in this room. Perhaps, I considered, I could concoct a spell to bar all memory of such events from this place.

As if she had some inkling of my concerns, Alice dismissed them with an unexpected laugh. "Not to worry. There are many rooms where the king satisfied his passion for his second queen, and more than one holds the distinction of being the *first* room."

"And yet there's the story of the heliotrope . . ."

"That's just a legend," Alice interrupted, and suddenly I knew why Alice included a single bead of coral among her strand of pearls. By building walls with their bodies, walls that yield to the ocean's vigorous ebb and flow, coral can withstand the fiercest storm. The ideal wearer of coral is practical and pragmatic. Thus far, Alice seemed to adhere to coral's sturdy virtues.

Alice told me a little more about the palace routine, promised to help me in any way I required, then left me to my solitude. Under ordinary circumstances, I would have relaxed after such a journey and so much stimulation, but just then I knew rest would not come easily. Not even the prospect of furthering my friendship with Alice or the greater prospect of being reunited with the queen could raise my spirits, so preoccupied was I with Frances Howard's dismal situation.

Inevitably, Frances's story reminded me of how dangerous it was to be a woman and how appropriate it was that the room I now occupied was named for yet another unfortunate maiden. Unlike a man, who might flirt with love or passion and remain free of scandal, a woman had everything to lose—not only her good name and her standing in society, but her very life.

What might Frances's fate be, and was it possible I had been called to Whitehall in order to subvert a catastrophe? Was this why I now found myself in the Heliotrope Room?

I looked down at Perseus. "Well, my friend, you heard as much as I did. It looks as if Frances Howard is in great danger. Do you know of any way to help her?"

To my amazement, Perseus directed my attention to the falling sun beyond.

"Sunset," I said, beginning to realize that Perseus and I had found a way to communicate. "Why is that significant?"

Perseus just stared, as if he expected me to puzzle the meaning out on my own.

I thought for a moment. Tomorrow night there would be a crescent moon. My monthly cycle had ended five days before. Tomorrow night I would again be able to communicate with Cordelia.

But tomorrow afternoon I was supposed to return to Lady Strange's house. By then it would be too late to both speak with Cordelia and help Frances Howard, for I would be miles away from Whitehall. Still awed by the communication that had passed between us, I was about to ask Perseus more, when someone knocked.

Answer it, Perseus said, speaking directly to some part of my brain.

The knowledge that we were communicating, without making any sound, thrilled the very tips of my fingers.

"Come in," I called.

The same footman who had admitted me into Elizabeth's presence now stood in the doorway. Beside him stood Frances Howard.

"The queen asked me to deliver this message." Although Frances's eyes were red, she was no longer crying.

"Please," I said. "If you have a moment, won't you come in?"

"Very well." Without showing any real expression, Frances dismissed the footman and stepped inside.

"What is the queen's message?" I asked.

"The queen has called a meeting of the Star Chamber," Frances explained, sniffling a little. "She will be preoccupied with official business for the next three days."

My spirits sank. "So I am to go home tomorrow without seeing her again?"

"No, you are by no means dismissed," Frances said heavily. "I'm surprised you don't understand that you are an important visitor, and the queen has been looking forward to your visit for some time now. Because of her unexpected obligations, she's requested that you extend your visit over the next week. Her Majesty has dispatched a messenger to your guardian, to inform her of the fact that you will not return home until next Thursday, at the earliest."

"Gracious," I said, feeling the room begin to spin. "This is all happening very fast."

"The queen is all-powerful," Frances continued. "An extra week at Whitehall could turn into two weeks, maybe even three. It all depends upon Her Majesty's schedule and to some extent on her whim."

Frances fiddled with the sleeve of her gown. "Will

your guardian be surprised to learn of this change in plans?"

"No," I said, resolved to write Lady Strange a letter as soon as time allowed. "My guardian understands all matters of court life very well."

Taken together, the change of plans and Frances's arrival confirmed my suspicions. I had official business of my own here at Whitehall, and that business must involve not only the harmonies surrounding the queen, but those around Lady Frances Howard as well. The lives of these two women, like so much I had been trained to study in nature, must be connected.

Recalling Lady Strange's first words to me regarding the white magician's role—*to use knowledge and enchantment to improve the lives of the people entrusted to her care*—I made the bold move of slipping my arm through hers. "Frances," I said, "would you be so kind as to take a walk with me in the garden?"

She fixed her sorrowful blue-gray eyes on me and shrugged. "I have no other conditions on my time."

With this lukewarm acceptance, we set off. Little by little, as we strolled among the shrubbery, occasionally pausing to admire the end of the season's roses, Frances grew calm, and we became more comfortable with each other. We spoke of daily life at Whitehall, and Frances told me of her responsibilities, her likes and dislikes.

To our mutual pleasures, we discovered we both liked reading, dogs, the scent of tiger lilies, and the taste of warm vanilla pudding sprinkled with nutmeg. We both disliked drafty rooms, runny eggs, scratchy underclothes, cruelty to animals, and overbearing people. Yet the real turn came when she discovered that both of our grandmothers had served Henry VIII's mother, Elizabeth of York, a Plantagenet heiress and granddaughter of the legendary Edward IV.

With Elizabeth of York's name on the tips of our tongues, I could not help but laugh grimly at Henry VIII's fuss about male heirs, for it was *his mother* who had brought an air of legitimacy to his father's reign. The fact that she was of royal blood went a long way toward cloaking Henry VII, the first Tudor king, with the mantle of entitlement, even as he usurped England's throne.

We walked on.

"To think our grandmothers were at court together," she said, walking more closely beside me. "My grandmother was the dearest person in the world to me."

With this newfound bond between us, it did not take long for me to coax Frances's troubled history from her.

The picture that emerged was of a young woman who had been only six weeks at court, inexperienced with men and society; a woman who had been carefully watched by her parents and who suddenly found herself thrown into the seething den of ambitions, alliances, and animosities that was the queen's court.

"I'm not in love with him," Frances confessed, the blue in her aura soaring so that her pale skin seemed to take on this melancholy tinge. "None of the other ladies-in-waiting would believe me if I tried to explain the circumstances, but the truth is, I did not willingly enter into the affair."

"Please," I said. "Tell me, if you can, how your entanglement with Edmund Seymour began."

Frances's lovely but sad features turned even more sorrowful. "Some two and a half months ago, the queen consulted an astrologer. On the strength of his recommendation, she gave a masked ball, believing that the Dionysian elements of her court needed to be given an ampler reign."

Such a thing shocked me, for why would the careful queen allow the forces of Dionysian anarchy to have any playing ground at her highly ordered court?

"The queen was a bit bored." Frances plucked a rosebud, then crushed it between her fingertips. "The astrologer thought a ball, on the eve of Taurus's crossing over into Gemini's twins, would inspire creativity," Frances continued, the blue in her aura almost completely stifling the rose. "In some respects it did; though what was created proved more dangerous than good.

"That night every one of the guests came in a disguise. Although I haven't said as much to anyone—not since what happened—ever since I arrived at court, ever since I laid eyes on him, I have been in love with Anthony Dervish."

I startled. "With whom?"

"Anthony Dervish." She seemed to caress the name, and for a moment the rosiness of her aura broke free of the blue, and her cheeks resumed their natural color. "He is the younger son of Lord Winchester. We are exactly alike, you see," she said, squeezing my hand. "More than anything, both he and I would like to live quietly on one of his family's smaller and more secluded country estates, dedicating ourselves absolutely to dogs, horses, and children."

For a moment she seemed to forget that her current situation ruled out any chance of such a life, and I trembled for her.

As if she detected my fear, she said, "Although the queen forbids us from entering into engagements while we are employed as her ladies-in-waiting, Anthony and I did speak of marriage."

Reminded once more of the dangers of women falling in love, I said, "Did you go so far as to formally commit yourself to him?"

Frances's features hardened. "Not officially, though it was understood that we had reached an understanding with each other."

"So Edmund Seymour knew about your feelings for Anthony?"

"Most certainly. You must understand, Mary, Edmund Seymour's ears and eyes are everywhere. On the night of the ball, I was on the lookout for Anthony. He told me he planned to come dressed all in yellow, and would wear a lion's mask."

Beware of the man who boasts of being the lionheart.

"Did you find him?"

"I thought I had," Frances said, and her tears once more began to fall. "I found a man dressed all in yellow and wearing a lion's mask. I was sure he was Anthony, even when he refused to speak with me."

Although I could already picture what happened next,

I remained silent as Frances led me deeper into her story.

"After two glasses of wine—more than I've ever drunk before—I followed this man out of the palace and into the garden. I should have realized that it was not my Anthony, for he could not have stayed silent for so long." Tears slipped down her cheeks. "How could I have known that Lord Seymour intended to make my unhappiness his pastime?

"Besides, I was so happy to be with Anthony, so ready to believe in the possibility of our future, I did not stop to think about deception," she confessed. "So I followed my enemy deep into the garden, trusting all the while that this was my Anthony, with whom I could feel absolutely safe."

"When did you discover your companion was not who he seemed?"

"After he kissed me." Frances's cheeks flushed a deep crimson. "Believing the man beside me to be Anthony, I kissed him back. Once I discovered the truth, it was too late." Frances lowered her eyes. "By that time he had already coaxed me to the ground. I wanted to cry out, and yet no sound found its way out. It was as if"—Frances stammered—"he used some enchantment to subdue my protest."

"Was this your only encounter with him?" I asked, convinced that it was Frances's love for another that made her vulnerable to Edmund Seymour. The words of the scholar Joan Lluís Vives, which I'd found squirreled away in a book on a dusty shelf in Lady Strange's room, echoed through my brain. *Romantic love confounds and blinds a woman of wit and reason so that she shall not see or know what is done.*

Frances lowered her head in shame. "It happened two more times. After that first time, you see, although my heart was not in it, I found myself going to him again. At least, my body did. My mind—my spirit—seemed faraway, as if a part of me were asleep."

Three was a powerful number. Three spoonfuls of treacle could cure melancholia. Three white rabbits brought fruitfulness to a house. Three citrine stones, properly arranged, could fill a gray day with sun. In Edmund Seymour's case, three must have been the number of seductions needed to bring Frances Howard with child.

Having confessed this much, Frances turned away.

"Please," I said, reminding her of the ties between our grandmothers, "I give you my word that you can trust me." I touched her hand. "Believe me, I want to help."

She turned to face me, her eyes brimming furious tears. "If you must know, he threatened to tell the queen I had willingly entered into the relationship. How could I dispute him? Edmund Seymour can be so charming when he wants to be. He has everyone fooled, even dear Anthony. Until that night in the garden, I genuinely admired him. That's what makes it all so ghastly."

"What is the source of his power?" I asked.

"His charm and his intelligence," Frances said without hesitation. "To the queen, he infuses courtly wordings into his phrases, lavishing her with praise and promising to do all he can to ensure Her Majesty's good reign, and she is deceived by him. Already the queen has given him valuable properties in the west country. Were I to try to defend myself, he would tell her that I offered myself to him, and he would be able to convince her of everything. Believe me, Mary, when I say I would be powerless against him."

"And the other ladies-in-waiting?"

"Because the queen is fond of me, some of the others view me as an obstacle to their own ambitions. A good number would like to marry Edmund." Frances's eyes bore into my own. "Most ambitious of all the queen's ladies is Vivienne Gascoigne."

A French lady-in-waiting. I knew not why, but the tips of my ears tingled at the name, and a picture of a white serpent rose before my eye. "Is Vivienne here now?"

Frances shook her head. "At present, she is on holiday with her family—they're always traveling to exotic places—but if you remain at Whitehall long enough, you're sure to make her acquaintance. What you need to understand, Mary, is that the women at court can be just as ambitious, and at times just as treacherous as the men."

"And Edmund Seymour?" I said at last. "He's left you alone since then?"

Frances bowed her head. "Yes."

Beside me, Perseus barked. I looked down at him and realized that he wanted to say or at least alert me to something. But what?

Again, Perseus barked.

Much to Frances Howard's exasperation, Perseus barked three times before he finally stopped.

"Is your dog in distress?" Frances asked, stroking Perseus's brow.

Instantly he quieted, as if my special friend had been affected by Frances's touch.

The number three? What, Perseus? What?

And then I knew. The number three—Edmund Seymour must know something about magic. Black magic.

"And now my story is finished, and so am I," Frances concluded, her head drooping on its long stem as her hand fell away from Perseus's brow. "For the time being, I shall continue my services to the queen, though I know it is only a matter of time before she discovers my condition and banishes or imprisons me." Tears continued to fall. "Either way I'm ruined."

"Isn't it possible for your family to help you?"

Frances laughed bitterly. "You are naïve, aren't you?" she said. "Don't you see? My parents forced me to come to court. They're ambitious, and their love for me is little more than desire for future advancement. I'm their beautiful daughter, and for this reason alone am I well-favored. In me, they see a chance to improve their circumstances. They'll never take me back in disgrace.

"If I had the courage I'd throw myself from the balcony and end things before the shame becomes public," Frances said, swaying a little. "In this state, I couldn't possibly face Anthony—"

"Don't speak that way," I said. "Perhaps you're mistaken in thinking the queen would not believe you if you told her the truth?"

"Whoever your guardian is, it's clear you have spent far too much time away from court to begin to enter into its complexities." Frances's words were as sharp as shards of glass. "Edmund Seymour is far too shrewd an enemy. What you don't seem to understand is this: I would never stand a chance against him. He would take the truth and twist it into a noose with which to hang me."

An image of Cordelia—her broken neck—flashed through my mind, and I shuddered at the perverse accuracy of Frances's metaphor.

"My own advice to you is this." The blue in Frances's aura glowered like a ripe bruise. "Leave Whitehall as soon as your seven days are up, and stay clear of this world, if you possibly can. You're no match for the Machiavellian forces at play here. If I could shift the hourglass, I would never have joined the retinue of the queen's ladies-in-waiting. How I would have preferred to live out my days as a farmer's wife or as a dairymaid. The life of the court is accursed. Mark my words: your presence here, like my own, will come to no good."

The moonlight found its way into my room, and I lay in the canopied bed searching for some way to help Frances. In the Canary Islands, I once saw a native witch doctor cast a spell on a woman who wanted to become pregnant. Although I never saw the woman again, about six months after we returned to England, a friend of Lady Strange's wrote to say that after more than a decade of barrenness, this same woman had been able to conceive and bear a healthy boy.

Is there a way to undo a pregnancy? I wondered, unsure of how the erasure of life would sit with my duties to help restore unities in a world currently out of joint.

Usually a child is a blessing.

Yet my birth had cost my mother her life.

And if an unmarried Lady Frances were to carry the child to term, her own life would be ruined, as would the life of her unborn child.

CHAPTER TEN

THE NEXT MORNING I ROSE EARLY. IN order to contact Cordelia, I had to put into effect the same ritual I had learned only one month ago.

I overrode the protests of my chambermaid and insisted on washing my white muslin underwear myself. Despite Alice Cavendish's raised eyebrows and the baffled looks of the other ladies-in-waiting, at luncheon I placed no meats or cheeses onto my plate, taking only vegetables and grains.

Yet there remained the matter of the herbs. Where was I going to find them?

I turned to Perseus, who motioned toward the windows overlooking the grounds.

 The queen's garden.

"Where are you going, Mary?" Frances called out, just as Perseus and I were about to set out along the least public of the paths that led to the garden.

Now that she had made me her confidante, Frances had decided to keep close to me.

Fortunately, Frances did not seem to find anything strange in my desire to pick a variety of herbs from the queen's stock. I suppose she was too preoccupied with her own unhappiness to worry much about other things, such as pillaging the end-of-season marjoram.

En route, we passed a youngish man with straw-colored hair, a too-sweet grin, and an aura like burnt sugar. The only odd things about his attire—he was costumed in an impeccable suit of brown velvet—were the many-colored splotches on his hands. "Does he have some sort of rare disease?" I whispered.

Motioning in his direction, Frances said, "You mean Henry Clifford?"

In a low voice I said, "I suppose so . . . but what is the cause of those strange marks on his hands?"

Frances laughed. "That's paint, Mary. Henry Clifford is one of the queen's favorite court painters."

Even Perseus seemed to snicker at my mistake.

I blushed and said nothing after that.

We walked on.

No sooner had we reached the garden than I heard a male voice call out, "Lady Frances!"

The slim figure who emerged from the shrubbery was in his early twenties. Tall and long-limbed, he had white-blond hair and the dreamy eyes of a happy child. Even his spring-green aura suggested innocence.

This must be Lord Winchester's son, Frances's beloved Anthony.

Although she took no pleasure in it, Frances made the introductions. The young man greeted me politely, but it was clear that both his attention and his concern were focused entirely on Frances, for his eyes almost never strayed from her face.

He loves her, I realized, and suddenly I knew what I needed to do. Despite my own mistrust of love, I needed to find a way to bring them together as husband and wife, and ensure that Elizabeth blessed their union.

Surely, Cordelia will be able to help me.

At precisely ten before two o'clock in the morning, I followed each step of the ritual. Lastly, I anointed myself with gold dust, then repeated the incantation nine times, as I had been originally instructed.

"Wise spirit of the other realm, come to me now, for I approach you with the purity of mountain water, and with all of the solemnity of winter. Wise spirit, I beg of thee, come."

Sure enough, after the ninth recitation, Cordelia's small face appeared, faintly at first, and then more clearly. We greeted each other, and I proceeded to tell her about all that had happened since our first meeting.

"You have done good work, Mary. In just two days you have learned a good deal about the first part of your mission."

"Edmund Seymour is the false lionheart, isn't he?" I asked.

Within her crystal orbit, Cordelia's eyes turned stormy, and she hissed her answer. *"Yes."*

Cordelia's fury alerted me to a possibility I had not considered. Was this evil person somehow connected with the sufferings in Cordelia's past?

As if she had heard the question, Cordelia said, "Remember, Mary, a person may be only a vessel in which a much older energy or spirit, whether good or evil, might find a dwelling place."

This statement frightened and intrigued me, but before

I had time to ponder it further, she asked me how I planned to aid Lady Frances.

I took a deep breath and said, "I must find a way to get Frances's marriage to Anthony Dervish sanctioned."

Cordelia's pale face brightened. "Very good. Do you know what you must do?"

"I must win the queen's approval, and I must ensure that Anthony will ask Frances to marry him, and she—accept."

"Yes." Cordelia rubbed her throat, and the burn marks seemed to glow.

For a long time, silence hung between us, causing me to wonder if Cordelia was thinking of a way to make such a thing possible.

"As you must already foresee, in taking these steps you will be alerting Edmund Seymour to your own power," Cordelia said at last. "It will not take him long to discover that someone acted against him. Soon he will identify you as his enemy, and you will have to conduct yourself with caution and absolute alertness."

"I understand."

Cordelia's grave face seemed to press more closely to the glass. "It's essential that you do, Mary, for Edmund Seymour is very dangerous and very powerful; and as you know, good does not always triumph over evil."

"I know this all too well." My eyes held Cordelia's. "Still, I am ready. Can you give me instructions for a potent and successful spell to help Frances?"

Cordelia proceeded to describe the steps and listed the spell's contents: a very young shoot from a tree with heart-shaped fruit, two whiskers of a cat, and an abandoned sparrow's nest. Then she said, "For the spell to work, you must understand the significance behind each object. You must complete each action faithfully, and you must complete the entire spell, incantation and all, before the end of the noon hour tomorrow, when Virgo, the goddess of relationships, is in ascendance. Be certain that you are standing on yielding ground, for it's difficult to predict the effect the spell will have on your body. Do you understand?"

No sooner had I spoken the word *Yes* than Cordelia began to fade.

"Wait," I cried. "Don't go yet. I have more questions."

But the image continued to wane.

"Remember," she spoke softly. "It is only a matter of time until the false lionheart knows who you are. Be on your guard. And never forget how dangerous and powerful he is."

Having spoken these most uncomforting words, Cordelia was gone, leaving Perseus and me to concoct the spell on our own.

For a good hour after meeting with Cordelia, maybe even two, I sat in the shadows of my room and contemplated all she had said.

Thanks to Lady Strange, I understood that the potency within Cordelia's spell derived from the cosmic conception of Heraclitus, one of the ancient philosophers. Heraclitus believed that nothing in nature is absolutely fixed. Put another way, all things can be made to change.

Acting on this principle, I was to do the following things in precisely this order:

First, take a very young shoot from a tree whose fruit resembles a human heart.

This was easy enough, for I knew that the fruit that resembled the heart was the apple. Although I would not transform the apple into a heart, the spell would draw upon the properties of the apple as a symbol of the human heart. It would induce in Anthony a love for Frances strong enough to compel him to issue a formal proposal of marriage. Simultaneously, it would induce a generosity of spirit in the queen strong enough to bring her consent, thereby overriding her rule about ladies-in-waiting not marrying while in her employ.

So too, the broken shoot would hearken back to Eve's eating of the apple and her taking on of knowledge. Only in this case, I would be "erasing" a kind of knowledge—the knowledge of Frances's pregnancy—from the minds of everyone concerned. At least, this is what I hoped would transpire.

Second, pluck two whiskers from a cat.

My main clue was that Cordelia did not specify a particular kind of cat. Therefore, I could assume that I was drawing upon the qualities in all cats, and in particular, those qualities related to the whiskers.

I turned to Perseus.

Cats are agile, he said, once again communicating with me in a language that did not require spoken words. *They have good balance.*

Agility and balance. This was a start, but still I did not have all the pieces. At least, not yet. I was righting the balance of things by fixing Frances's situation because Anthony truly loved her and she him.

A fine beginning, but you're not all the way there, Perseus said.

I decided to try again. Not only would I be righting the

balance, but I would have to act with care and agility, as if I were two people, or at least one person with a pair of eyes in the back of her head.

This is better, but you must think further.

A cat's whiskers. Source of that intrepid creature's grace. Pluck two whiskers, and the balance of the cat would be awry, at least temporarily. Of course. By making a love marriage, I would be tampering with the basis of the marriage system. Thankfully, very few people married for love. There could be consequences.

Voilà. Perseus bowed.

I contemplated the third component of the spell.

Place the shoot from the apple tree and the cat's whiskers in an abandoned sparrow's nest.

Finding a nest was not going to be easy, but it was possible on a property as large as Whitehall. Then I had to understand why I needed a nest.

The possibility of a new life: a new start?

At precisely two minutes before noon on the following day, I stood beneath a weeping willow tree, cradling the nest in my hands. Within lay the shoot of an apple tree and the whiskers of the cook's fat marmalade-colored cat.

I repeated the incantation seven times.

All of these things I managed to do despite the pouring rain. Within a few seconds, my hair, my gown, my entire person, were soaking wet.

After I finished, Perseus uttered a low groan.

I looked up, and in the distance, hidden within a grouping of trees, I saw a human face watching me through the branches. Who it was, or even of what sex, I did not have a chance to see, for in the next moment I lost consciousness and fell to the ground, instantly understanding why Cordelia had insisted that I recite the spell on yielding earth.

CHAPTER ELEVEN

Iₙ ᴛʜᴇ ᴅʀᴇᴀᴍs ᴛʜᴀᴛ ꜰᴏʟʟᴏᴡᴇᴅ ᴍʏ ꜰᴀʟʟ, ɪ
found myself in a wood of ebony shadow. Wherever
I turned, voices cried out, their shrieks penetrating
to the very marrow of my bones. Yet the voices did
not seem to belong to bodies. Instead, they stut-
tered through the branches of crippled trees, cutting
through me as if they would hiss me to my grave.
Little by little, I began to understand that the voices
that clung to my rib cage and clawed at my ears were
the chaotic cries of evil struggling to triumph over the
good energies I had cast into the world.

I fled, pursued by the voices and a pale, silent serpent that sported a precious, incredibly bright jewel in
 the very center of his head. No matter where I hid, the

stone's light exposed me, and I had to keep running, had to keep hiding, again and again, groping my way through the darkness, for the serpent possessed the only source of light. Meanwhile, the cacophonous voices continued to chatter their ominous news.

Let fear be a teacher, I told myself, resolved to fight them.

No sooner had I spoken, when a thin stream of sunlight poured through the trees, and each leaf and branch seemed to regain its luster. I managed to find my way out of the woods, and the voices lost their strength. Soon I reached a high cliff overlooking the sea, the only sound, the rush of water crashing against the rocks.

The voices ceased their pursuit, and for a moment I almost believed I heard one of those voices fall headlong into the water.

I regained consciousness only to find myself lying in bed in my grand room at Whitehall. To my relief, there at the foot of the bed was Perseus.

Welcome back, Mary, he said, his wise blue eyes focused on my own.

Alice Cavendish and Frances Howard were also in attendance, having curled themselves into chairs at my bedside. When they saw my eyes flutter, they rose and brought their faces closer to my own.

An old, stooped man with a benign peach-hued aura, who I took to be a doctor, also drew near.

"Good morning, young lady. I'm Dr. Browne. You've had a good, long rest," the old doctor said. "Is it possible for you to tell me what day it is?"

I shook my head, for in truth I had no idea.

"Monday morning, precisely eleven o'clock," Alice replied, her face a wide plate of concern.

I sat bolt upright. "Are you telling me I've been unconscious for three days?"

"That we are, my dear," the doctor said, coughing a little so that I smelled garlic on his breath. "Until this morning, your body burned with a low but steady fever. You've had the palace terribly worried."

Frances took my hand, sparkling with an airy lightness I had not seen in her before, the blue in her rosy aura having been subdued to lavender. "I'm so glad you're feeling better," she said, speaking with such happiness that all self-knowledge of her precarious situation seemed to have left her, including any trace of our last conversation.

Alice passed me a glass of water and licked her lips. "Frances has news of the highest order. Shall I inform Mary of your circumstances?" she asked Frances. "Or shall you?"

"Ladies, ladies," the doctor protested. "Perceive you not

that the Lady Mary is just recovered? I beg of you not to overwhelm her just yet."

"No," I insisted. "I feel well enough. Please, Frances." I leaned toward her, aware of the spinning sensation in my head. "Tell me your news."

Frances held out her left hand. On her ring finger twinkled a trio of perfectly cut rubies set in gold. Taken together, three stones of praise become an emblem of devotion.

"Frances!"

"That's right. I'm engaged to be married. Lord Winchester's son proposed to me last night in the garden. I was walking by myself among the roses when he called out to me. The next thing I knew, he was down on one knee asking me to be his wife." She squeezed my arm, and her blush deepened. "Oh, Mary, I am standing on the pinnacle of happiness, for the queen has given her permission. Most extraordinary of all is that Her Majesty did not punish me for entering into courtship while on duty."

Alice fixed her sharp eyes on my foggy ones. "In all honesty, I do not believe the queen would have consented so readily had it not been for your illness. I think the prospect of losing you kindled her good will."

"Must you present my betrothal in such a light?"

Frances spoke crossly; yet light danced behind her eyes.

The spell worked, I realized.

And neither Alice nor Frances have any memory of Edmund Seymour's actions, Perseus added, speaking to me in silence from his place at the foot of the bed. *Of course, the baby is still growing inside her.*

"The outcome of the matter is this," Alice said bluntly. "In ten days' time, Frances is going to relinquish her duties as one of the queen's ladies-in-waiting, for none of the ladies are allowed to have an allegiance higher than her loyalty to the queen."

"After I am married I will belong utterly to Anthony," Frances said, her voice dreamy.

Alice told me next that the queen wanted me to take Frances's place at court. "Will it please you to become a permanent member of Her Majesty's circle?"

"The opportunity pleases me," I replied, thinking entirely of my calling. As lady-in-waiting to the Queen of England, I would now live within the volatile heart of the court's intrigues and ambitions.

CHAPTER TWELVE

THE NEXT MORNING I LINGERED IN BED, relishing the success of my first spell and filling in the gaps in my knowledge.

What happened to me after I fainted? I asked Perseus.

You fell into a pile of moldering leaves. With more forethought, you would have worn a cloak over your thin gown.

But you fetched Alice immediately, I said, grateful to Perseus, whose swiftness ensured I did not catch cold.

Alice fetched two of the strongest men. Believe it or not, the portrait painter helped carry you to your rooms.

Henry Clifford? I asked, astonished.

The very one.

Perseus, I said, striking a much graver note. *There were some very odd elements in my dreams.*

141

Perseus raised his head and listened more carefully. *Go on.*

There was a serpent, and it was entirely white. The creature pursued me through the gloom. Whenever I thought I'd found a hiding place, the light in its forehead exposed me. The source of light was some sort of jewel.

Ah yes, Perseus said knowingly. *The Demonius of the Dead Sea.*

You know it, then?

Yes, though only in legend. Supposedly, in ancient days, there was a rare white serpent who possessed a sapphire with the power to cast out demons and cure all sorts of illnesses. The creature spent months healing the sick in the hopes of being accepted into human society, but as you know, human beings hold long-standing prejudices against snakes.

Goodness found itself misunderstood, I said.

Precisely.

So the serpent fell into the black arts and used its power for evil?

So the story goes. Perseus gazed at me thoughtfully. *Most intriguing that you would dream of the serpent now.*

What happened to the jewel? I asked. *Did the serpent keep possession of it?*

According to legend, some crusaders killed the serpent, plucked out the jewel, and brought it back to Europe. But the truth may tell a different story. I do know that the descendants of the white serpent still exist, and to the misfortune of all the benign snakes, they are most venomous and deadly creatures.

We talked on until the time came to begin the day. I rose and bathed my face with lavender water, dressed in my best gown, and pinned my mother's amethyst brooch to my bodice. I arranged myself in this finery because I was to see the queen.

"Your dog accompanies you everywhere, doesn't he?" Alice asked when she came to fetch me, and found both of us ready and waiting.

"Yes," I said. "He's my constant companion."

"I'm not overfond of animals, although I certainly understand your attachment to this one. We were all rather dumbstruck by the way he came bounding into the palace on the day you fainted. He eluded all of the servants as he ran through the halls in the direction of my own chamber, as if he knew exactly who he was seeking." She paused, then stood there scrutinizing Perseus.

When her eyes returned to mine, she said, "It was as if Perseus knew you were in danger, and the person he needed to come and find was me."

I looked down at my companion. "Perseus is very intelligent."

Indeed I am, Perseus said, wagging his tail for Alice's benefit.

I expected more wit and banter from the sharp-tongued

Alice. But that afternoon she seemed subdued, and even the amber of her aura seemed paler. With very few words, she led me to the queen's privy chamber, then deposited me just outside the doorway. "Here's where I take my leave of you. Good luck," she said, pressing her warm lips to my cheek.

"Is anything the matter?"

A seam creased Alice's brow. "Nothing of great importance. It's just that the books I was expecting still have not arrived, and now one of the ladies-in-waiting, Vivienne Gascoigne—you haven't met her yet—is delayed returning to court, and so I've been saddled with her responsibilities. The truth is, I just wanted to spend the morning reading."

Again that name—Vivienne.

But before I had a chance to say anything further, Alice touched my shoulder and said, "Don't delay. Her Majesty expects you."

Alice left me then, and the same servant led me into the grand room where the queen and I had met. Again, I knelt before Elizabeth. There I breathed in the powdery scent of her gown and stared at her hem until she signaled my rising.

As soon as she did, I noticed a golden falcon with emerald eyes pinned to her breast. The falcon, I knew, had been her mother's symbol. (I felt sure that Anne Boleyn had chosen it, because in this creature of prey, the female is the larger bird.)

"My dear Mary." The queen held out her hand and drew me to her. "You have given us all quite a fright. I trust you are now feeling quite well again."

"Yes, Your Majesty, thank you for your concern."

She noticed my brooch, and in an instant her entire manner gentled, a puzzling billow of rose immediately appearing within the regal purple of her aura. "You are in possession of the amethyst. Are you aware of the origin of this gift?"

"No, Your Majesty, I know only that it belonged to my mother."

Elizabeth smiled almost girlishly, and the rosy billow increased. "It was the very first birthday present I gave her."

My hand flew to my heart, and I steadied my legs to keep from falling. "Your gift?"

"That's right. I chose the amethyst because at that time she was new to the 'purple': new to the life of a royal. So too, I wanted to share a secret with your mother. You could say that I felt compelled to give her a cryptic warning."

I leaned closer. "A warning? Of what sort?"

Elizabeth's smile increased, and her features took on a

mischievous expression. "Although not everyone is convinced of this power, according to the alchemists, the amethyst can act as an amulet against intoxication in love."

My heart seemed to double in size, so that it throbbed against my breast. The queen knew about the virtues. But of course! All those pearls. Purity and nobility. Such a thing only made sense. The fact that my queen understood and shared the symbolism I had so closely studied made my own secrecy regarding my true role in her court easier to bear.

Once again aware that she was awaiting my reply, I said, "But why did you want to protect my mother against intoxication in love?"

"Isn't it obvious?" Elizabeth said, swallowing hard. "Duty compelled me to love my father. Nevertheless, I'm perfectly aware of how difficult he made life for his wives. Don't forget, Mary, I knew his fifth queen, Catherine Howard, an ancestor of the beloved Lady Frances. Catherine was nineteen at the time of her marriage to my father. He was no longer in his physical prime and could therefore not satisfy his young queen."

"Catherine Howard's sexual appetite was the reason she became intoxicated by men other than the king," I said, recalling the unfortunate young queen's naïve trysts with other courtiers, trysts that ultimately cost the unruly woman her life.

"Precisely." The queen shuddered. "I was eight years old when Catherine Howard went to the block. Foolish creature though she was, I remained devoted to her, for I valued her kindness in spite of her promiscuity. At the time of your mother's marriage, I gave her the amethyst as a secret sign. I didn't want her to fall in love with someone else and lose my father's favor."

And her life, I almost added, for I knew my mother had been in love with someone else all along, my father. At the time Henry VIII was trawling about for a new wife, considering, though not yet settling, on my mother, Thomas Seymour was making his first dangerous impression on her heart.

"To see this beautiful gem again after all these years pleases me immensely," Elizabeth said gently. "You see, I thought my gift was lost."

"After my mother's death, the Duchess of Suffolk salvaged it," I told the queen.

"The dear duchess." A look of sorrow flickered across her features. "You do know that she was lady-in-waiting to your own mother when she served as England's queen?"

"I do," I said.

The queen's voice grew warmer, and her gaze deepened, as did the rose in her purple aura. "What else did the duchess tell you, I wonder?"

"I know that the duchess and my mother grew up together and were tutored by the same masters," I told Elizabeth, sticking close to safe subjects.

"Very true," said Elizabeth. "But only your mother was a woman of great learning. As I told you that first day, I shall never forget the sincere interest she took in my own education. She helped me with my translations and encouraged my own interest in poetry." The queen's face turned thoughtful. "To be honest with you, my dear, given your mother's extraordinary precedent, I have always regretted that I was not able to be of more help to you when you were in the duchess's care."

"I'm afraid I don't understand."

Elizabeth's face turned pale, and in an instant the rose in her aura vanished. "To speak plainly, the duchess was not the most fitting guardian for you. Although she was a good woman, she was also very young when the Duke of Suffolk took her as his wife. As you probably know, the duchess was originally intended as the bride of the duke's son. When the young man died, the duke decided to marry her himself."

"Yes," I said, reminded of the single time the duchess confessed to me that her own life would have been happier had she married a man closer to her age. Instead, she found herself the very young bride of a man who had been Henry VIII's playmate.

"After the duke's death, the dear duchess became rather careless." The queen eyed me significantly. "You might say that she gave way to fantasies a more levelheaded woman would never have allowed. Frankly, my dear Mary, falling in love with one's Master of the Horse is not a wise thing to do."

"No," I agreed. "It isn't."

"I'm relieved to hear you say so, for I was afraid the duchess might have tainted your views on love. My firm belief is that a woman must be governed—in all things— by her head and not by her heart. Do you agree?" she said, regarding me carefully.

"I agree fully, Your Majesty," I replied.

Elizabeth's voice relaxed, and she began to toy with an enormous pearl ring on her left hand. "Again, I am relieved. I would not like to see your life crippled by the mistakes I have seen other women make."

"I do not intend to be crippled by mistakes when it comes to men and love," I said, trying hard not to speak too severely before my queen.

"Very good," Elizabeth said, and in her look I believe I saw a hint of understanding play about her lips.

Mustering my courage, I said, "Your Majesty, may I pose a bold question?"

Elizabeth's eyebrows rose. "Is it a question essential to your own well-being?"

"Yes." After all, my well-being was England's, for was not the future of England, in the person of Elizabeth, entrusted to my care?

Elizabeth's hazel eyes flickered over my face. "Then I give you leave to ask."

"It has been six years since your own accession to the throne. Since we are speaking of marriage," my voice faltered a little, "may I ask you if it is in your plans to wed?"

Still fingering the ring, the queen turned away, then walked over to the window and looked out at the gardens. The sun shone on her person, illuminating her auburn hair and the pearls at her throat. At that moment, she looked both majestic and infinitely far away.

"Bear in mind that I would think such words, spoken by another of my ladies, very bold and very imprudent," she said at last. "But since it is you speaking, I will answer your question."

"I am grateful to you," I said, bowing low and trying to steady my furious heart.

"Today my answer is no, I shall never marry, unless I find a man fit to rule at my side." The purple in her aura blazed. "A man willing to be king but simultaneously a man with no desire to rule me."

"That is quite a challenge," I replied.

"It may very well be an impossibility," the queen said. "You see, Mary, I have already learned more about the relationships between men and women to last me a dozen lifetimes, and in nearly all cases, the woman has been at a great disadvantage." She shuddered. "Even if a woman's marriage is a happy one, there is always the great risk that she may die in childbirth or the complications that often arise afterward."

"Very true," I said, thinking of my own mother, who died of a fever just six days after I was born.

The queen fell silent, and I wondered if she realized the unintentional hurt of her words.

"Since you are only just recovered, I think it best that you do not exert yourself during the next few days," she said. "In a week's time, you can return to Lady Strange and fetch what you will need to establish yourself here."

"I am to go home, then?" I replied, unable to hide the joy in my voice.

"For a short while." Again the sharp gaze. "So that when you return, you will be able to serve me with your entire head and heart."

I breathed deeply and my whole being relaxed, for although I could not share my real work with anyone here at court, I would at last be allowed to share my experiences with my guardian.

"Now, I recall my promise to you," she continued, and again that hint of rosiness made its presence felt. "Regrettably, I have as many official responsibilities on this Monday as on the day you first arrived. As much as I would have delighted in your company, and in the fresh air, we will not have time to stroll through the garden, for I have to meet with my dear 'spirit,' and the other members of my council again at three o'clock."

"Spirit?" I glanced at Perseus, wondering if it was possible that Elizabeth, too, communed with the other world.

"A nickname." Elizabeth laughed, and pink suffused her white cheeks. "William Cecil is such an old, wise soul that I dubbed him thus. He began his service during my father's time, you know."

"But of course," I replied. Nevertheless, my shoulders

slumped a little, for how could my queen dismiss me so soon?

She stepped over to me, her luminous silk skirts rustling as she moved. Then she raised my chin. "Do not look so grim, my dear Mary," she said. "I am by no means sending you away. I still plan on sharing with you the memories of your mother that I have cherished for almost two decades."

"Oh, Your Majesty," I said, feeling tears begin behind my eyes, "I am so grateful."

Elizabeth raised me, and then linking my arm through hers, we left this room and passed through a heavy mahogany door that led into an even more private sitting room. Here, long windows flooded the space with light. The walls were of pale yellow and the furniture was inlaid with an exquisite Venetian gold. There was even a silver-topped table encrusted with jewels. On it rested a crystal vase of red roses in full bloom.

"When I was twelve years old, I translated Margaret of Navarre's *The Mirror of the Sinful Soul* for your mother," she said, her tone wistful. "Do you know it?"

"No," I said. "I'm afraid I do not."

She opened the uppermost drawer of a beautiful desk of lacquered wood and retrieved a small book, which she handled lovingly. "Margaret of Navarre was a devout woman who died just a short time ago. Like your mother, she became a great model for me," Elizabeth said. "Her book is a meditation on the soul's yearning for God. Because your mother was one of England's most devout and learned women, I thought my translation to be an appropriate gift.

"Take note of the cover," she said, placing the exquisitely bound book in my hands. "I designed it myself."

I gazed at the splendid volume with its cover of purple satin, the emblem at the center a copy of my mother's badge—a crowned maiden rising out of a Tudor rose. Carefully, I opened it. There, on the first page I read:

To the most noble and virtuous Queen Katherine. Elizabeth, her humble daughter, wisheth perpetual felicity and everlasting joy.

Here, too, a much younger Elizabeth had written:

I hope that no one else shall see it lest my faults be known by many, for it is incorrect and imperfect.

Once, Elizabeth had been a sunless child who watched her father marry one woman after another, as he single-mindedly quested for a son. Now she stood before me decorated with pearls and diamonds, her purple aura radiant. How radically Elizabeth's life—and the life of England—had changed. In Elizabeth's queenship the impossible had come to pass. A woman had become both king and queen.

From a high dresser, Elizabeth fetched a small jewel box, then opened it. "For my fourteenth birthday, your mother gave me this necklace of pearls with a single ruby at the center."

"How beautiful," I gasped, admiring the tear-shaped ruby. The jewel of praise had been cut to echo the pearl as emblem of a tear from heaven. In this perfect gift, my mother had brought her stone of choice together with Elizabeth's.

"I have always loved this simple necklace. In the politic world into which I was born, friendships are not necessarily based on good will," the queen said solemnly. "As one of my ladies, you will need to keep a sharp look about you."

"I will."

"Good. I have no wish to frighten you," she continued. "It is just that you have lived your whole life away from court. As you return to take your rightful position, you will need to be shrewd."

What did the queen mean when she referred to my

"rightful position"? Was it her intention to make me a full-fledged member of her court? Or was she alluding to the fact that I was a queen's daughter? For I knew that she could have no knowledge of my role as white magician, a person sent to keep watch over and strengthen the ordering goodness of her reign.

She unfastened the clasp. "Today I give you this necklace to wear as a sign of your mother's love, for I know that she awaited your birth with quickening joy. I speak the absolute truth when I say that your mother wanted you more than anything else in the world. She would be immensely proud of you, Mary, for you are a daughter worthy of such a mother's praise."

Overwhelmed, I bowed my head and allowed the queen to fasten the ruby necklace around my throat. Did she understand the significance of her action? My queen, she whom I was destined to serve and honor, was repairing the connection between mother and child. As the jewel relaxed against my heart, I felt as if that ruby were a lifeline. I thought, too, of the rose that had crept into Elizabeth's aura and wondered if perhaps the shade I had always associated with romance and foolishness might not be linked to tenderness as a kind of strength, as well.

CHAPTER THIRTEEN

On THE EVE OF MY RETURN TO MOONSWAY, there was a grand dinner and concert for the courtiers and ladies-in-waiting. In the queen's words, the evening was to be "a celebration of the changing of the guard."

On this occasion, Elizabeth intended to toast the going away of one lady-in-waiting, Lady Frances, with the coming of another, *me*. The event was remarkably well-timed, for early the next morning, Frances Howard, too, intended to leave the palace for her much longer journey, a good two days of northward traveling to her parents' estate in Wiltshire. Her marriage to Anthony Dervish, I learned with relief, was to take place within a fortnight. If all went as planned, Frances's baby would be born without any question of legitimacy.

The "ambrosial banquet" the queen insisted upon was to consist of more than three hundred dishes. By early morning all of the palace's three kitchens were in full operation. From one of the servants I learned that the dinner would require two horse loads of oysters, several thousand smoked herrings, forty-four loaves of white bread, many more gallons of white wine and beer (the queen's preferred drink), several bushels of lettuce, an even greater quantity of apples, pears, and hazelnuts, fifty pounds of butter, as well as more than four dozen rabbits, two hundred quails, capons, partridges, pheasants, and pigeons.

Usually, during the late morning I stopped in at one of the kitchens to fix myself a cup of tea. The cooks found my habit peculiar. "Why does one of the queen's ladies wish to heat up her own water?" they asked. How could I explain how much I missed the cookery sounds of home, where so many rooms did not seal this part of the house off from the rest?

This morning, however, I passed on my cup of tea.

Although my official post as lady-in-waiting to her Majesty, the Queen of England, was less than a week old, I now understood the full meaning of a recurrent phrase around court: "The queen is as good as gold. Yet she exacts a great deal for the gold she gives." From the boy who cleaned the stables to the women who cared for her jewels, Elizabeth expected superlative and sometimes exhausting service.

Once she learned of my knowledge of herbs and folk remedies, an interest I shared with my mother, the queen asked me to be the sole creator of the elaborate facial creams that kept her skin blemish-free. Therefore, as soon as I came downstairs with Perseus, we made our way straight into the gardens to procure lavender, clary sage, and chamomile, the herbs that soothed any irritation and worry in the queen's face so that it glowed, at least temporarily, like the fresh skin of a well-favored child.

After gathering the herbs, I went to the henhouse, an incredibly noisy, incredibly smelly turret in which lived the queen's three hundred hens, prized and fed the finest grains because of their laying abilities.

"Three eggs today, Lady Mary?" the keeper, a boy of twelve, asked.

"Exactly, Thaddeus, thank you."

From behind his back he immediately produced a trio of perfect eggs, delicately packaged in a woven basket. "Will these do?" he said, smiling at me.

"Perfectly." Though I returned his smile, I worried he had taken a romantic interest in me, for his innocent green aura always bore a disturbing trace of rose in my company.

Mary dear, Perseus said, *do not be so sure the presence of rose in someone's aura is always such a simple thing to read.*

Isn't it? I frowned.

Not always. You must learn to recognize that there are more subtle gradations of feeling.

I hoped Perseus would explain his point further, but he only held my gaze cryptically. Like my guardian, on most occasions he expected me to puzzle matters out for myself; a practice that sometimes irked me. Still, it was a practice that made sense when it came to making connections, whether those involved the aspects of a person's character, or the concocting of an effective spell.

Once I returned to the palace with the herbs and eggs, I went next to a small trio of rooms just beyond the kitchen. Here stood the queen's personal pharmacy. From the cupboards I retrieved poppy seeds for purification, as well as alum, borax, and a powder made from the iridescent inner layer of an oyster's shell. These last three ingredients helped preserve the whiteness of the queen's complexion.

After measuring exact amounts of each ingredient, I poured them into a bowl and stirred the mixture exactly one hundred times. Only then did I crack the eggs into the bowl, separating each yolk and laying it aside. The queen's creams required only the delicate and highly nutritious white. The yolks I gave to the cooks to use in the rich puddings all of us adored.

I poured the cream into a special pink glass, then rang a small bell, and Kate, one of the sturdier housemaids, immediately came into the room.

"You've got Her Majesty's lotion ready, then?"

"Yes." I handed Kate the glass. "Have you seen the queen this morning?"

Kate's round red face reddened further, and she grinned broadly. "I have. Her Majesty certainly is no morning person, for she's in as foul a temper as ever I've seen her."

Ordinarily, I would not have been comfortable with such loose talk, but Kate was the exception. When we first met, she showed me a small pendant shaped like the moon, one of the queen's symbols, for it linked her to Diana, the virgin huntress. Kate always kept this pendant pinned to the inside of her cotton smock. I knew she was loyal to the queen.

After Kate left, I climbed the staircase to the queen's wardrobe.

I stepped through the doorway, and Frances's features instantly brightened. "Oh good, you're early. I hoped you would come soon. I'd like to steal away for a while." She blushed, the rose in her aura shining. "You see, I'm to meet Anthony."

"Let's get to work, then," I said, for I, too, was eager to head outside and meet, not a man, but the sun.

Frances's chief responsibility involved caring for a portion of the queen's clothing. Now she was passing this esteemed and rather taxing duty on to me. "Who else cares for the queen's clothes?" I asked when I saw the great size of this first locked wardrobe.

Frances frowned. "Let me think a moment: there's Lavinia Hilliard, Olivia Teerlinc, and Amelia Gowland. Every once in a while Alice Cavendish helps out, but she's not terribly interested in clothes, as you've probably noticed."

"What about Vivienne Gascoigne?" I asked, for I knew that this lady's return to court was already overdue.

"Never," Frances replied, but when I tried to coax the reason from her, she absolutely refused to tell it to me.

"Well then, will any of the other ladies be joining us this morning?" I asked, as Frances placed a bejeweled key into the lock, then opened the heavy wardrobe doors to reveal no less than forty gowns.

"Amelia may come, but she's always too late to be of

any real help, and unfortunately, Lavinia and Olivia do not possess sturdy constitutions and typically have colds."

"So you usually do most of the work?"

Frances shrugged. "I don't mind. I love clothes. Besides, for a going-away present, the queen gave me one of her own dresses. A lovely gown with black piping around the neckline and tourmaline stitched into the bodice. Wearing it"—she twirled, and her skirts swirled around her—"I shall feel almost like a queen."

Tourmaline's peculiar virtue was forgetfulness. Was it at all possible, I wondered, that somewhere in the hinterlands of consciousness Elizabeth had some inkling of Frances's plight and wanted the best for her? Eager to see the gown, I asked, "Is it among the ones gathered here?"

Frances shook her head. "No. The queen keeps her black-edged gowns in the sixteenth wardrobe in the next room."

Sixteenth! Dizzy, I leaned against the wall.

We spent the next several hours carefully removing the cuffs, collars, and other detachable items from each of the gowns. Because the gowns were frequently heavily jeweled and made of exquisite yet hard to care for fabrics like velvet and silk, they could not often be laundered. To prevent their getting dirty, the queen wore silk or cotton underthings that were washed regularly with a mixture of soap, warm water, and lavender, as were the detachable items with which we concerned ourselves.

Until I actually held one of the queen's gowns, I never understood exactly how heavy a velvet dress encrusted with rubies and pearls could be. Just then, I became less aware of their symbolic value and more aware of their weight. If I handled a dozen such dresses three times a week, I would be as strong as the laborers who unloaded heavy barrels from the horse carts. I said as much to Perseus.

Surely, Mary, you exaggerate.

I glowered at him. *Want to try this work and see?*

No, thank you, he said, then went back to genteelly licking his front paws beneath the room's only sunlit window.

Two hours later, once we had finished the painstaking separation process, a pair of housemaids came to fetch the basket of things, then carried them off to be cleaned.

The final step, which Frances explained with remarkable specificity, involved coating the gowns with two layers of a fragrance that smelled like cloves and oranges.

Only once we had finished our labors and emerged smelling like clothes preservative, our hair and skin covered with a white dusting, did we shut up the doors to the room and escape.

On the verge of parting, Frances touched my arm, and her blue-gray eyes glistened with tears. "I'm glad to have met you, Mary. We may not have another chance alone like this, and there's something I wanted to tell you."

I leaned closer. Was it possible that Frances had any recollection of my spell and all that came before? I wondered.

"I feel as if you've done me a great service." Frances's face lost all color, and her expression grew serious. "Although the nature of it is something I cannot pinpoint."

"There is one thing. I am relieving you of being mistress of Her Majesty's wardrobe." I glanced down at my powdery arms. "Is that not a service?"

"Yes, of course." Frances took hold of both of my hands. "But in seriousness, I hope you enjoy your time here as a lady-in-waiting. The queen has been very, very good to me. Still"—a flash of rose—"I look forward to the day when it's just Anthony and myself. I have learned a great deal here at court, and I have cherished the responsibility of tending to my queen's wardrobe. Thanks to my efforts, Her Majesty is the noblest-looking monarch in all of Europe. Nevertheless, I'd rather have babies to care for."

A picture of Frances tending to the child she would believe to be her husband's rose before me. "You and Anthony will be very happy," I said, willing the words to be true.

"Yes." Again the flash of rose. "Mary," she said, keeping hold of my hands. "I wish you such happiness also."

"Thank you." As on the day when Frances initially told me about her feelings for Anthony, I refrained from speaking my true feelings about marriage and romantic love.

There was only one thing left to do.

That day, I had been appointed to carry the queen's new set of gold toothpicks upstairs to her private bathroom. Normally, a housemaid would take care of such an office, but because these toothpicks were encrusted with jewels and came as a special gift from some rich landholder who hoped to gain a title from Elizabeth, the job fell to me.

At last, just as the clock struck one, I finished my work.

In the kitchen, I snatched a few apples and a brick of cheese; and for Perseus, a very thick, very juicy slice of roast beef.

Then I flung open the back doors, and Perseus and I

set off across the grounds. The fresh air felt like ambrosia. Unlike the stuffy palace, the out-of-doors was cool and clean and scented with leaves, moist grass, and the coming apples of autumn. Relishing the uninhibited movements of my body, I loosened my stays, and for a long time I just walked, my feet carrying me farther from Whitehall, the tightness in my neck and shoulders loosening, the breath moving more energetically through my body.

For a little while at least, I was a liberated woman.

Eventually, Perseus and I reached a green meadow abloom with late September wildflowers. All around me, red poppies waved in the breeze. Goldenrod grew high, while the white lace flower made a pattern against the grass as lush and beautiful as the finest tapestry. I kicked off my shoes and walked barefoot through the dewy carpet, instantly reminded of the ease and safety of my life at Moonsway.

Tomorrow I will be home.

I thought of Jack's big paws, his sloppy kisses, and his gentle eyes. I thought of Lady Strange's serene warmth, not to mention her wisdom. And of course there was Bess's playful banter and the calm of my silver room. As these thoughts of home swirled through me, my body bubbled up with longing.

CHAPTER FOURTEEN

LATER, WHEN THE MOON PEERED THROUGH MY windows, it came time to face the glittering world of the court, the ambitious circle within which my own mother once moved. In the privacy of my room, I bathed and dressed in a simple gown of yellow linen, a gift from the queen, hesitating a little because the bodice was a bit too fashionably low cut for my own taste. To cover myself, I wore a long white shawl. In addition to the opal, which I always wore beneath my camisole, I clasped the ruby and pearl necklace around my throat, allowing it to shine in plain view.

For the first time since my arrival at Whitehall, fear, like a pair of icy hands, reached for me, and for a moment I could not move. I could not explain it, but somehow I knew the night's events would complicate, possibly even imperil, my work at Whitehall.

I'm frightened, I told Perseus. *Though I cannot say why.*

When I have fears, I think back on words and episodes that have been fortifying, Perseus said, considering me thoughtfully. *Is it possible for you to recall any such things now?*

The icy, grasping hands still clung to me, and at first I could only shake my head no.

Don't be so quick to protest, Perseus said. *Concentrate.*

I focused and simultaneously tried to relax, and eventually the words of Lady Strange's father echoed through my mind, soothing me like balm.

"When the time is ripe, you will avenge these crimes, not with any violence, but with the white magic that is your birthright."

Perseus watched me closely. *Am I right in concluding that you have found what you need?*

Yes, I replied. Still, although I had mastered the moment's fear, in the furthest reaches of my mind and body, a dank foreboding kin to the terrible secrets buried in a traitor's cellar lingered.

Downstairs, with Perseus at my side, I stepped into one of the great halls, a luxurious space crowned by a fretwork ceiling with intersecting ribs and pendants trimmed in gold. As I joined the gathering, I became aware that this room brought together more of the country's nobility than I had seen since the queen's coronation day.

Courtiers strolled along passageways lined with painted columns topped with heraldic beasts. They spoke of growing tensions with Spain, the rising cost of importing tea, well-founded concerns regarding a long winter, as well as a popular debate on the possibility of fate versus free will.

Meanwhile, many of the queen's ladies sat together in tightly knit groups, laughing and talking. Although their conversation was less of political matters, they, too, circled around the day's pressing events.

At the very center of the room, perched on an elaborately bejeweled throne on a dais, presided the queen. Dressed in an elaborate gown of silver and gold, around her throat she wore a dazzling array of diamonds and pearls, and in her auburn hair sparkled hundreds of other jewels, each with its own virtue. Every once in a while, accompanied by one of the most handsome and dashing of her courtiers, she rose to dance, moving along the gleaming parquet floor with great energy and precision. Each of her ladies knew how much she adored this form of entertainment, for it was one of the only socially acceptable—and trap-free—flirtations between the sexes in which the Virgin Queen might joyfully and exuberantly participate.

Not far from Henry Clifford, the impeccably dressed court painter who always had paint stains on his hands, I spied Mary Hastings engaged in heated conversation with Sir Cuthbert Naunton, a young man with an unabashedly red, meaning an unabashedly ambitious, aura, whose star was on the rise. Every once in a while Mary's cheeks crimsoned, and she batted her eyelashes at him. Did she have her marrying eye set on Naunton? I wondered. And if she did, what would the queen have to say about it?

The burly Sir Christopher Hatton, head of the queen's bodyguard and possessor of a responsible chestnut aura, stood close beside one of Elizabeth's other favorites, Lord Robert Dudley, who, thanks to her, occupied a very high place in her court, and had been gifted with wealth and property.

Dudley had been away during my first days at Whitehall, so this was the first time I'd seen him. I was immediately struck by Dudley's rare burgundy aura. Burgundy was a close cousin of crimson, the sign of ambition and intrigue, my father's own color. The presence of red in Lord Dudley's aura did not surprise me, for he was the son of the treacherous John Dudley, Duke of Northumberland, who had tried to place another son, Lord Guilford, and poor Lady Jane Grey on England's throne immediately following the death of Henry VIII's son, Edward.

Burgundy proved a more difficult color to assess than red because burgundy was also related to the regal purple. Clearly, the mixed nature of Dudley's history and his aura convinced me that I would have to follow his movements closely.

In another corner of the room hovered a motley party of courtiers and ladies that included the sleepy yet spiteful Lord Teasewell, as well as Lady Helena Devereux, a widow with two grown sons at court. There was also Lady Rothschild, who at age forty-two was still beautiful, for she possessed large, mild, gray eyes and the milkiest complexion I had ever seen. People often spoke of the miraculous fact that Lady Rothschild had nursed many a poor soul through the smallpox without contracting the deadly and disfiguring illness herself. Lady Rothschild's mild green aura attested to the youthful benevolence that continued to thrive in an aging body.

Beside her stood a tall, willowy young woman dressed

in a gown ablaze with jewels—many of them diamonds. The woman's hair was of an almost transparent blondness that made her skin seem even paler. This creature should have been attractive, for each of her features was perfectly shaped, from her narrow nose, wide blue eyes, and generous mouth, to her full lips. And yet there was a twisted quality to her face. Her aura was yellowish, though hers was not the yellow of the sun. Rather, it was the chalky yellow of a fried egg yolk left to spoil in the air. I sensed something sick about her, and remarkably, the image of the white serpent flashed through my mind.

You must discover who she is—immediately, Perseus stressed.

I found old William, one of the queen's most trustworthy servants. "Who is she?" I asked, indicating the willowy lady.

"Lady Vivienne Gascoigne. Surely you know her."

I shook my head, and William must have realized how new I was to the queen's circle of ladies-in-waiting. "But of course you don't, m'lady," he said, bowing in apology, for despite his humble origins, he was as genuinely courteous as the greatest of the great courtiers. "Lady Vivienne has been away these past few weeks. She's only just returned, many days overdue."

So this is the dangerous Vivienne Gascoigne about whom Frances warned me, I said to Perseus. *How is it that she dares to wear so many diamonds in the presence of our queen?*

Clearly, she has a very high opinion of herself. An overreacher, probably. Do not let her stray from your sight, Perseus warned.

I nodded and focused more closely on Vivienne, discerning a nascent sixth finger growing from the side of her left hand. Anne Boleyn had possessed such a deformity; one of her accusers had singled it out as evidence of her sinful nature. Was it possible, I wondered, that the queen bore Vivienne some affection because of this perverse similarity?

A nudge from Perseus told me that Vivienne had caught me staring. Quickly, I looked away.

I continued to make my way through the increasingly warm room, nodding to familiar faces, expertly avoiding Lord Teasewell's barbs, and only occasionally making the acquaintance of someone new and self-important.

At the center of another group of courtiers, I spotted a man whose exceptional looks compelled my attention. The stranger's eyes were almost black, and something about the shape and the sharpness brought to mind both a wary stag and a creature of prey, a wolf, perhaps, or a lion. In contrast to his eyes, his skin was as fair and creamy as the first light of dawn. Queerly, his coloring and features recalled my own father. Once the comparison registered, I wondered not that my mother would have singled Thomas Seymour out for his physical attractions.

And yet, despite the similarity, there remained a subtle but important difference. From the single cameo portrait still in my possession, I knew that my father's hair had been as dark as his penetrating eyes, but this man's hair was a rich shade of gold. So too, it was the rare and luxurious texture of a lion's mane.

I tried to focus on the other people and activities swirling around me, but in spite of my efforts, my gaze was inevitably drawn back to him.

The man eventually caught me glancing his way. Raising his goblet to his lips, he seemed to toast me with it. When he shone on me a darkly handsome smile, I knew what had troubled and not just intrigued me all along.

I could not detect his aura.

Dizzy, I sought the solitude of a breezy corner. Protected by shadows, I stood before the open window, and with closed eyes allowed the cool air to bathe my face and throat, my thoughts moving in a disjointed whirl. Who was this courtier, I asked myself, and why didn't I discern an aura?

How much time passed, I do not know. All I remember is a smell like that of peat mixed with burning leaves, followed by a voice whispering in my ear, "Why are you here alone?"

Slowly, I turned to find myself face-to-face with the very one who both unnerved and compelled me.

"You startled me," I said, wrapping the shawl more tightly around my shoulders.

He bowed. "My apologies. All evening, I have wanted to introduce myself. When I caught you looking my way, I found I had the right opportunity—at last."

I frowned, forcing any former recognition from my eyes. "Was I looking your way? I recall no such encounter."

He smiled a flirtatious yet unsettling smile. "You did look my way, and you looked more than once. I raised my glass to toast both your beauty and our connection. How can it be you have no recollection of such a tribute?"

I stepped away from him. "I do not remember, and in all truth I have no idea what you mean by a connection." In a clear voice I said, "You are a stranger to me, sir."

"You can disavow the look that passed between us," he said, surveying my face and allowing his eyes to travel down to my throat. "But you cannot disavow the connection."

Struck again by the golden luxuriance of his hair, the prophecy returned.

Beware of the man who boasts of being the lionheart.

Edmund Seymour. This must be the very man who had tried to destroy Frances Howard. I knew then that he must be very powerful, for he was already alert to the presence of an adversarial magician.

I could not suppress my own aura now, or he would suspect something. Still, I knew the silver would surely alert him to the uniqueness of my nature.

Trying not to betray any emotion, I swallowed hard, comforted only by Perseus, who drew closer to me.

"I learned only today of your arrival and of your appointment as lady-in-waiting to our queen." He reached for my hand, and I had no choice but to give it to him. "I congratulate you."

Ever so slightly, I inclined my head toward him, taking note of the large sapphire he wore on his ring finger. How had he come into possession of such a valuable gem?

With studied courtesy he returned the gesture. "I wanted to introduce myself because as I said, we *are* closely related, though strangers to each other. I am Edmund

Seymour, the eldest son of the late Duke of Somerset, Lord Protector under our late King Edward. And you are my young cousin, Mary, daughter of my late uncle."

"I am pleased to meet you, sir," I said, bringing a distinct chill to my voice. "However, I identify myself more closely with my mother's family, having had very little contact with or knowledge of the Seymours. After all, your father gave the command that brought the headsman's axe down on my father."

In spite of my fear, I forced myself to hold his eye.

Refusing to acknowledge this last remark, he continued to study me, even allowing his eyes to travel to my breasts, so that I wished for a heavy cloak and not just a thin shawl. "You do have your mother's mark upon you," he said at last. "How I wish I had known the late and highly esteemed Katherine Parr. Even today, when her name plays upon another's lips, it is always with respect."

I raised my head high. "My mother was a great woman."

Edmund scanned my face. "I do not argue with that. Yet it remains to be seen if you are a great woman also."

"I did not know that I was being put to any test," I said sharply.

He laughed. "You like a good challenge. I can see that."

Edmund drew closer, and a sharp heat unlike the warmth I felt in Elizabeth's presence flashed through me. Thankfully, Perseus chose this moment to position himself between my cousin and me. With Perseus beside me, the air seemed to relax, and so did I.

"Well, my dear cousin," he said, pressing my hand to his lips. "Now that you have come to court, we shall see a great deal of each other." His gaze held my own. "I will seek you out at every opportunity."

With a bow, he relinquished my hand and departed.

I could feel the blood rushing to the tips of my fingers and even to my toes. As for my aura, its silveryness seemed to waver, though it remained thankfully clear of any impurities such as rose or blue or the tremulous yellow-green.

He's a terrible, evil person, I reminded myself. *Think of all that Frances revealed. You cannot possibly find any pleasure in his company.*

And yet I had.

Do not lose your resolve so easily, Perseus said. *You have had very little interaction with men. That is all. Fortify yourself by recalling those strengthening words and episodes.*

I tried, once more calling forth the words of the scholar Vives, words that had imprinted themselves on my memory so many years before: *Romantic love confounds and blinds a woman of wit and reason so that she shall not see or know what is done.*

I expected the words to have a fortifying effect on me. Like a tonic or bracing, winter air. But the hypnotic presence of my dangerous cousin remained before me.

I was about to despair, until at last, Lady Strange's words reverberated through me: *Remember, you are a white magician before anything else.*

Inspired by her faith in me, I stilled my trembling, then fetched a glass of water from a table. Although I would not own the reason to myself, I secretly vowed to wear the protective amethyst at all future gatherings of the court.

I was about to reach for another glass when Perseus growled, giving me just enough time to recollect myself. I looked up to see Vivienne Gascoigne approach in that bedazzled gown far too fine for her position, those splendid diamonds glinting in her hair. Yet as she came closer, I saw that they were diamond chips, as if someone had taken a much larger diamond and cut it into bits, thereby weakening the virtues of the gem.

"I caught you staring at me earlier," she said in the most impolite tone imaginable. "We have not been introduced. You are—"

I inclined my head, but I did not bow. "Lady Mary

Seymour, daughter of the late Katherine Parr."

"Ah, yes," Vivienne said dismissively. "The last wife of Henry the Eighth."

"Henry the Eighth's last *queen*."

"And a short-lived reign it was" she sneered. "She did not bear the late king a child."

"No," I said. "But even you must be aware of the equally great service my mother rendered her most royal husband. Surely, you are educated just enough to know that my mother cared for our good Queen Elizabeth after Henry the Eighth's death."

"I heard something about that," she yawned, the sickly yellow of her aura glowing like fog on an overheated day on the Thames. "But such things are ancient history. There was some scandal with your father, was there not?" Her tone became a glinting knife.

Absolute honesty was the only way to curb her edge. Without batting an eye, I said, "My father was executed as a traitor."

Vivienne laughed, and the diamonds in her hair seemed to wince at such rudeness. "So now we have a traitor's daughter at court. What will be next, I wonder?" Again she laughed, waving the hand with the superfluous finger, so that its wriggling movement recalled a tiny snake. "The

Scottish princess who even now vies for our queen's throne? I cannot possibly imagine what could be worse for Her Majesty's reputation," she hissed, her thin nostrils flaring. "But first we must of course suffer Thomas Seymour's brat."

I could see how badly she wanted to list my father's supposed crimes, but I could see, too, how shrewd she was in her decision to keep silent. Vivienne knew some of my father's supposed crimes, specifically his alleged seduction of our queen, could not be mentioned in this court.

Vivienne's eyes narrowed, and she came closer, a threatening protectiveness creeping into her voice and features. "I see you have made the acquaintance of Edmund Seymour."

"Yes," I said neutrally. "He is my cousin."

Vivienne's yolk-yellow aura seemed to choke the surrounding air, and I found myself gasping for breath.

I stepped away from her, but before I could get away, she plunged her sharp nails into my wrist.

"Release me!" I cried, as one or two other courtiers turned to stare.

"Mark my words, Mary," she said, her breath hot on my throat, "I intend to be the most prominent and the grandest of the queen's ladies, and I will bide no competition."

"Release me," I said again, more calmly this time.

"If you have any wit at all, you will keep away from Edmund Seymour," she continued, her nails still piercing my skin, her voice a low snarl.

Perseus growled, then butted his head against her very hard, so that she at last let go.

"Stupid dog!" she howled, and then her eyes met Perseus's, and she drew back.

In the next moment she was gone.

I rubbed my wrist and stared at my loyal friend.

I couldn't attack, Perseus said. *Then she would have cause to distort what actually happened, and despite the queen's fondness, I would be forced to stay in your rooms. She is one to watch. She may even have some connection to magic, for I think she saw the awareness in my own eyes.*

My thoughts whirled wildly, but just then I did not even have time to gather myself, for Frances Howard was coming my way. Dressed in a petal pink gown as rosy as her aura, she looked happy enough. Yet her face wore an expression of puzzlement.

"I've just had the most unsettling conversation with Lord Seymour," she said. "He was rather malicious, and seemed to speak absolute nonsense. Something about a bastard child—my bastard child." The puzzled expression deepened. "I cannot understand it."

Frances's speech was proof of my spell's power, for unlike my cousin, she had truly forgotten any trace of their former relations, as had everyone else—chiefly my friend and necessary ally, Alice Cavendish.

"Why do you suppose he said such things? Is it possible that he's losing his mind? Or perhaps he's had too much to drink. The wine *is* very potent tonight."

"I do not know my cousin's character," I said. "But I do know the Seymour men are changeable. It's best not to dwell too long on it. After all, tomorrow you will be gone to begin a new life. Why think unpleasant thoughts? Soon the intrigue of the court will be behind you."

Frances beamed and squeezed my hand. "I suppose you're right."

No sooner had she spoken when Anthony hurried to her side.

"My congratulations," I told him. "You are a fortunate man."

"I am indeed, for she is a goddess," he said in absolute sincerity. "I am in great haste to marry her."

"Yes, best not to let her go," I said, understanding that Anthony's haste must be a part of my spell.

"I wish you much joy," I told them both.

Anthony bowed, and Frances kissed my cheek.

Then, hand in hand, the two hurried off together, and I stood by myself in the center of the room, fiercely hoping joy would indeed be their lot.

There were assigned places at the meal, and I found myself at a table that included Henry Clifford and another of the queen's favorite painters, one or two of the more subdued ladies-in-waiting, and a number of aspiring courtiers. Surrounded by this motley crew, I sat wedged between a dyspeptic Lord Cuthbert Naunton and a peculiar young man named Philip Sidney, who talked only of poetry. Fortunately, it was a subject I was interested in. During the first two courses, we discussed the sonnets of Petrarch. Like the Italian poet, we found that we were in agreement that harmonious words helped shape a harmonious soul.

Unfortunately, the peculiar young man did not seem to possess the talent of his Italian predecessor. Midway through the meal he revealed to me his plan to write a sonnet sequence "full of so much emotion that even the queen's hounds will weep." When he recited a few painful rhymes that turned on *hart*, *dart*, and *fart*, even poor Perseus covered his ears.

It took everything in my power to prevent breaking into

laughter during the soup course, an action that would have been the height of bad table manners.

At long last, after more than six courses, each one more elaborately prepared than the one that had come before, the meal reached an end, and we rose to go. Before parting, Philip Sidney caught my arm. "I've so delighted in your company I may even write a sonnet in your honor," he said, blue eyes dancing.

Oh dear, Perseus said. *What a way to go down in history.*

"Please, sir," I said, scowling at Perseus, "such an honor is not necessary. You must not squander your gifts on me."

"How could I be squandering my gifts if I was to celebrate a lady as serenely and cerebrally—"

Perseus roared with laughter, though no one but me heard him.

"—lovely as you."

Trying my very hardest to keep a straight face, I said, "If you want to be a great poet, I would seek out the *Hamonis* stone. It's gold in color and comes from the Far East. No stone, howsoever precious, can transform you into a great writer," I added, revealing a bit more of my knowledge than was perhaps wise. "But the *Hamonis* possesses the virtue of eloquence."

"Thank you, Lady Mary." He bowed. "Are you sure you

would not like a sonnet composed in your honor?"

"Please," I urged. "No." As quickly as possible I escaped to the music room.

Yet Philip Sidney proved the least of my problems, for it was there that my cousin approached me a second time.

"I have spoken to the queen about you," he said, his dark eyes making of themselves two caresses, his voice charming me in spite of myself.

I steeled myself against him. "Why the great interest?"

"Because you are my pretty younger cousin," he said, once again drawing disturbingly near. "You, Lady Mary, are a woman with whom I would like to have a very close association. It is universally understood here at court that I am of a most refined nature and choose to keep company only with those whose stars are on the ascent."

Impulsively I hazarded, "But are you not close with the star called Vivienne?"

My cousin's eyes narrowed to points. "Vivienne is a falling star. Her reigning nights are over."

"Is that not politics and self-interest rather than refinement," I said. "And is it possible that you believe the court to be the universe?"

Again he caressed me with his eyes. "It is good to know you are well-favored and smart," he continued. "For I find you quite irresistible, my dear young cousin, and I would not like to be tempted by someone with whom I could not have an honorable, intelligent relation."

Beside me, Perseus uttered a low growl.

I raised my chin a little bit higher. "Well-favored, how?"

"Our very good queen tells me that she intends to restore your mother's lost properties to you. Every house and garden that was seized from Katherine Parr after she married your father, Her Majesty acknowledges as rightly yours." He spoke these words slowly, pausing after each word in order to measure my response and, perhaps, to gauge my own ambitions.

I furrowed my brow, simultaneously struggling to make sense of the words, but Edmund Seymour only continued. "Chelsea Manor and Wickham Manor, even your father's place, old Sudeley Castle. You are to be a grand lady." He allowed his eyes to travel to the tear-shaped ruby at my throat. "I see you are already in possession of some of her jewels."

Realizing I had to collect myself, I said, "If I am to be so grand, then I shall have little time to stand about and make loose conversation." It took all of my self-control to refrain from covering the necklace from his invasive eyes.

Before I could pull away, he seized my hand and pressed

my palm to his lips. The sapphire on his own finger seemed to blind me with its light.

"Let go of my hand," I demanded.

Edmund Seymour spoke gallantly, but he did not loose his hold. "My dear cousin," he purred, "you are to be so grand as to have all the time in the world, for you will soon be one of the richest as well as one of the most comely young women in all England. When that occurs, I hope that you will waste your time with me alone. In fact, I intend to make it my vocation."

Sweat prickled the back of my neck as I found myself disturbingly reminded of my father's own self-interest in my mother.

Edmund took a step closer, and the peaty, burnt-leaf smell I had breathed in earlier intensified. I could hear my heart pounding, and the same humiliating heat rose up from deep within me, so that my limbs grew heavy, and although I knew this was all terribly wrong, my traitorous skin now craved a caress.

Edmund was about to say something more when Perseus butted his head against my cousin's legs, causing him to let go.

"Quite a protector you have in your dog," he said, scrutinizing Perseus in the dim light.

"Yes," I replied, regaining, or at least feigning, composure. "Dogs, unlike men, are absolutely loyal."

It was not until the concert began that I found time to gather my thoughts and communicate with Perseus. *Does he suspect anything?* I asked.

Perseus's eyes flickered. *He suspects something, for he knows someone must have come to Frances Howard's aid. Yet he does not suspect you. Not yet. Nevertheless, you must be very careful.*

What's our next step?

But Perseus did not reply. The wisdom I usually saw in his eyes had vanished, and he assumed the noble but simple countenance of a loyal dog.

Perseus, I said again, *what's our next step?*

This time Perseus warned me. *He's watching us.*

The message sent shivers up and down my spine. For the remainder of the concert I sat stiffly in my chair, my eyes fixed on the expert hands of the musicians. My greatest fear at that moment was that Edmund would find a way to separate Perseus from me. If I lost him, I knew I would crumble. After all, Perseus alone knew who and what I was. Only to him could I confide every aspect of my work.

Do not reveal your weaknesses, not even in thought, a voice seemed to say. But whose voice? Who was trying to communicate with me?

Did you speak, Perseus? I asked.

No, came my friend's reply.

I did not flinch, keeping my gaze riveted on the harpsichordist. And yet my spirit rose slightly, for I believed that somewhere in this room I must have an ally. Someone else knew who I was.

CHAPTER FIFTEEN

In the early morning there came a knock, and then Alice Cavendish stepped swiftly into the room, wearing a simple dress of dark blue that flattered her complexion. In her outstretched arms she carried my tea tray. "Morning," she called.

"Where's Molly?" I asked. "She usually brings me breakfast."

"I wanted to talk to you before you depart, so I volunteered to bring your toast and jellies. I even managed to find a rare dish of gingered pears."

"That's very good of you," I replied, surprised to see Alice act the part of chambermaid, especially at the early hour of eight a.m.

 "It's not just generosity that brings me here," Alice

said, as Perseus and I eyed each other knowingly. "I also bring a message."

A disturbing image of Edmund Seymour flashed through my mind. "What sort of message?"

"The queen would like to speak with you before you leave."

Instantly I rose.

"Relax and eat your breakfast," Alice said, settling into a chair after helping herself to the pears. "You're not expected for at least another half hour. I came a bit early so that we could chat. Honestly, Mary, I'm going to miss you. Palace life is much more pleasant since you arrived."

"Thank you," I said.

"I only speak the truth."

We appraised each other approvingly.

"Has Frances Howard departed yet?" I asked.

"Just after dawn. I'm rather worried about her, though. Frances was very sick during the night. Vomiting."

A chill swept through me. *Morning sickness.* "Is she often ill?"

"Frances is the picture of good health. And yet, it's most odd." A fogged look came into Alice's eye. "I seem to have forgotten much about Frances of late. My memory is usually superb. I cannot understand it."

"Pray, tell me," I said with a certain reckless calculation.

193

"If your opinion of Frances has gone foggy, what is your opinion of me?"

Alice squinted. "Do you really wish to know?"

"If I did not wish a truthful answer, I would not hazard the question."

Alice did not hesitate. "Well then, I find you intelligent, trustworthy." She raised a biscuit to her lips, all the while keeping her nearsighted eyes on my face. "But I also find you secretive. I cannot put my finger on it, Mary Seymour." She straightened her glasses and looked straight at me. "Something tells me that you are not quite who you appear to be. Put another way, I suspect that the face you wear in public is very different from the face you wore during your walk through the woods yesterday."

I laughed a bit nervously. "Is it not true that each of us presents a mask to the world, especially to the world of the court?"

Alice's face grew thoughtful. "Perhaps. But you have a scheme afoot, some secret, although what that secret is, I haven't a clue."

Struggling to maintain my composure, I turned toward Perseus. *Help me.*

You must give Alice some clue. She must value the confidence, but you must not reveal your real vocation in any way.

In other words, I must satisfy her and simultaneously remain opaque?

Precisely.

But what sort of a clue?

Allow Alice to ask you a question. Let her believe she is in control.

"Alice," I said. "I give you leave to ask me one question, and I promise to reply as truthfully as possible."

Her face brightened with the possibility of new knowledge. "Well then, my question already lies on the tip of my tongue."

My body stiffened. "Yes?"

Alice crossed one leg over the other, then clasped her hands together at her knees, and grinned too broadly. "What is your impression of your cousin Edmund Seymour?"

Stilling the jumpiness inside myself, I said, "I think his public face is not the face he wears in private. I think he keeps secrets."

"Given his position, this comes as no great surprise." Alice said, her eyes not once leaving my face. "Yet he certainly seems taken with you."

Cold fingers pressed against my spine, but I tried to shrug away the signs. "You make too much of trifles. He is flirtatious and worldly, that is all."

"True enough, but in your case I believe his interest runs deeper." Alice spoke confidentially. "I believe he would like to entwine his future with your own."

The cold fingers remained on my spine. "What are you talking about?"

"Last night, long after you left the party, I overheard Edmund Seymour speaking about you—in the most glowing terms—to the queen's own favorite, Lord Dudley." She righted her glasses, and an almost wicked smile swept across her face. "I believe your cousin admires and desires you."

Had this been our first meeting, and had that most undependable of gods, Sagittarius, been on the rise instead of balanced Libra, I do believe I would have suspected Alice of some witchery, but then I realized Alice had mentioned Edmund Seymour to me before my spell took effect.

Still, how could she be wishing or even talking about marriage to me, especially given all that she had said about her own value of education and freedom? What had happened to her sympathy for the royal wives Anne Boleyn and poor Elizabeth Howard, who had lost their heads because Henry VIII believed they were adulteresses who needed to die for their crimes?

Unfortunately, my distressing conversation with Alice proved to be the smaller of the two surprises that awaited me that morning. No sooner had I come into the queen's presence than she, too, began to speak to me of Edmund Seymour.

"Your cousin thinks very highly of you, Mary," she said, the pearls in her hair catching the light. "Indeed, he is all in favor of your permanent presence at court and would like to see you in a high position among our ladies. In Edmund Seymour you have a worthy and important advocate. He is wealthy and well established." She paused, clearly taking close measure of my response. "And I believe, I feel absolutely confident, that he will only continue to rise and prosper at court. The young woman who becomes his wife would do very well for herself. Her own star would shine brightly from the heaven that is England."

Unsure of how to respond to this elaborate and rather grandiose metaphor (even for a sovereign queen), I remained kneeling and said absolutely nothing. I dared not believe that my own queen, she who I was supposed to serve, she whose healthy reign I was supposed to ensure, could possibly be suggesting that I think of Edmund Seymour as a suitor, especially after all that she had said to me about her own concerns when it came to marriage. How could the queen have forgotten that she herself had said that women always had the disadvantage after they wed? And why did she suddenly sound like Alice?

And yet, was it at all possible, I wondered, as the queen's pale face glowed with misguided admiration, that Edmund Seymour had come by her affection in an honest fashion, or had he put some sort of spell on her? And did the sapphire he wore on his ring finger have anything to do with it?

"No need to speak of your own desires now," Elizabeth told me at last, waving her hand and indicating that I should rise. "As planned, you will leave Whitehall and return to Moonsway. Surely you will want to have a few days with Lady Strange, so I shall not expect you back for a week."

Thinking it best to remain silent (at least for now), a second time I knelt before my queen, bowing even more deeply this time as I kissed her hand. Still, I could feel my whole body quaking with all the contradictory plots that, in less than ten days' time, seemed to have been set afoot.

CHAPTER SIXTEEN

So eager was I to return home, the journey away from court, though only a few hours, seemed to last forever.

At last, just before sunset, Perseus and I arrived at Moonsway. As soon as I saw the pink house that looked a shade closer to coral in the falling light, and breathed in the fragrance of the end of the season roses, I felt more at ease.

Bess opened the door. "Welcome back, Lady Mary," she said, pressing me close. "Thank goodness you've arrived safely."

"It's good to see you, Bess," I said, grateful to feel her affectionate, uncomplicated arms around me; to take in her yeasty, fresh scent. "Where is my guardian?"

"In her sitting room, drinking her habitual cup of verbena tea, where else?"

I kissed Bess, then said, "I must go to her."

I found Lady Strange curled up on the sofa, surrounded by a sea of cushions, her violet eyes glimmering with anticipation, her golden aura aglow. Stretched at her feet lay Jack. As soon as his eyes lit on me, he leapt into my arms and covered me with wet kisses.

"I am glad to see you, Mary," Lady Strange said, once Jack and I released each other, and my favorite hound set about sniffing Perseus, much to my noble spirit's dismay. (*The indignity of it all*, Perseus's eyes said. I could not help but relish this moment—just a little).

"You have been daily in my thoughts," Lady Strange said, hugging me close. "Now, do sit down, and in good earnest tell me all that has happened."

After she poured me a cup of tea and offered me a few of Bess's almond cookies, I curled up beside her and told her almost everything. In particular, I relayed Frances Howard's circumstances and the spell I had cast with Cordelia's instructions, the three days of unconsciousness that followed. So too, I relayed the story of the queen's professed affection for my mother as well as the story behind the amethyst amulet. "The queen gave me this gift from my mother," I concluded, my fingertips sparking as I placed the ruby-and-pearl necklace in her hands.

Lady Strange admired the necklace. "This is a very good sign," she said. "As I hoped and believed, you are already close to the queen's heart. This will aid you immensely in your work at court, for the queen's gift attests to the fact that she trusts you. As her white magician, Mary, you will need that trust in order to see clearly into her motives."

"Meaning, Elizabeth's trust will enable her to speak to me in confidence so that I won't have to peel through so many layers to find the truth."

"Very good, Mary," Lady Strange said. "I see you are beginning to put into practice all that you have learned."

At such praise, I beamed.

"The necklace so perfectly unites the rubies of your mother with the pearls of Elizabeth," Lady Strange continued, tapping her teacup with the tips of her long fingers. "What a stunning union. What a sign that you are already beginning to order the chaos of our queen's father."

"Yes," I agreed, although at that moment my thoughts were focused more on my mother than Elizabeth. This had been my mother's gift to Henry VIII's neglected daughter. That's what made it so special. When I wore the necklace I felt closer to her.

We stayed silent for a while, until at last I said, "I have a confession to make."

Lady Strange's eyes rested on my face. "Yes?"

"The court is a complicated, often frightening place." As I spoke, my thoughts whirled with all that had passed. "At times I was greatly afraid."

"Fear is natural," my guardian said. "Still, as Cordelia told you, fear should not become a power in its own right. Fear should be a guide, a friend, but fear should not govern you."

"Yes, I know. Nevertheless, at Whitehall I felt constantly on my guard. Finding out who I can and cannot trust, measuring just how much—and no more—to say; these things are more exhausting than anything I've undertaken." As I spoke, I wondered if my guardian had any idea that I was circling but not actually alighting upon the most disturbing element of them all.

"Surveillance is a necessary condition of your work, Mary," said Lady Strange, refilling her teacup and giving me no sign of how much she understood. "But remember you have Perseus with you, and he will always be a great helpmate in warding off evil."

It was true. Already he had helped me to twice evade my cousin on the night of the queen's party. Beside me,

Perseus sighed, and I stroked his head and then Jack's. (Thankfully, by now my old friend had given up sniffing Perseus.)

"Do you find it disturbing that Edmund Seymour seems to possess a number of the same dark qualities as my father?" I asked her.

"Perhaps," Lady Strange said thoughtfully. "Your cousin's character will inevitably pose a great challenge to your own. It would not surprise me to learn that he is the one pressing the queen for the return of your holdings."

I startled.

"Think about it, Mary. Such an inheritance would increase his own wealth and power, were he to capture you as a wife."

"Of course he stands no chance of capturing me," I said boldly.

"No," Lady Strange agreed, her violet eyes unreadable. "That he does not."

"And yet he and I are strangely matched, for he allowed evil to take root. And I allowed good."

"A very concise way of seeing things," Lady Strange considered. "What you must do is remember your present advantage and make the most of it."

It was then that I told Lady Strange of the sapphire Edmund Seymour wore on his ring finger. "Does the history of his sapphire connect with your own?"

"If it is a true sapphire, it must, for all the gemstones find their same point of origin."

It was not long before the discussion of gems—and their abuses—brought us to the subject of Vivienne Gascoigne, who I could still see drenched in the light of the hundreds of diamond chips overwhelming the pale gold of her hair.

"What do you know about her family?" I asked.

"Not a great deal, but what I do know is unsettling. In the twelfth century, the Gascoignes came over from France when Eleanor of Aquitaine married Henry the Second. They are a mysterious clan, one driven by their passions. During my grandmother's day, one of the Gascoigne women murdered a man who betrayed her in love. If I remember correctly, the woman was ultimately torn to bits by violent dogs."

Trying my utmost to shake off the ghastly image, I said, "If they are passionate and mysterious, are they also involved in magic?"

"Almost certainly. One of the Gascoignes, the Lady Genevieve, served as a lady-in-waiting to Eleanor of

Aquitaine. She accompanied Eleanor to the Middle East and learned about the magical arts there."

Memory of the Demonius of the Dead Sea and of my dream of the white serpent seared my mind. Were the two connected? Without wasting another second, I described both to Lady Strange.

"It is possible, though improbable, that Vivienne's ancestor somehow laid her hands on the Demonius."

I drew closer to her. "Why improbable?"

"Because the Demonius happens to be the largest sapphire in the world. Were someone to possess it, that person would be immensely strong, perhaps all-powerful. Given Vivienne's petty vindictiveness, I cannot believe that she can really claim much power, or she would not behave in such a mean way."

"But what about the diamonds in her hair?"

Lady Strange laughed so hard the teacup shook in her hands. "You have answered your own question when you said that cutting a large diamond weakens its potency and therefore, its virtues. If memory serves me correctly, I do recall hearing that the Lady Genevieve brought a diamond back from the desert, a gift from a great Mohammedan who hoped to make her his wife. Most likely, her descendent, the Lady Vivienne, is a far less noble person and has curbed the diamond's power by chopping it up in order to adorn her person. Pure vanity, my dear."

Lady Strange's eyes held my own. "Nevertheless, if Vivienne is a magician, she must not discover the source of your strength, for she might try to cripple or even destroy you, and although she has not your birthright or your virtue, we both know that good does not necessarily triumph over evil."

"Too true," I said, struck more forcefully by the reality of Cordelia's violent death.

It was then I told Lady Strange of Perseus's warning about Edmund Seymour's watchfulness during last night's concert. I told her how, afterward, someone else spoke directly to my mind and warned me not to show any weakness. "That person, whoever he or she was, knows who I am. Does that not mean I have an ally, a fellow white magician, at court?"

Lady Strange considered my question for a moment. "Possibly," she concluded, "though you must remember a key point of your training: things are not always as they appear to be."

"You're saying that someone who initially appears to be evil might in reality prove to be good, and vice versa?"

"That I am, Mary. The more time you spend practicing the magical arts, the more you will discover that there are many people and creatures, as well as objects, involved in the same arena. You must not immediately assume that the voice you heard is a good one. The best advice I can offer you is to remember your powers of observation and contemplation. Question everything and assume nothing."

"What about auras?" I asked. "Aren't they always right?"

"In my experience, yes," Lady Strange said. "That said, if a magician is very powerful, he might manipulate his aura or that of another person. Therefore, there may be times when not even an aura can be trusted."

Daunted by the scope of my task, my body seemed suddenly heavy. And then there was the absence of Edmund Seymour's aura, overwhelming proof of his unreadability and his simultaneous threat.

"Listen, Mary, part of your work will be to learn to recognize good from evil; both evil and good can take many forms. Above all, you must be careful, especially in your own practice. As you have already seen, each spell has its consequences. It's absolutely crucial you understand as much about a particular magical action as you can, well before you undertake it. Consequences, levels of energy—

all these things must be carefully evaluated. Never, my dear Mary, act in haste."

From there, we turned to the ominous subject of my inheritance and the queen's desire to elevate me. "The last thing I want is to be made an heiress," I said plainly.

"I am relieved to hear you say so. Were you to become an heiress, your position at court would become more complicated, for you would suddenly be a wealthy young woman with a revered mother's memory behind you. Many a man would try to marry you, and, as we both know, your official, albeit concealed, reason for being at court never shall be marriage or social prosperity. The accumulation of suitors would only cloud and misdirect your energies."

Suitors. Marriage. I pictured a lurid cave from which there was no escape. "How am I to prevent the queen's action?"

"With all the grace of your station and birth. You must be sure to appear genuinely grateful, but you must also convince her that it would be doing you and she harm, were she to make you rich."

CHAPTER SEVENTEEN

KNOWING ALL THAT LAY IN WAIT FOR ME upon my return to Whitehall, I relished this time at Moonsway. For a few delicious, equinoctial days with Perseus and Jack as my companions, I took long walks through a meadow blooming with yarrow, cowslip, and a few surviving primrose. Later, curled up in the shade of some stately tree, I ate a simple lunch of bread and fruit; then allowed myself to sit back and dream of the life I had led before going to court. Back then I could dream about my destiny without actually endangering myself by living it.

Sometimes Lady Strange joined us, and it was just like the old days. We gathered big bunches of September goldenrod and Queen Anne's lace and plucked small, tart lady apples from the trees, talking all the while about the properties of stones, the significance of auras, and countless other aspects of the expansive realm of white magic. For dinner, Bess made sure Cook prepared all my favorite dishes, including creamed asparagus soup and luscious cheese soufflé. Then, in the hours before bedtime, with Perseus's or Jack's head resting in my lap, I drank spiced cider and read poetry or drama aloud beside the fire.

Time seemed almost to stand still.

But of course this was all illusion. While I dreamed away the hours in the company of Perseus and Jack, the greater world continued to move. At Whitehall, I knew Alice Cavendish and the other ladies-in-waiting were busy making sure the inner circle of the queen's court revolved with polished elegance. Meanwhile, Vivienne Gascoigne plotted her petty machinations.

I did not like to imagine what my dark cousin was up to.

On the eve of my departure I received a message emblazoned with the royal seal. Secretly hoping my return had been delayed, I opened the paper and read:

On the morning of your expected return, Lord Dudley will be traveling through the environs of Moonsway. Her Majesty has entrusted your passage to his safekeeping.

from Elizabeth, Your Queen

I groped for the chair. I had just begun to contend with Edmund Seymour, and now here I was on the brink of encountering the powerful and possibly dangerous Lord Dudley, son of the traitorous Duke of Northumberland who had forced his own son's and Lady Jane Grey's rule on England during the two days that followed Edward's death. After Mary rallied her armies and had the duke and his conspirators put to death, the surviving members of the Dudley family were imprisoned in the Tower. Afterward, they lived within the dingy mantle of disgrace.

Until Elizabeth came to power.

Toward midmorning I heard the crunch of Lord Dudley's carriage on the path.

My reprieve at Moonsway had ended.

After smoothing my hair and straightening my gown, I left my room and proceeded down the staircase, only to hear Bess say to herself, "My word, the great lord is as dark as a gypsy."

Indeed he was, though I had never thought of him that way. The olive-complexioned Lord Robert Dudley had auburn hair, a reddish beard and mustache, an arched nose, and heavy-lidded eyes. Tall and muscularly built, he wore tight-fitting clothes that showed his long legs off to expert (and I suspect, well-calculated) advantage.

I came toward him, and he looked up from beneath his complex aura of burgundy, smiling in such a way as to seem truly sincere.

I must learn to see if he is closer to the red or to the purple, I told Perseus.

Absolutely, my loyal friend agreed. *It's of the utmost importance that you discover upon whose side—if anyone's—he stands.*

"My dear Lady Mary," Lord Dudley said, bowing deeply. "I have instructions to escort you to Whitehall. To both of our surprises, and I hope to our mutual pleasures, we shall spend the next several hours solely in one another's company."

"Sir," I said, choosing my words with care, "I am grateful to you for carrying me back to the palace."

"Do I find you well?" Lord Dudley asked. "And are you ready for the journey to court?"

Stepping swiftly into the room, it was Lady Strange who answered. "Mary is quite well," she said. "And yes, she is prepared. I, however, require a few minutes alone with her."

"Lady Strange," Lord Dudley said, bowing, so that I saw a lapis lazuli—the sapphire of the ancients—adorning a ring on his left hand. "It is a pleasure to see you again. It has been a very long time. I think the last time was at Katherine Parr's coronation?"

With her unwavering grace, my guardian greeted him politely, but she said nothing about the last time they'd met.

I felt his eyes upon us as Lady Strange and I ascended the stairs with Perseus quick at our heels.

"I am not easy about our separation," I confessed, once Lady Strange closed the door to her room.

"It's true that good thoughts and memories alone will not sustain us," she said, stroking my hair. "I have therefore made some further provisions for our communication during the time we are apart."

This pricked my ears. Beside me, Perseus, too, seemed to stand at attention, eager to hear what Lady Strange had arranged.

"You have learned that each spell, each instance of magic, must be carefully planned for," she said as she stepped over to the window and gazed out at the drive, where we both knew the carriage waited.

"Under normal circumstances, our communication

should therefore take the usual form of letters. The exceptions to this rule are as follows: one, a life-threatening situation; two, an absolute breakdown of the magic; and three," she said gently, "extreme homesickness."

I was grateful for this last promise, for I suspected that I would often fall prey to missing Lady Strange and Jack.

"Mind you, Mary," she said, her lower lip quivering just a little, "you must not abuse this third condition, for the raven's assistance comes at great personal cost."

"Of course not." Preoccupied with our impending separation, I did not want to think about the costs. "Tell me about the raven," I said instead.

Lady Strange drew me toward her and, in hushed tones, told me about a mysterious raven who could fly seven times as swiftly as an ordinary bird of his kind. "Speed is not the bird's only gift. He can also carry information. If you need me, you need only call for him, give him your message, and he will find me—wherever I am."

"How am I to call him?" I said. "Surely there is a particular incantation."

"Yes." Lady Strange closed her eyes. "Repeat after me: 'Raven, raven, swifter than a shooting star, more deadly than a bolt of lightning, and darker than the darkest night, I seek thee.'"

Once I had committed this string of words to memory with absolute precision, I scanned the room, hoping to find the raven hidden there. "But where is he?" I pressed, eager to meet this new helpmate.

Lady Strange's face remained solemn. "You won't find him here."

I frowned. Perseus's own stillness throughout the conversation should have alerted me to this fact. "I'm sorry, Mary, but the raven will not appear casually. As I said, he is a bird whose assistance comes at great price."

I wanted to discuss this further, but before I could do so, Lady Strange held a finger to my lips and said, "Ask me not what that price is."

I yearned to know more, but Lady Strange just shook her head. "It's no use," she told me. "I cannot reveal such things, or I will damage the enchantment's efficacy."

With these words I understood I was leaving my guardian, wrapped ever more deeply in a curtain of magic that I was only just beginning to understand.

CHAPTER EIGHTEEN

OVER THE NEXT SEVERAL HOURS, LORD Dudley and I were entirely alone. At first we talked of such things as the changing fashions at court—*"My sister swears lace-edged doublets will be the very thing next season"*—the forecast for a plentiful harvest—*"Apples will be especially bountiful"*—and a bitter cold winter—*"Some say the Thames will completely freeze over. The last time it did so was half a century ago. The old folks say one could literally walk across the river and peer down at the fish and other water creatures preserved within the ice."*

But by the time he offered me a sip of sherry from his flask, we had entered into conversation of a far more personal nature.

"You may not realize it," Lord Dudley said, "but the queen and I have known each other since the time we were very small children. My own birth, on June twenty-fourth preceded hers by just under three months."

"I had no idea you were so close in age," I replied, sure his desire to create a connection between himself and our queen signified something.

"We are indeed," he continued. "My nurse says that she and the other caretakers used to bet on which of us would cut a tooth first."

"Pray tell me, Lord Dudley, which of you did?" I asked, struck anew by his lapis lazuli gemstone, and determined to learn why he would choose to wear the sapphire of the ancients.

"Our good queen, of course," he said.

For the next few minutes we sat without speaking; I listened to the horses' hoof beats and tried to catch Perseus's eye, but my good spirit remained focused on the countryside beyond.

"What you may not realize is this," Lord Dudley said at last. "At court, you and I shall see a good deal of each other. I serve Elizabeth with my whole heart. You, too, will be expected to do as much."

His words immediately recalled to me the virtues of his

preferred gem. Like the sapphire, lapis lazuli embodied devotion and bravery, although in lapis these virtues were present in a less potent form. If Lord Dudley adhered to these values, then he spoke truly. Yet it was possible that he defied the virtues of his gemstone.

"I do not shrink from the responsibility of serving my queen," I told him.

"Your loyalty was never in question. I trust that you are a woman of the highest virtue, for you are Katherine Parr's child."

Unsure of his sincerity, I was about to speak, when Perseus looked away from the window and caught my eye.

Measure your words carefully, he advised.

As if he sensed what had passed between Perseus and myself, Lord Dudley considered me and said, "It is wise for any courtier to be cautious. Yet I have watched you from a distance. In the garden, for example, you are all boundless energy. And then there is your friend Alice—"

"Alice is a trusted, female companion," I emphasized. "My first true friend at court."

"Mind, I would never jeopardize your virtue," Lord Dudley said. "Still, I would like to better understand why you are so reserved in my company."

How could I tell Lord Dudley that his presence at

court inevitably recollected the memory of his traitorous father who had tried to manipulate Henry VIII's son, Edward, when the boy became king?

"If you will not tell me, then I shall hazard my own answer." He leaned toward me, and I saw his ink-dark eyes widen. "Do I have your permission to do so?"

Newly aware of how closely Perseus was following our conversation, I replied, "I suppose."

"You fear I am the fruit of a bad seed."

I swallowed hard, yet tried my best to give no outward physical sign of his words' impact.

When I did not reply, he pressed, "Am I right in supposing this to be the reason for your caution?"

My eyes met his. "Yes, sir," I said at last. "It is."

"Well, my dear Lady Mary, I hope my actions will convince you of my trustworthiness. However, let me say that although you are Katherine Parr's child, your own father, with the exception of his prudent decision to marry your mother, was a man of doubtful character. You would not like to be judged by his model, would you?"

"No, sir," I said, drawing myself up slightly, aware of the virtuous opal concealed beneath my camisole and simultaneously puzzled as to why Lord Dudley would call such an alliance prudent unless he, too, was determined to realize his ambitions through a woman. "I would not."

"And yet, we have that in common, too. Both of our fathers lost their lives because they plotted against the crown, and as a result, our respective families suffered great misery. I am very well-informed about your own early childhood, Mary," he said, with too much intimacy. "I know how poorly you fared in the Duchess of Suffolk's company once she entered into that unfortunate liaison with her Master of the Horse. Katherine Parr's daughter, the babe who once slept on satin sheets, turned into a seamstress's apprentice—"

"What do you know about my history?" I said sharply. "What can you possibly hope to gain by such words, by such unwarranted intimacy?"

"I only hope to make clear that good is not always distinct from evil," Lord Dudley said, tugging at his reddish beard.

I was about to say more when a severe glance from Perseus alerted me to the necessity of controlling my emotions.

"Listen," Dudley continued, "I do not say these things to hurt you. I volunteered to escort you back—"

I dug my heels into the floor of the carriage. Not once had I considered this possibility. "You volunteered?"

"Yes. Nothing would please me more than to count you among my friends," he said, with what appeared to be true sincerity. "I would like to be assured, too, of your good opinion of me."

"Well then, sir," I said, my gaze level with his own, my faith in my calling guiding me. "You must prove yourself worthy of my good opinion."

During the remainder of our journey, Lord Dudley did precisely that, recalling the years of Queen Mary's reign, those despondent years of persecution for England's Protestants. And as he spoke, the purple in his burgundy began to outshine the red.

"Henry the Eighth may have begun the Protestant Church in England," Dudley explained. "But when Queen Mary came to power, she not only reinstituted the authority of the Catholic Church, she went so far as to forbid the practice of the Protestant religion in this country. In 1554, Mary went a step further when she made plans to wed the Catholic Prince Philip of Spain."

I thought of the costly war England had entered into on the side of Spain, the draining of money and lives, all because of the foolish queen's fanatical devotion to a husband who did not return her affections. Yet when I spoke, it was not the private disaster I dwelled upon but the public; for a woman who falls disastrously in love is one thing, a queen who does so is another. "And interference," I said, "especially Spanish interference, is something the people of England cannot abide."

Folding his arms against his chest, Lord Dudley leaned back in the carriage seat. "Precisely. As you can conclude, Queen Mary's unpopular reign presented our Protestant Elizabeth as her natural successor. In 1554, our present queen was implicated in two plots to overthrow her half sister. First, during the winter months, Mary accused Elizabeth of consulting with an astrologer in order to determine the best time for such an action."

Cautiously, I asked, "What was the outcome?"

"Fortunately, this charge proved false. Although Elizabeth did meet with the astrologer, her purpose proved to have a more private cause. She'd had a proposal of marriage and wanted to consult the stars." Dudley's face lost all color, and real sadness seemed to creep into his eyes. "As Her Majesty's history attests, the stars were against such a match."

"And the second charge?" I asked, curious to learn if Lord Dudley had been Elizabeth's disappointed suitor.

"The second charge was far less easy to dismiss.

Although Elizabeth did not play a part in the matter, that same year the headstrong poet Thomas Wyatt concocted a plot to rid England of Queen Mary. In her place, he wanted Elizabeth to rule as a Protestant monarch alongside Edward Courtenay."

"The Black Prince Edward the Fourth's great-great-grandson," I said, recalling all the hours Lady Strange and I had spent poring over family trees.

"The very man. Although Courtenay was not a natural leader, he had Edward the Fourth's legendary memory to buttress any flaws in his character."

"What happened during Wyatt's rebellion?" I asked, for although Lady Strange and I had already discussed the event, I wanted to hear Dudley's version.

"Wyatt managed to assemble a small troop, and in the dead of night they marched on London." Dudley's face turned very pale. "The talented man was caught within two hours of his party's entry into the city and quickly executed. Unfortunately, Wyatt's capture and his confession of Elizabeth's absolute innocence did not convince Queen Mary to let the matter rest. No, once Queen Mary discovered the plot, her suspicious and unhappy mind lost itself in the details of the conspiracy. Although Elizabeth had always behaved as a true sister and loyal member of her half sister's court, Queen Mary became convinced of her guilt."

"She had Elizabeth taken to the Tower," I said, reminded of a long ago conversation I'd overheard at the duchess's funeral.

"Yes. A terrified Elizabeth arrived by river in the dead of night. You can only imagine what she must have felt, for the episode brought back all the anguish in her mother's history. Within those same thick, stone walls, Anne Boleyn was beheaded." Dudley shuddered. "For three long months, poor Elizabeth suffered the captivity of an airless room. Each day she feared the executioner's axe."

Here was another parallel between the queen's history and my own, I realized; for it was my father's brother who convicted, then condemned my father to a traitor's death. Feeling the tears beginning, I was about to ask Lord Dudley for a handkerchief.

But then my eyes met his. He, too, seemed on the verge of tears. A man crying? Now, this was suspicious. What if Lord Dudley was attempting to lull me into sympathy in order to manipulate me?

"Why are you telling me all of this?" I said. "What do the queen's long ago sufferings have to do with your friendship?"

He did not flinch. "Absolutely everything."

"Pray, sir," I said, forcing myself to hold his gaze. "Explain."

As if he had read my thoughts, he said, "I will tell you so that you do not believe that I am only trying to sway your emotions. And yes, Mary, I can see you are suspicious of me. Such suspicions—given the life at the court—are well-founded. What you have probably not considered is that I, too, was once a prisoner in the Tower. After my father's execution and my older brother's, the surviving members of my family remained in the Tower—even my beloved sister, who later nursed our good queen through the smallpox.

"We, too, feared for our lives. Queen Mary was in an insecure and vengeful mood. Elizabeth's time in that prison, and my own, overlapped. During these terrible months when we knew not if we would live to see another week, Elizabeth and I managed to comfort each other." Dudley's voice turned almost tender. "So you see, I shared this terrible memory with Elizabeth, and it became a great bond between us."

A great bond. There were those who spoke—in hushed tones—about the real reason for the queen's solitary state. Some said Elizabeth loved Lord Dudley, a man without a drop of royal blood, a man with a disreputable family history, and therefore a man unworthy of a sovereign queen. And yet she had raised him a little higher, time and time again, gifting him with lands and titles, until he rose very high in her court to be among its most esteemed and wealthy members. Had she also given him the rare gift of lapis lazuli which he now so proudly wore?

"Upon my release from the Tower, I had everything to do with persuading Elizabeth's half sister, Queen Mary, of her innocence."

I did not say so, but I found it difficult to believe that Dudley, the Protestant son of the traitorous Duke of Northumberland, could have convinced the paranoid Catholic Queen Mary of her Protestant half sister's innocence. Nevertheless, the sincerity with which he professed his loyalty—coupled with the deepening of the purple in his burgundy aura and the steadfast presence of lapis—I could not doubt.

"I have been loyal to Elizabeth ever since," Dudley concluded, the purple now shining. "It is for my loyalty and friendship, and for nothing else, that our good queen has rewarded me."

CHAPTER NINETEEN

No sooner had we arrived at White-hall than I spotted Alice Cavendish strolling along the grounds, her spectacles perched unsteadily on her nose, which was buried in a thick book. At the sound of our approach, Alice looked up from her reading, waved, then hurried over. Once the carriage came to a hault, Lord Dudley helped me to step down as the driver unloaded my luggage.

"Welcome back, Mary," she called, hugging her book to her chest.

Until that moment I don't think I realized how much I needed to see Alice's plain, intelligent face again. Whereas court life had proven itself to be a maze of innuendo and caution, Alice presented things as she saw them, and although (thanks to my spell) she was deluded when it came to Edmund Seymour's character, she remained clear-sighted insofar as other matters were concerned.

She curtseyed to Lord Dudley, who in turn bowed to her.

"You are a loyal friend to come out and meet Lady Mary's arrival," he told her.

"I have missed Mary immensely, sir." She squinted at Perseus. "And her remarkable dog also."

Then, foregoing etiquette, Alice flung the book to the ground, threw her arms around my neck, and in most un-lady-in-waiting-like fashion, kissed me on both cheeks.

Beside us, even Perseus seemed to beam.

When it came time for me to take my leave of Lord Dudley, I allowed him to clasp both of my hands between his own. Just out of Alice's earshot he said, "Am I correct in assuming that you and I have reached an understanding?"

"You are, sir." My words were few, but I infused them with genuine warmth.

While Molly unpacked my bags, Alice briefed me on all that had happened at Whitehall in my absence. She told me that Frances Howard had arrived safely at her parents'

house. Also, that plans were being made for a winter garden to be laid beyond the orchard.

Once Molly departed, however, Alice's revelations turned more confidential.

"You have arrived in the midst of a host of entertainments. Tomorrow, there will be music and singing, and then on Friday, a play. Drama may be a commonplace here at court," she continued, tapping her fingertips together in an almost conspiratorial fashion. "Still, the subject of this particular play is most noteworthy."

"Go on, then," I said. "Tell me about it."

Alice beamed, and her spectacles slipped down her nose. "I knew you'd be interested. The play takes as its point of departure the seasons. As September draws to a close, Virgo will be replaced by Libra. Virgo is the queen's astrological sign. The thing is, some say that the waning of Virgo, its symbolic role within the play, is a clandestine message to Elizabeth to marry."

I startled. "How does this news strike you?"

"As a grave surprise as well as a grave disappointment," Alice confessed. "Much of my admiration for our queen stems from her independence. 'I allow myself to be governed by no one,' I heard her say once. Such words I could take as my own creed."

"And yet you seem to be in favor of my cousin's supposed affections toward me?" I could not resist adding. "Is that not a contradiction?"

"Really, Mary," Alice frowned. "I do not believe it is. Your cousin is a respected member of the court. For you, such a match would be an immense opportunity. Imagine all you could do to improve the lives of our sex as wife to such a husband. Why, you might even found a university exclusively for women."

"But why must I marry to have the means to do such a thing?" I said, trying my utmost to keep a level tone. "Can't you see that your reasoning is flawed?"

"No," Alice said while her spectacles fogged.

"Yet you would never consider such a thing. Is that not true?"

"True," Alice stammered. "I would not."

I decided not to press the matter further, for it would only lead to a squandering of my energy, which I definitely needed to conserve. Besides, I had begun to wonder if Alice's resoluteness on this point might not be a sort of residue from my previous spell, for was there not a connection between her amnesia and her certainty that Edmund would make me a good husband?

Turning my attention back to the predicament of the queen, I asked, "Has a suitor presented himself?"

Cautious as always, Alice hurried to the door to make sure no one was listening.

I fixed my eyes on Perseus. *I had no inkling of any of this. The queen with a suitor?*

At court, change can happen very swiftly, Perseus said. *In the blink of an eye.*

Once she felt assured of our privacy, Alice returned to my side to finish her story. "Yes," she said, her cheeks reddening. "There is a suitor."

"Is it one of the courtiers?" I asked, as the conversation with Lord Dudley crackled through my memory.

Alice stared. "Certainly not. The queen with a commoner. What an idea!"

I stifled a laugh, for such things had happened before. "Who is it, then?"

"It is the French King Charles."

The French king? I turned to Perseus. *Am I too late?*

Just as Alice said, the morrow brought a full evening of exquisite entertainments. Venetian minstrels strolled through the gilded rooms, serenading the court with Italian love songs. Others played a series of golden flutes, each of which reproduced a different animal sound. And everywhere I glimpsed elaborate silver trays of delicacies: shrimps and herrings, oysters and pickled vegetables. Decanters of wine were poured. High spirits flowed.

I caught sight of Edmund Seymour engaged in conversation with Vivienne Gascoigne, and noticed a pipe in his hand, a pipe very like the ones I'd seen sailors smoke. Instantly I understood his peaty, burnt-leaf smell was that of tobacco. He soon noticed me staring, raised his glass, and smiled a disarming smile meant for me alone.

Vivienne watched it all. In her face I saw a look that was impossible to mistake: one of pure hatred. I gave thanks that I had worn both the amethyst brooch and the ruby-and-pearl necklace. More than ever, I needed the strength of my jewels. As always, the opal was pressed against my heart, an ever-present reminder of who I was and the virtues I had to live up to.

I spotted Lord Dudley standing close beside the queen, who was engaged in conversation with a foreign-looking man in an elaborately embroidered doublet and the most unusual and rather ostentatious gold-tipped velvet shoes; their color, aubergine. Was this the French king?

When Elizabeth caught sight of me, she sent a servant over to fetch me.

I joined my queen's group, then bowed and kissed her hand.

"Welcome back, Mary," she said, allowing her hand to rest within my own for just a moment. "Your presence here at Whitehall has been sorely missed."

"Who is this lovely young woman?" asked the stranger, speaking English with a thick French accent.

"Lady Mary Seymour, the daughter of the late Katherine Parr, my father's last and most devoted wife. She is the newest of my ladies-in-waiting." The gold in her hazel eyes seemed to darken. "I have the greatest hopes and intentions for her future."

"It is an honor to meet you," he said, taking my hand as if I were a fragile object: a porcelain vase or a silk tapestry, and not a woman who stood a full hand's breadth above him. "News of your mother's beneficence and intelligence has traveled as far as France. And now that I see you, I must assume you are the very print of your mother in goodness as well as beauty.

"Allow me to introduce myself. I am Jean de Lys, Count of St. Anseilles." He bowed dramatically and swept out his left hand, revealing a lozenge-shaped citrine topaz, emblem of courtesy and manners.

He's silver-tongued, Perseus said.

"He is a most choice courtier, skilled in the shrewd arts of the court and in the artificial pleasures of love," Lord Dudley said, not even trying to choke down his disapproval.

"Mend your words, my good sir," the count said. "I am an ambassador from King Charles, sent to woo and to win your radiant and supremely intelligent queen's hand."

Lord Dudley made a little coughing sound but did not reply.

For a time I remained within this close-knit circle, listening with discomfort and some pain (for he did make a travesty of the English language with all his ornate phrasings) to the count's professions of love on behalf of his thirteen-year-old king.

"Do you believe the queen seriously intends to marry him?" I whispered to Lord Dudley, moving away from the count's potent perfume.

Drawing his finger to his lips, he said, "It's safer if we speak outside."

He took my arm, then led me into the garden. Among the cool scents of lavender and thyme, Lord Dudley told me that in times of trouble the queen often played the courts of Spain and France against each other.

"As ruler of England, she must be careful not to lose the friendship of the one if she is out of favor with the other. As a woman, she has license to use her feminine charms to forge these alliances." He grinned at me, as if by sheer virtue of my sex I understood these tactics. "Why, just after Elizabeth came to the throne, King Philip had the gall to ask her to become his wife." He chuckled. "We both know that our good queen most politely and most politically refused him."

"Are you telling me the queen is inviting the French king's attentions in order to secure an alliance with France against Spain?"

"That is precisely what I am telling you," he said, lowering his voice. "Take care you don't broadcast this knowledge around the court."

I raised my finger to my lips, reminded of one of the cardinal rules of a lady-in-waiting, that she not dabble in politics, a rule that conflicted with my real role of white magician. In this realm, politics and the well-being of England went hand in hand. "Why is the queen out of favor with Spain?" I asked.

Lord Dudley grinned. "Because she refused Philip's offer of marriage. That pompous fool actually possesses the vanity to believe that only by marrying him—and converting to Catholicism—can Her Majesty save her soul and the souls of her subjects."

"Such a proposal is most preposterous," I agreed. "Yet what of the French king? Do you not think there's a chance she will accept him?"

"That child? Elizabeth may be a virgin queen"—a secretive look came into Dudley's eyes—"nevertheless, Her Majesty does value the chess game of courtly, not carnal, love, but only with a worthy player. No, my dear Lady Mary." He stroked his mustache. "I would stake my reputation on a firm but utterly captivating refusal."

"Why does the queen, why does England, need France's friendship now?" I asked.

"You are dabbling in politics," Lord Dudley said, studying me.

I stared back at him. "I correct you, sir. I am only trying to educate myself on the situation."

"You are bold, Lady Mary Seymour," he said, a new attentiveness penetrating his voice.

"Perhaps," I said. "But if you want to make an ally of me, you must understand that I require the entire story before I come to a decision."

"Fair enough," he replied, the purple in his burgundy aura shining brightly.

I stepped a bit closer. "Why do you scrutinize me so?"

"I am marveling at the strength of your will. You

present yourself as the epitome of a demure lady, but given the chance, you manifest the most resilient convictions. In this way I do believe you are like your mother.

"True," he said, noticing my slight start, "I did not know her well. Still, I do remember the way Katherine Parr held fast to her own beliefs. Once she even went as far as to distribute her prayers among soldiers going to war, despite the king's dangerous conviction that she had overreached her bounds."

"I hope I am patterned after my mother in most things," I said, strangely touched by the accuracy of Lord Dudley's memory. "But please, tell me why the queen longs to make France an ally."

"I speak to you in the strictest confidence, you understand?"

"Of course."

"Well then, I will tell you because I trust you," Lord Dudley said. I inclined my head, acknowledging the compliment. "Her Majesty wants to safeguard the proposed trade route to Russia because there is much piracy on the high seas, as well as an unofficial tradition of plunder between the English and the Spanish."

"So the queen is inviting the suit of the French king

because she hopes the French will protect our ships en route to and from Russia?"

"Precisely."

"But won't she have to go through Sweden in order to reach Russia? Will she not need to secure the permission of the Swedes?"

"Very good, Mary. Unlike most of your sex, I see you know your geography."

"Of course I do," I said, grateful to Lady Strange for the thousands of hours of study, and simultaneously smarting for all the women who had not had my opportunities.

"To return to your question, when the time is ripe, Elizabeth will convince the Swedes of the value of granting England permission to open such a route."

"How?" I blurted out.

"She has her methods," he said with calculated slowness. "You see, Mary, another one of Her Majesty's suitors is King Erik of Sweden."

For the first time, I truly understood the peculiar advantage of a woman monarch in a world governed by men. She could dangle the carrot of marriage in front of their eyes—not just treaties and trade agreements, but marriage, the most binding of all alliances.

"Who is to lead this first expedition?" I asked, my

heartbeat steadily increasing, my hands suddenly clammy.

"The queen has not yet come to a final decision. Sir Walter Effingham, one of England's finest naval officers, is the favorite." Lord Dudley hesitated. "But there are other competitors for the post. Chief among these is your own cousin, Edmund Seymour."

Unable to conceal the shock that flickered across my face, I tried to retreat into the shadows. "He would like to go to Russia?" I said, concentrating on an overblown but fragrant rose.

"So he tells the court." More cautiously, Lord Dudley said, "I hope I did not upset you. Would you be very unhappy if your cousin were to go far away?"

"Of course not," I replied, meeting his eyes. "What a question."

From the way he looked at me, I could tell: rumors had been set afoot. Meanwhile, without furthering the impression that I longed for my cousin, I wanted to understand why Edmund would be drawn to that part of the world. Surely, there must be something very great at stake here.

"Why do we seek trade with Russia?" I asked.

He laughed, then plucked a newly opened rose from the same bush. "I am not at liberty to fully answer that question," he said. "At least not at present. I can tell you only that Russia is a fertile market for many of our country's goods. And Russia opens up the possibility of additional trade with Persia and other Far Eastern countries."

"Our chief competitor, or at least our chief threat, is Spain?"

"Yes, although the Spanish have less chance of success," he said, taking the liberty of placing the rose behind my left ear. "The menacingly devout Philip and his tiresome relatives do not possess the charm of our queen."

"You do not mean to say the Russian czar also seeks Her Majesty as his bride?"

Again Lord Dudley chuckled. "Not yet, no, and to such a marriage I know the queen would not consent. The last thing she wants is a marital alliance with a distant, snow-banked country where the favored drink is vodka.

"I tell you this only so that you will understand the way the queen's charm figures into her international dealings."

"I am grateful for this confidence," I replied, curtseying.

Lord Dudley bowed and kissed my hand, then gallantly took his leave.

No sooner had he gone, when my cousin stepped forth from the shrubberies. My heart rose to my throat, and my palms, even the soles of my feet, broke into a feverish sweat. How much had he heard? I wondered, hurrying to find an escape route. I looked left to the miniature spruce and right to the flower beds, but it was no use.

I was cornered.

The next thing I knew, Edmund was standing close to me and raising my hand to his lips. As disturbing as these actions proved, even more disturbing was that again he seemed to have suppressed his aura. Edmund's lips pressed the back of my hand. Fortified by the cool resolve of the amethyst, I pulled away.

"Why do you avoid me, Mary? You do not seem so unfriendly to Lord Dudley." His eyes rested on the rose in my hair. "Is it possible you favor him over me?"

"I do not know what you mean," I said formally.

"Lord Dudley escorted you back to Whitehall, did he not?"

"He did," I replied, still seeking escape, "but it was at the queen's request."

Perseus moved closer to me.

"Ah, my young cousin." Edmund plucked the rose from behind my ear and seemed to want to nuzzle in close. "Why can't you see that you are wasting precious time in avoiding me? Don't you understand that I should have everything to do with your present and your future? Together, we could drink from life's most ebullient cup.

Do you not see how much power we could command, could enjoy together? Picture Katherine Parr's daughter with another Seymour."

"I cannot picture such an alliance," I replied, moving farther away from him, fighting the urge to yield to his touch.

"Do not be so certain I am entirely the devil you believe me to be," he said, again drawing near, as did Perseus. "Have you never wondered at the ways in which a person's surface might conceal other aspects of his character?" His eyes held my own. "Think of your own mother's history."

"Do not dare to speak to me about my mother."

But Edmund Seymour continued in a lulling, lyrical way I could not so easily resist. I could not explain why, but despite Perseus's nearness and the amethyst brooch, my body betrayed me. I exerted all my efforts at self-control. Still, that quickening fire coursed through me. Then, to my absolute horror, a seam of rose appeared in the very center of my silver aura.

My cousin must have noticed this, too, for he pressed forward more confidently. "You must see that your mother fell in love with Thomas Seymour because she was hungry for life. He brought your mother adventure and pleasure of a kind no aging king could ever give. He brought her his own beauty and devotion." Edmund brought his face very close to my own and lightly touched my hair. "Do you not long for these things, too, Mary?"

"No!" I pushed away from him, then fled.

CHAPTER TWENTY

I SPENT A SLEEPLESS NIGHT IN MY BED-CHAMBER.
Every time I drifted off, my cousin's face—whispering
in my ear in that strange, lulling way—startled me
awake. My body's responsive yearning both astonished
and disgusted me. So, too, I was disappointed by the
failure of the amulet to protect me. Was it somehow
defective? Given that it had been a gift from Elizabeth,
this fact I doubted. And yet the amethyst could not
steel me against my cousin. What gave him so much
power? Was it the sapphire in his possession?

Careful not to wake Perseus (how ashamed I would
have been had he seen me in such a state!), I filled my
washbasin with warm water. Recalling a recipe
 Persephone had used to protect herself during her stay

in the underworld, into the pure water I placed a compost of fennel and marjoram, herbs prized for their purifying properties, as well as a stalk of poisonous and hairy worm-wood, a potent plant valued for its repelling qualities. At two a.m. and again just before dawn, I washed every patch of my body, all the while reciting an incantation I hoped would cure me of this madness.

Come morning I felt groggy and out of sorts.

Still, I could not hide in my room. There was the queen's facial cream to prepare and a number of her less elaborate gowns to attend to. Most pressing of all was the queen's request that I dine alone with her in her private chamber.

When the time came for me to go to the privy chamber, Alice did not escort me. Earlier, while walking among the ornamental hedgerow, she told me that she planned to help Vivienne Gascoigne with her lines in Friday's play.

"She actually asked for your help?"

"The haughty Lady Vivienne never asks for anyone's help," Alice corrected. "Still, I've heard her recite passages aloud on other occasions. Her diction needs improvement, so I volunteered to coach her. I couldn't bear to sit through a botched performance." She squinted, then stooped to pluck a weed from the path. "I guess you might say I'd do anything for art."

I wanted to question her further, but Alice had little time for conversation when her intellectual powers were needed elsewhere. So I went about my business, and when the luncheon hour arrived, I found my way to the queen's rooms, accompanied by Perseus alone.

A trio of three young men stood posted just outside the dining room. When we sat down to the meal, this same trio served the queen and then myself, offering us each dish as they remained kneeling at the tableside, their eyes downcast.

I would have liked to ask the queen about this most peculiar custom, but no sooner had the beer been poured and a luncheon of capons, pears, and hazelnut cream pudding been served, than Her Majesty turned immediately to her point. "I would like to restore you to your proper station, Mary."

"That is very kind and generous," I said, mindful of Perseus so that he could guide me in my responses. At the very least, I trusted Perseus to tell me when I had spoken out of turn.

"Your responsiveness gladdens my heart." Elizabeth

lifted the glass of beer to her lips and drank deeply. "Although I do not have the papers here before me, I intend to return to you your mother's property of Chelsea Manor as well as Sudeley Castle."

Shuddering, I shrank back. "But Sudeley Castle belonged to my father."

Elizabeth considered me thoughtfully. "Surely, Mary, you are entitled to your father's property as well as your mother's."

"I mean no disrespect, Your Majesty," I said with firm politeness, "but I would prefer not to take ownership of Sudeley Castle."

Astonishment erased most expression from the queen's face, and the forkful of pear fell from her hand and clattered to her plate. "How can that possibly be? Is it not an unnatural thing to refuse your inheritance? Besides, your mother is buried there. I have visited her grave many, many times. Surely, you would like to possess the land that contains her final resting place."

"True, my mother died at Sudeley Castle, but what good to me is her crypt when I have lost the one person I should have grown up to respect and love? The one person who should have been my childhood's all?"

Elizabeth remained so gravely silent that I could hear

the furious beating of my heart ten times magnified. Perseus, too, seemed a bit stunned and sent me messages of warning.

Yet was it not my duty, both to myself and to my queen, to speak the truth?

I watched and waited, until at last she said, "You have pressed very close to my own history. I know too well there is no substitute for a mother's love."

I was just about to rejoice when Elizabeth said, "Still, you must remember that you were born at Sudeley Castle. You have a right to the property."

"No right." Despite my queen's rigid posture and menacing silence, I pressed on. "Was my father not executed as a traitor? Did he not commit the highest crime, that of treason? And for these reasons, did he not lose all of his lands and holdings?"

"These are strange words," she said at last. "To remind your sovereign of your father's crimes. Equally strange is the bold way in which you speak to me." Our eyes met. "A sovereign queen is one whom you should revere, even fear."

Despite my trembling, I could not back down.

"No." Elizabeth pursed her lips. "I cannot encourage such outspokenness."

Perseus and I exchanged concerned glances.

"My intuition tells me that you are not the young woman you appear to be, Mary," she said at last.

I looked down at my hands, absolutely without a clue as to what the queen would say next, yet trusting silence as my most potent ally.

"If your father's legacy is so abhorrent to you, then I will gift you only with the one house to which you have every right: Chelsea. It was my father's gift to Katherine Parr, and it was the house in which she was the happiest." In an almost peaceful voice she said, "During the months following my father's death, I spent many joyful days there with your mother. It is a beautiful place. You were conceived there. You cannot possibly refuse this offering."

"Your Majesty, this gift I would be most honored to accept," I replied, understanding the meaning that this house must have held for my mother.

"I could do more for you, Mary," the queen said. "I would like to do more."

In her eyes, I saw how much my queen wanted to do for me—and how dangerous it might be to refuse.

A subtle sign from Perseus prompted me to use the tools of grace and charm in which I was well-schooled.

Into Elizabeth's listening ear, I poured the following words, not feigning a drop of sincerity: "The necklace you have given me—my mother's gift to you—is worth more to me than all the jewels or properties in the world. With this gift you have created a chain of relationship between my mother, Your Majesty, and myself. I am satisfied with this treasure and therefore seek no greater wealth or position."

Elizabeth stared, and for a long time a thick silence hung between us.

"You are a riddle to me, young Mary Seymour," she said at last, her voice kinder and more personal than before. "If you do not seek wealth or position, what do you seek?"

Temperately but clearly I spoke the words of my vocation as her white magician. "I seek only to serve you, and to see that England thrives under your good reign."

"Very well," Elizabeth said, at the corners of her lips the trace of a smile, "for the time being, you shall have your wish. You shall take possession of Chelsea, and you shall remain an untitled lady-in-waiting."

I bowed my head, rejoicing as best as I could in this partial triumph.

CHAPTER TWENTY-ONE

FRIDAY CAME, AND BEFORE I KNEW IT THE GREAT clock struck nine o'clock, and the hour of the play arrived. Beyond the palace, stars decorated the purple sky. Within, every member of the court gathered in the Great Hall dressed in his or her finest costume. The men wore velvet doublets with richly embroidered patterns. The women wore shimmering silks in pale rainbow colors. Pearls gleamed. Everywhere, the musky scent of perfume blended with the courtiers' perspiration. Not quite ready to join the swirl of conversation, I lingered for a time in the shadowy corners. Here I could observe a great deal without being myself observed.

 I spotted Alice Cavendish speaking with Malcolm

Cuffe, one of the queen's most esteemed scholars. Whatever the topic, it delighted and enthralled her, for Alice's cheeks were flushed, and her eyes blazed.

Perseus directed my attention to Vivienne Gascoigne. I found her standing close to Henry Clifford. Vivienne tended to speak only to those in power, so it astonished me to see her talking, in a most confiding fashion, to the queen's portrait painter, with his velvet suit, his paint-stained hands, and his wishy-washy, burnt-sugar aura. Nevertheless, there she was, and whatever the cause, her words seemed to please him, for he almost leaned against her, his expression both vacuous and dreamy.

Perseus and I traded puzzled but intrigued glances. What was going on?

Before we had a chance to find out, we were called into the adjoining chamber to view the performance. Vivienne hurried away to prepare herself for one of the lead roles, and Henry Clifford's eyes followed her as she fled. He seemed to be blushing.

The theatrical depicted the plight of two goddesses, the virgin huntress, Diana, and the goddess of marriage, Juno. Each tried to persuade a nymph named Zabeta to follow her example. It ended with Juno warning Zabeta that she should not heed Diana—and remain husbandless—

but should find more reason to marry, like Juno.

"When I choose a man, he will be a person of incarnate charm, noble parts, and a velvet tongue," Zabeta said at last.

Zabeta was clearly a near anagram of the queen's name, and the performance contained an underlying message that was, without question, directed at Elizabeth.

With Perseus at my side, I watched the performance, all the while remaining alert to the expressions of the other people in the room. The French ambassador was clearly delighted with a spectacle that seemed to applaud his own royal master's bid for the queen's hand. Meanwhile, the queen's face, whitened with powder, betrayed nothing of her true feelings.

My eyes lit upon Lord Dudley, who viewed the performance with an unwavering frown. (Only later did he pronounce the whole affair "a trivial entertainment not fit for a queen's audience.")

Edmund Seymour sat so still that not even his eyes seemed to move. I could not help but wonder if his own interest in the play did not, at least in part, stem from the fact that Juno was played by Vivienne Gascoigne. Even though he had begun to snub her these days (his interest having transferred quite obviously to me), I knew they were powerfully connected. My cousin's aura remained a mystery. Still, a violent sort of red-blue-black energy seemed to pulse between them.

The performance ended when Zabeta gave herself in marriage to the noble, velvet-tongued charmer who sought her out. The closing image found the nymph in her new husband's greedy arms, as he covered her lips with kisses.

There followed a great round of applause.

While most celebrated the performance, I alone remained stunned by what I had witnessed. How could Elizabeth's courtiers be so ready to force her into a married state? Did they not appreciate the strides she was making as a single ruler? She had no husband to accommodate, no foreign power. As for her need of an heir, Henry VIII's notorious history had already proven that such talk could become a deadly obsession. Besides, when the time came, I felt certain Elizabeth would appoint a proper successor to the throne.

Once the applause ended and the audience began to disperse, I quit the stuffy interior of the palace. Accompanied by Perseus, I strolled out into the quiet of the garden.

How long we sat there, I do not know, for I allowed myself to get lost in visions of a peaceful life at a manor house somewhere in the countryside. I pictured a verdant meadow with a gurgling stream, days spent reading or just lying in the sun. There would be no queen's reign to safe-guard, no enemy courtiers, no vindictive ladies-in-waiting, no marriage plots, or other forms of treachery. It was a delicious, perfectly unrealistic daydream, and there in the cool night air, surrounded by autumn's fragrant flowers, the wind swoosh-ing through the leaves of the trees, I relished every bit of it.

Until someone screamed.

Perseus bounded across the lawn. I followed close behind as monstrous, torn images flashed before me, chief among these, Cordelia, her slender neck broken.

Amid a tangle of leaves and broken branches, we found Vivienne Gascoigne's crumpled body—her sickly blue eyes wide open in a horrible, terrified stare; her mangled throat bared so that I could see the bruises someone's hands had left behind.

Forced to think of Cordelia—and of my own connec-tion to her—I felt my body weaken and knew that I was in danger of collapse.

Everything is not as it seems, a voice warned.

I looked up. Partially concealed in the shadows of the trees, I saw a man. We locked eyes, and an iron band clutched my insides. Should this man attack, I would be defenseless against him, for I carried no weapon, and we were out of earshot of the house.

"Murdered," my voice chattered. "One of the queen's ladies has been murdered."

Perseus drew nearer to me and uttered a low growl.

"Who is it?" I cried. "Announce yourself immediately."

The man who stepped out of the shadows was Henry Clifford, the portrait painter I had spied in Vivienne's company just a few hours ago.

"You!" I cried, an uncanny sort of relief intermingling with my terror. "You're the one who communicated with me during the concert. You warned me."

He smiled, and yet his smile was like no other I'd seen before, for it seemed to cover me like a heavy blanket.

The blanket grew heavier.

"I am so relieved to have found you," I said, not quite certain I believed my own words, yet powerless against uttering them, for the blanket was so warm, so thick. "Still, we must alert the guard to what we've discovered."

My eyes met Perseus's.

Do not be so sure of this image, the voice warned again. I looked at Henry Clifford questioningly.

Compelled by his smile and the insinuating boldness of his movements, I allowed Henry Clifford to take hold of my arm and lead me away from the site of the murder, as

Perseus followed close behind, chiding me with disapproval and concern.

We drifted further into the night. For a while the chirping of crickets seemed a familiar comfort, but then their chorus ceased suddenly, and he tightened his hold on my arm. The blanket fell away, and in that instant all of his former charm and trustworthiness vanished. I had been mistaken. Henry Clifford had not been the one to warn me on the night of the concert. I now knew that he was not my ally.

Perseus lunged toward Clifford's throat.

Clifford drew his sword. Perseus was in midair when the painter plunged the blade into his shoulder so that my poor, loyal friend fell to the ground.

I tried to break free of Clifford's grip, but it was as if some vise of spells wound around me, brutal and firm and absolutely unrelenting.

In the distance I heard voices, people approaching. "Here," I cried out. "Help me, we need help over here!"

But Clifford's paint-stained hand covered my mouth, silencing my cries.

In the next instant I felt my body thrown to the ground, and then my mind went blank as the blood drained out of my head and I lost consciousness.

CHAPTER TWENTY-TWO

WHAT PASSED IN THE INTERVENING HOURS, I
do not know. As if someone were speaking to me
across a great distance, I heard words, voices, but I
could not make any sense of them. It was as if I had
lost my ability to both understand and to care, for
even Perseus's wounding ceased to occupy me. I did
not wonder if he was all right or injured or even dead.
I simply allowed myself to float on a strange, numb-
ing sea of fathomless depths, as gannets circled over-
head and a faint image of the white serpent pulsed in
the distance.

When at last I awoke, I found myself in my bed at
Whitehall. My brow throbbed with a headache. My
body felt leaden, heavy. I did not want to move.

Beside me sat Alice Cavendish and Dr. Browne, who had nursed me through my first collapse in the garden.

My eyes traveled over the room. There was no sign of Perseus anywhere.

Tears slipped down Alice's cheeks, and she pressed my hand to her wet face. "Thank God!" she cried. "In good earnest, Mary, you've had us all terribly frightened."

I tried to find words, but my tongue lay like a stone on the muddy riverbed of my mouth.

"Whatever it was you saw in the garden, it certainly gave you a fright," the old doctor said.

Smiling a little, Alice said, "Otherwise, we'll have to assume you are a new marvel, prone to losing consciousness."

Finding my voice at last, I said, "How many days have passed?"

"It is late afternoon, the day after the pageant," Dr. Browne said.

I breathed a deep sigh of relief, grateful I had not lost more time.

Alice leaned in very close. "What happened to you? We heard your screams from inside. Nearly a dozen of us, including myself and Lord Dudley, ran toward you, but when we arrived, we found you lying on the ground unconscious, Perseus nowhere to be found."

"I do not remember," I said, despite the fact that I did remember. I just couldn't put my memory into words. Speech required so much effort, and just then I felt like a sleepy cow in a field: heavy, passive, longing only to dream among the milkweed. And yet, despite my stupor, I remained peripherally aware that my grazing land was ringed round with a deadly barrier, observed by some predator, a wolf or a fox.

"How are we to remedy her state?" Alice asked the doctor.

"Whatever Lady Mary saw frightened her so much that she has blocked all recollection from her memory," the doctor said. "We will need to give her time to rest. Perhaps in a few days the events will return to her."

"And if they do not?" Alice asked, her eyes wide with worry, her amber aura radiating the most sincere concern.

"Then we may have to assume that her forgetfulness is for the best," the doctor replied, his mild expression still fixed on me.

Unable to think further on the subject, my lids closed and I drifted back into sleep, finding myself once more on those perilous seas.

In dreams, the full picture of what I had seen played over in my mind. Only this time I was Vivienne Gascoigne, and a man—who I took to be Henry Clifford—had grabbed hold of my neck and began to choke me. I struggled as the vise of his hands pressed the breath out of my throat, blocking the passageway to and from my lungs, but my energies were of no use. The hands were too powerful. Before my eyes, the fingers turned into ten white snakes that coiled around my delicate throat. I found myself suffocating, and—

I awoke screaming.

Still at my side, Alice immediately took hold of my hand. The doctor frowned and waved a vial of smelling salts beneath my nose. Beside them, I was greatly amazed to see Lord Dudley.

I bolted upright, a cold sweat prickling my brow.

Lord Dudley leaned forward and touched my shoulder. "What is it, Mary?"

"I saw Vivienne Gascoigne's body in the garden last night," I said, each word feeling like an enormous effort. "She'd been strangled. I do not know if Henry Clifford committed the crime, but I do know he had some part in the matter. He must be arrested and interrogated."

"Slow down, Mary," Alice pressed.

"Don't you see?" I insisted. "Henry Clifford stabbed my dog. He must be stopped."

"Delirium," the old doctor muttered, once again waving the salts.

"No such terrors have happened," Alice said soothingly.

"Mary." Dudley's voice was almost severe. "You are making wild and dangerous accusations."

"You may have dreamt a murder, but you did not witness one," the doctor added.

Still swimming in that black, depthless sea, I asked, "How do you know?"

"Because Vivienne Gascoigne was at breakfast this morning," Alice replied. "She is perfectly well. Indeed, she was laughing heartily at one of the Fool's jokes made at another lady's expense. And Henry Clifford manifests his usual politeness and delicacy," she said thoughtfully. "In no way does he behave like a man who has just committed a heinous crime. Isn't that correct, Lord Dudley?"

"It's true," he told Alice, though he kept his eyes on my face. "Vivienne is her malicious, vivacious self, and that sycophant Clifford is up to his usual flattering portraits and nonsensical sketches of the palace gardens."

"So you see, my dear, you have just had some disturbing nightmares," the doctor said, patting my forearm. "It is nothing more than that. What troubles me more than the seemingly boundless depths of your imagination are these fainting spells you are given to. Not only are they disruptive, but they could be hazardous. What if you fell from a balcony and tumbled into one of Her Majesty's ornamental ponds? What if you were out strolling along the periphery and a band of gypsies found you? What if . . . ?"

"Doctor," Lord Dudley said, shaking his head.

"I'm sorry," the doctor said, recalling himself. "Still, I think we will need to bleed her with the royal leeches, or prescribe a long rest in one of the country's secluded, former nunneries."

"The royal leeches," Alice protested. "Surely not!"

"Do not treat me like an invalid, for I have fainted only twice in my life," I burst forth, certain there was some dark magic afoot.

The doctor patted my forearm a second time, then poured some water into a glass and spooned in honey and a dollop of white powder that smelled like ground-up oyster shells. This vile concoction he tried to pass to me.

"No, thank you," I said, pushing the glass away.

"But Mary," Alice interrupted.

"Please," I pressed. "Can you at least tell me what's become of Perseus? He was with me the night of the party. Each of you knows how loyal he is. Always at my side. Is it not strange that he is not here now?"

Alice furrowed her brow. "Perseus's absence is very strange."

"I'm afraid we have not seen him," Dudley confessed.

"Such peculiar attachment to a dog," the doctor added, noting it down as a symptom in his great black book.

My whole being sank. *Perseus.* How could I proceed without him?

Once they left me alone, under the doctor's orders to rest in bed, I reviewed what had happened. If there hadn't been a murder, there had at least been an illusion created whereby I—and I alone—had seen Vivienne's mangled body. And Henry Clifford was somehow involved. At the very least, someone had taken Clifford's shape—but who? To assume the shape of another human being, one must possess great power. This much I knew.

Even without any evidence, I suspected that Edmund Seymour had played the chief part in these Cimmerian matters. Perhaps Vivienne's body was a kind of warning to me.

And yet something about the picture did not make sense, for my cousin had been all warmth and graciousness at the party. He was attracted to me. I knew this. Definitively.

Time sneaked by. I continued to try to formulate a plan, but whatever magic had been performed had rendered my body and mind lethargic. I did not have much energy for thought.

Mostly I yearned for sleep.

When I awoke it was dark, and someone was tapping on my door.

I dragged myself out of bed and trudged over to the doorway.

"Who's there?" I called through the heavy wood.

"Alice," came the muffled reply.

I opened the door to find her dressed in a starched white nightgown, the sleeves so stiff they gave the impression of an angel's wings. Alice held a book in each hand, and her spectacles perched unsteadily on her nose.

"It's late," I said, rubbing my eyes. "Why are you here?"

"Because I could not forget what you said earlier. While preparing for bed, I found myself seized with the feeling you should not be alone tonight. Just to be safe, I plan to spend the wee hours in your room."

"But I need to sleep," I protested, already hearing my bed's call as pictures of cow pastures abloom with wildflowers danced through my drowsy head.

"Not to worry." Alice held up the books. "I plan to read."

"I am immensely grateful," I said. "But why this turn of good faith?"

"Perseus," she said, already arranging a place for herself on my sofa. "You could have dreamt the monstrous things in the garden, but nothing explains Perseus's absence. I know the dog's loyalty to you, for he sought me out that first time when we found you beneath the willow tree. Had Perseus not found me, you might have caught a terrible cold lying in that pile of moist leaves. No," Alice concluded, "your dog's loyalty is greater than any husband's. He would not have abandoned you in your distress. There is some foul play at work here. Of this I can have no doubt."

"Thank you, Alice," I whispered, laying my hand on hers, tears springing to my eyes. In Alice Cavendish I had an irreplaceable ally. And in Perseus I had a remarkable friend—but where was he? The grisly scene in the garden sprang into my head.

But then I yawned, and my anxiety dissipated. "I'm sorry, Alice, but a huge heaviness has settled into my brain. My thinking is no longer lucid. In the morning, I hope I will be clearheaded, and then we shall be able to speak."

My last image, before I fell back into my languorous dreams, was of good, loyal Alice with the starched white nightgown wings reading by firelight. If only Perseus could have sat beside her, then all would have been well.

CHAPTER TWENTY-THREE

O<small>N THE THIRD MORNING OF MY RECOVERY I</small>
rejoined the queen's household. I found things just as
Alice said: no visible sign of foul play anywhere.

Instead, within the sumptuous rooms of the palace,
the queen's Fool beguiled everyone with his caustic
wit, chiding Henry Clifford for his inability to render
nature with accuracy, Mary Hastings for her perpetu-
ally roving matrimonial eye, and Alice Cavendish for
her overwhelming interest in bookish learning.

Beyond the palace, a group of artisans were at work
repairing the superb sundial adorned with fanciful
beasts and capable of telling time in thirty different
ways. In the gardens, local men and women labored
from dawn until dusk to ensure that the marigolds,
roses, and other flowers bloomed, while the oak and

chestnut trees grew strong and straight. There were several retainers hard at work, laying out a new group of boxwood hedges. Others harvested the end of the season's tomatoes, beans, and potatoes. The kitchens continued to operate on their normal schedule, churning out enough meals to feed the hundreds of people in the queen's employ, without giving a single sign that anything was amiss.

Everywhere, ladies-in-waiting gathered in small groups to oversee household matters, from the distillation of the queen's special cordials and the making of her favorite preserves, to the polishing of a series of enormous silver tables adorned with garnets and other precious stones. A goodly number had even devoted themselves to repairing some of Whitehall's older and more fragile tapestries. Their bowed heads gave the impression of studied concentration. Meanwhile, councilors strolled in and out of the endless, splendid rooms, deep in conversation.

As I passed by, I actually overheard one group discussing the gory details of the killing of a stag. "In the end, we set the whole pack of greyhounds loose," one of the men said. "How swiftly they finished savaging the prey."

Immediately I thought of Perseus—and of that ghastly sight in the garden. Almost mistrusting my own sanity, I hurried away as quickly as I could.

Throughout this time, the French ambassador, Jean de Lys, Count of St. Anseilles, still hovered at the queen's side, wearing his gold-toed slippers, determined to convince her of the virtues of marriage to his king. As the citrine topaz glistened on his left hand, he spoke of the French king's undying love and devotion, and dished up other filigreed phrases from his dusty books on courtly love. On behalf of his absent and supposedly smitten (with power!) monarch, the French ambassador gave the queen small but expensive gifts: a bottle of the finest ambergris perfume, a gold bracelet encrusted with emeralds, even a very rare bird with feathers the color of ripened apricots; and finally, a ring adorned with a single perfect amethyst, proving with this last gift that he knew nothing about the gem's more subtle virtue—to protect the wearer against intoxication in love.

The queen continued to grant the count an audience. Still, it was clear to those who could read the signs that she had no intention of making this foreign marriage.

After breakfasting with several of the other ladies-in-waiting,

I strolled into the garden. Here I found Henry Clifford sketching plans for a large painting of the queen walking among the autumn flowers. "Good day to you, Lady Mary." Clifford's voice was warm, and his boyish face seemed open and friendly. "Splendid day to be outdoors, is it not?"

"Good day, and yes, it is lovely weather," I replied, then stopped to watch him mix the paints, waiting for the telltale signs of shaking hands or a slantwise glance.

But there was nothing, just the usual smiling politeness of a velvet-clad portrait painter determined to flatter yet another of Her Majesty's—his patron's—ladies-in-waiting.

We chatted for a while, talking about little things like the weather, the delicious currant scones we had enjoyed at breakfast, and Lady Montague's new hairstyle, as well as the forthcoming portrait of Her Majesty sumptuously outfitted in white satin and pearls with the garden flowers as a backdrop—until I took my leave of him, convinced that Clifford did not retain any knowledge of what had happened that night.

Had Vivienne Gascoigne concocted a spell in order to gain possession of his body? Recalling their unprecedented closeness on the night of the play, the way her hand lingered on his arm, I sensed that the answer was *yes*.

That same morning, I also learned that Vivienne had been granted leave from Whitehall for a few days. Was the disappearance of Perseus connected with her absence?

Again, I could not help but feel certain it was.

I must get Perseus back, I realized, but how?

Cordelia.

I could contact my good spirit only once my monthly cycle had ended, and once the moon assumed the shape of a perfect crescent. The trouble was I could not recall the shape of the moon. So concerned was I with finding Perseus that I had forgotten to keep watch over its changes.

In my desperation I thought of the raven.

As quickly as my feet would carry me, I hurried back to the palace, making polite smiles at the other ladies-in-waiting and members of the court, but not daring to waste a single moment in politic conversation.

At last, after almost tripping on the great staircase (I took the stairs two at a time despite the disapproving frown of Prudence, one of the queen's strictest ladies), I reached my rooms.

Only after locking the door, then checking all my compartments to be sure that I was completely alone, did I close my eyes and recite the strange incantation. "Raven, raven" I said, "swifter than a shooting star, more deadly than a bolt of lightning, and more tenebrous than the most tenebrous night, I seek thee. . . ."

A light wind picked up, and the curtains began to flutter. In the next instant, it was just as Lady Strange promised: a gleaming blue-black shape flew swiftly through my window, then settled on the writing table.

I hoped for conversation, but the raven remained silent. The yellow points of his eyes told me that he was immune to the questions I wanted so desperately to ask.

I wrote to my guardian, the ebony-feathered bird looking on with no particular interest. In as concise a way as possible, I explained all that had happened. Most pressingly, I detailed my desperate need to find Perseus as well as my fears about Vivienne Gascoigne's allegiance to Edmund.

Once I finished, I rolled up the letter and secured it with a hot-wax seal. "Carry this message to Lady Strange as quickly as you can, my dark friend."

Immediately, the bird took hold of the paper, then escaped through the window.

Within seconds he became a pinpoint on the horizon, then was gone.

Some half an hour later I left my rooms, still shaking from what I had done, and simultaneously eager to discover the status of the moon.

Magic always has consequences.

Hurrying through the palace hallways, I caught sight of old William. Surely, I thought, he will know the status of the moon, for this most faithful of the queen's retainers had grown up on a farm and still took a great interest in the agricultural activities at Whitehall.

With trembling hands and a hushed voice, I managed my question. "Do you know the current status of the moon?"

Old William smiled. "But of course, Lady Mary. Tonight the moon will assume a shape found on your own pretty hand."

Frowning, I scrutinized my fingers, my palm, my every knuckle.

"Have a look at the white of your thumbnail, m'lady," old William offered.

"A perfect crescent," I said, exhilaration mounting. "Tonight the moon will be a perfect crescent."

"That's right." Old William stared at me with mild concern. "Still, I cannot understand why you're so gleeful about such a thing. Perhaps," he continued in a soothing

tone, "you're not well enough to be up and about yet."
He patted my hand. "Perhaps you ought to be back in bed."

"Not at all, good William," I replied. "I'm feeling very well now." And to his great astonishment, I reached up and planted a kiss on his weathered cheek.

Certain I had not squandered my precious opportunity, I hurried away, eager to prepare for my meeting with Cordelia and confident that she would be able to help me find Perseus.

After returning to my rooms, where I washed my best muslin underthings by hand as the ritual prescribed, I hurried outdoors and made a beeline for the queen's gardens. Here I planned to gather the necessary herbs for my bath. *Lavender is for tranquility; thyme is for patience; marjoram is for wisdom; heal-all is for the cure.*

"A pretty lady-in-waiting among the queen's flowers," a voice whispered in my ear, the scent of tobacco following.

Edmund Seymour.

Realizing he must have been lurking in the shrubbery, I instinctively hid my basket of herbs behind me and stepped away from him.

"Busy among the herbs and flowers, I see," he said, trying to scrutinize the basket's contents.

"That's right." I resolved to keep my reply as emotionless as possible.

He ran his fingers through his golden hair, then stepped closer. "So little warmth from you still, Lady Mary?"

"So little time. I'm very busy today," I replied. "No need to read more deeply into my actions."

He reached around and took hold of the basket, then peered inside. "Quite an assortment," he continued, gazing at me with impertinent smugness. "Are you aware that Hecate wooed Hercules with an herbal concoction made from a number of the plants you have gathered here?"

"I'm not interested in Greek mythology at the present," I said, snatching back the basket.

"Still, what will you do with these potent herbs, I wonder?" He lit his pipe and considered me thoughtfully. "Not going to cast a spell to make me love you? Of course, to do that you'd need to sprinkle kisses into the belladonna." He spoke playfully, even proved bold enough to caress my bare arm.

Alarmed at the way my cousin's words penetrated to the magical heart of my activities, I backed away from him. "I am gathering these herbs for the queen. I have no time to be idling about in foolish conversation."

"The queen requested thyme and marjoram?" His voice was still warm, but his eyes were suspicious. "Is she ill? In need of some tonic? Somehow, I cannot but believe that you are doing far more with marjoram, thyme, and heal-all than making mere cosmetics."

"I wish you wouldn't pry into the queen's private affairs," I said, affecting a shock I did not feel. Like my cousin, I, too, was intimately involved. Whereas he sought only intrigue and personal gain, my own involvement stemmed from a desire to ensure Her Majesty's good reign; and that good reign could not thrive without Perseus as my adviser.

Edmund Seymour touched my hair. "I would not dream of prying," he said. "Still, I doubt the innocence of your own activities, cousin dear. I believe you spent some time in the queen's gardens gathering herbs with Frances Howard just before she went away. And then there was that mysterious and sudden marriage of hers, not to mention the bizarre amnesia that followed." He laughed so hard that tiny tears sprang to his eyes. "Don't think I'm not grateful to you for transforming Alice Cavendish, formerly my sharpest critic, into such a strong ally. Such a remarkable and unprecedented change." His eyes shone. "Not even I could have conjured anything better."

His eyes met my own, and I knew he not only suspected me, he *knew*. Instinctively, my hand leapt to the opal concealed beneath my clothes. Mentally, I recited each of its virtues.

"Well?" he said, tamping the bowl of his pipe. "Have you nothing to reply?"

I continued to stare back, my own gaze piercing, cheeks flushed. In the most resolved voice I could muster, I stilled any signs of trembling and replied, "Nothing."

Edmund sighed and tried to take hold of my hand. "How I wish you would come over to my side," he said in a dulcet tone. "What a delicious pair we would make. Think of your parents' precedent: a Seymour and a Parr."

"My mother died shortly after childbirth," I said. "Afterwards, my father lost his head when he was executed for treason under your father's authority. At that time, I, their only child, became a pauper and an orphan. Not much precedent in that."

This time he succeeded in seizing my hand, then brought it to his lips, his eyes resonant with an emotion I dared not return. "That's where you're wrong, Mary," he said, stroking my fingertips. "We could find a way to make that precedent sing."

I looked away, freeing my hand from his.

"Have you no feeling at all for me, Mary?" he asked, his tone almost tender.

I shook my head.

Nevertheless, something must have betrayed me, for he said, "Ah, I thought I'd find feeling there."

I startled. Had I smiled? What?

And then, despite the amethyst brooch pinned to my heart, I noticed the rose creeping into my perfect silver.

He brushed a strand of hair away from my eyes and brought his mouth very close to my own. "For now," he whispered, his breath on my lips, "*this* will have to be enough."

CHAPTER TWENTY-FOUR

I N THE PRIVACY OF MY ROOMS, I CURSED THE rose's appearance in my silver aura. How could I—a white magician schooled in the most serious of subjects, a white magician committed to ennobling my queen's reign and my country's future—be susceptible to romantic, pitiful, unworthy rose?

I could deny it, and yet despite the virtues of my opal, virtues I held as my standard, and the amulet of the amethyst, the proof had been there. The very possibility that I was prey to the same feelings that destroyed my mother when she fell in love with my father brought bile to my mouth.

I removed the amethyst brooch and examined it for some flaw—but found none. As I suspected, the fault did not lie in the jewel. I realized that no matter how potent, no object, no external force, could absolutely safeguard one from danger.

Strength must come from within.

Perhaps this is why no one and nothing could have saved my mother from falling in love with Thomas Seymour. The strength to resist would have had to come, not from an external source of authority, like a king's daughter or from a powerful gem, but from inside.

But what of my strength? Was I somehow unworthy of my destiny?

"I must cease this train of thought and prepare for my meeting with Cordelia," I said, hoping that speaking the words aloud would steady me. "I must grind the herbs for my bath," I continued. "I will scrub away any trace of rose as I bathe in the purifying properties of lavender, heal-all, and the others. I will meet with Cordelia, I will get Perseus back, and I will never ever allow myself to falter again. Unlike my mother, I will be as resolute as the most unyielding gem. I will make myself invincible."

Just before nine o'clock, when the moon sliced through the

cobalt sky, its shape a perfect silver crescent, the raven returned with Lady Strange's message.

Be not convinced that the Woman of the Fogged Aura and the Man Unworthy of His Gem have conspired together and are jointly responsible for Perseus's capture. Remember all that I said of the Gascoigne women. The Fogged Woman may love the Man Unworthy of His Gem and so be extremely dangerous and entirely responsible. Beware of her, Mary. BEWARE.

At last the clock struck two, and the time came for me to contact my good spirit.

Once Cordelia's pale face appeared in the crystal, I told her everything. I narrated the subject of the play, recounting the encoded plot urging Elizabeth to marry. I told her, too, of the scream in the garden and the uncanny appearance of Henry Clifford, then the wounding and disappearance of Perseus, and the sleepy apathy into which I myself had slipped. I even told her of Edmund Seymour's interest, though I revealed nothing of my own roseate and shameful feelings.

Once I finished, Cordelia stayed quiet for a long time, her eyes solemn, her mouth a tight bud, so that I almost feared I had violated some principle in speaking so directly.

When at last she found her voice, I was relieved to hear kindness and not judgment there. "Since our first meeting, I have waited for a sign that would prompt my own confession, and now that Perseus has disappeared, now that you are facing real danger alone, I must believe that sign is here, perhaps even woefully overdue."

"I'm afraid," I stammered. "I don't understand."

Cordelia's pale face glimmered from within the crystal. "In plain terms, the moment is ripe for me to tell you a part of my own story."

"Really?" I said, coming closer to the glass.

"Yes. It may help you to understand the craft and motivation of those who hunger for a distorted kind of power, one to which they have no right. And such knowledge may help you to protect yourself."

"Please," I said. "Go on."

"As I began to tell you during our first meeting, in mortal time I had two sisters; each was bent on securing power for herself; each hated me. Ultimately, after seizing my father's kingdom, each became convinced of the loyalty and love of one Edmund of Gloucester, the bastard son of their father's councilor, whom they elevated and fawned over like a pair of bitches in heat."

"What happened?" I asked, struck by yet another tale of family division and female frailty when it came to men.

"Edmund used his influence with each to better his own fortunes. Ultimately, my sisters, once the staunchest allies, became bitterly pitted against each other. In the end, my sister Goneril poisoned my sister Regan in the hopes of keeping Edmund for herself."

The breath drained from my lungs as I asked, "Did she succeed?"

"Yes, but her success proved short-lived. She tried to flee, but within hours of the crime she was captured and charged with murder."

"Was she executed?"

"No," Cordelia said, her hand caressing her damaged throat. "In order to escape punishment, my miserable sister took her own life."

I shivered. "And Edmund? What happened to him?"

"His good half brother, Edgar, challenged him to a duel." Cordelia's eyes seemed to turn to flame.

"So Edgar became ruler? Good triumphed?"

"Yes," Cordelia said. "But by this time, much blood had been shed."

"What about you?" I asked, emboldened by the necessity of my circumstances. "What part did you play in this story?"

Cordelia hesitated, but seeing the urgency in my own eyes, she eventually spoke. "Long before the confrontation between the brothers, my sisters coveted my father's land and power. They hated me because I truly loved him, and so they worked very hard at convincing my father that I was a disloyal child. Among the things they coveted was a fine sapphire. That gem"—Cordelia continued to stroke her mangled throat—"was to be a part of my inheritance."

"Did they seize the sapphire?"

"Foolish women that they were, they quarreled over it. Goneril won, and she gave the sapphire to Edmund."

"And with that transaction were you lost?" I asked, knowing the sapphire's power.

Cordelia laughed an eerie, ephemeral laugh, kin to January wind raking through bare trees. "No. Even without the power that the sapphire would have bestowed upon me, good people hurried to my aid."

"So you were not forsaken?"

"No. After my sisters convinced my father to disinherit me, I lost all, including the suitor interested in my no longer existent dowry. Still, fortune shone upon me, for I was ultimately blessed by marriage to a prince who truly loved me." Cordelia's eyes seemed to rest on something in the far distance. "In another story," she said, "my life could have been a fairy tale."

Her violated body proved her story did not have a happy ending.

"Afterward," Cordelia spoke in a low voice, and again her features glimmered and turned pale, "my husband's army went into battle with the armies of my sisters."

Straining to hear her, I leaned even closer so that my face almost pressed up against the glass. "What happened?"

"We lost," Cordelia whispered, already turning away from me toward the inner world in which she moved.

"Cordelia," I pleaded. "Please continue."

For a long time she remained with her back to me, so that I feared she would not reveal all, but at last she turned around, her eyes wet and wild. "Had Edmund possessed an ounce of goodness, after my capture he would have treated me with dignity."

"But he didn't," I said with certainty.

"No. Fearing the people's allegiance to me, Edmund ordered me to be killed. Edmund's command caused these marks." She bared her throat. "I died in a prison cell, hung by a common soldier's hand. Despite my virtue, my death was that of the lowest form of criminal."

Inadvertently, my hand crept to my own throat. "And the sapphire?" I asked, shaking. "What became of it?"

"After Edmund's death, it vanished." Cordelia came very close, so that I could see, all too clearly, the misery in her eyes and the gruesome scars that still seemed to cut into her throat. "I tell you my tale not to reawaken a ghoulish history and set terror running loose in your heart, Mary, but to warn you of the danger of the passions," she said. "Given all that you have said, I fear that Vivienne Gascoigne and Edmund Seymour were formally in league together. Now he has betrayed her—most certainly because he sees in you a chance to rise."

I made an attempt to say something, but Cordelia overrode my interruption. "Do not marvel at his interest. You are a queen's daughter after all, and the present queen wishes to make of you a wealthy heiress. Besides, Edmund Seymour may even love you insofar as such a man is capable of loving. . . ."

"Impossible," I cried. "Such a man could never love."

"Improbable but not impossible," Cordelia corrected. "Even the Edmund of my own history proved vulnerable to love. Had it come soon enough, my own fate might have been averted."

Again, I saw my cousin standing beside me in the

garden, but onto that moment I superimposed the vigorous cleansing efforts that followed. "But I have battled him at every turn."

Cordelia's pale face turned even paler. "You may battle him with your will, Mary, but are you sure that all of your heart resists him?"

Memories of treacherous rose seeped into my thoughts.

"Well?" Cordelia asked me again.

"Yes," I managed, remembering my vow. "Each part of me resists him."

Cordelia managed a faint smile, though no color returned to her cheeks. "If this is as you say, your resolve will be a great strength."

Eager to leave the subject of my feelings for Edmund Seymour, and desperate for a way to recover Perseus before Cordelia ran out of time, I asked her how to go about seeking him.

"To recover Perseus's body will not be so difficult, but to restore his spirit will be a terrific challenge. My feeling is this: if Vivienne captured Perseus, she created the strongest barrier around his spirit, for she knows that this is where the source of his power lies."

"I do not understand."

"Simply this. Vivienne is less interested in imprisoning

his dog's body and more intent on keeping his spirit captive, for it is Perseus's spirit that links him to the powerful, good energy. The only spell I know, the only spell strong enough to return Perseus to you, will bring you his body. His spirit, you will have to find a way to recover on your own."

"How can one separate the spirit from the body?"

"Without too much difficulty if you are an enchantress," Cordelia said.

Discouraged that Cordelia's abilities extended only to Perseus's body, I nonetheless copied down each step in a spell designed to bring the borzoi back to me, if not in mind, at least in body.

Then, without further warning, and in spite of my protests and anxiety, Cordelia began to fade.

"Please," I begged. "I am still so uncertain."

"I'm sorry," Cordelia called, touching her fingertips to the glass. "My time has run out."

I rose before dawn, then spent the next four hours search-ing for the ingredients Cordelia had named: fur from a rabbit's nest, a triolet of wild mushrooms, the bark of a young birch tree, the dew from a white rose.

Once I had each item, I arranged them on a table in my

room. As on the previous occasion, I knew that for the spell to be effective, I had to understand the symbolic value of each ingredient.

A rabbit's nest is lined with fur. Symbol of safety and nurture. By bringing Perseus back to me, I would be returning his body to safety, and I, in turn, would feel more secure.

The triolet of wild mushrooms I had been directed to find was poisonous if eaten. Yet the mushrooms were also soft and beautiful, with brown caps and delicate gray spots along the stems. The mushrooms were there to remind me to beware beauty, to not be too trusting of appearances alone. Was it possible that this applied to my own feelings also? I behaved one way on the surface; yet down deep I harbored unconfessable, poisonous feelings.

In spite of the discomfort such an answer caused me, I knew it must be right.

But why a triolet of mushrooms? Why the number three?

I searched my memory and my imagination, hazarding all sorts of possibilities, until realizing at last that the answer was right in front of me. I had to banish my poisonous, rosy feelings so that my inner emotions matched my outward composure. Only then could I restore Perseus's spirit to his body. Only then could Perseus and I be together again. The necessary trio: spirit, dog, and white magician.

I laughed aloud, so certain was I that I had found the answer.

Fortunately, the dew of a white rose was easy. The dew symbolized tears: my tears shed for Perseus's absence, with the sincerity of a white rose.

Next I studied the papery bark in my hands. One can write on birch bark. Perhaps I would find some message written on a tree? I was carried back to the moment I discovered my destiny written on the ancient tree in the deep forest beside Lady Strange's house. Or did I metaphorically need to peel away the bark and go even deeper? Somehow, I trusted the second—go deeper. After all, my destiny had not been written *on* tree bark. All those many years ago, Lady Strange and I had stood in that darkened wood, and my destiny emerged *within* the patterns of the ancient tree's bark, once I performed the proper ritual; and that first ritual, like this one, involved calling upon the powers of the sisters who wept amber tears.

Confident I had puzzled out the truths, I spoke the incantation Cordelia taught me.

"Ancient spirits, hear my plight, for although young, I am of your wise order. Let the sisters of Phaëthon shed amber tears pure enough to bring my gorgon slayer back to me."

Be sure to perform this spell in the privacy of your rooms, for you will lose consciousness once again, and it would be far too suspicious for you to faint among the members of the queen's household for a third time.

Who will waken me? Perseus? I asked, just before fainting to the ground.

In dreams I found myself within a wooded landscape, vaguely illuminated by a few lonesome stars. In the far distance I could just make out a gloomy stone house obscured by ivy. The house had three high turrets, and red and yellow flowers covered the surrounding grounds. Walking through the woods, I searched for Perseus, certain I would find him here.

But where? I saw no caves, no underground hiding places. Where could he be? And more important, where was I?

I awoke to a feeling of wetness.

Bending over me and covering my face with sloppy dog

kisses was Perseus, his pale blue eyes like the December sky. My whole body surged with joy as I threw my arms around the dog's shaggy neck and wept. *I've missed you, my friend.*

I spoke the words again in my mind.

But it was just as Cordelia had predicted. Perseus had returned to me as a loyal dog. Nothing more or less.

All evidence of the wound to his shoulder was gone.

This was indeed worth my close observation. Had the wounding been solely a part of the spell, too?

The only clue Perseus carried was the crown of late-blooming red and yellow yarrow he wore about his shaggy head. I thought of my dream—the house, the wooded landscape, the flowers.

Perhaps Perseus's spirit had placed these flowers around his body's head as some sort of clue, a sign for me to follow.

CHAPTER TWENTY-FIVE

Early the next morning Lord Dudley sought me out, finding me at last in one of the palace's many sitting rooms. "You are a difficult lady-in-waiting to track down," he said. "I have been searching Whitehall these past two hours."

"I'm sorry, sir," I said. "I have been quite busy this morning."

His gaze traveled from me to Perseus, and his posture softened. "I see your friend has returned."

"Yes," I said cautiously. "Last night."

In the past Perseus had comported himself like an aristocrat: head held high, intelligent eyes alert. Now, without the spirit to guide his dog's body, Perseus gnawed on one of my old slippers. He even attempted to sniff Lord Dudley's feet and ankles—as well as his more private parts.

Lord Dudley averted his eyes and said, "There has been a change in your companion. Is something wrong with Perseus?"

"Not that I know of," I stammered.

Lord Dudley clearly expected me to say more, but I lowered my gaze, hoping to avoid any further embarrassment and to bring him to the point.

"Despite the pleasure I always find in your company, Mary, today I did not seek you out for conversation alone. The truth is, I am gravely in need of your assistance."

"I hope I can grant what you need," I said loudly, for I was trying to drown out the slurping sound Perseus made as he licked his underbelly.

Lord Dudley glanced about the room, then circled the perimeter, checking behind doors and curtains. After ascertaining our privacy, he said, "Surely you remember our conversation about the Russian expedition."

"I do."

"After successfully negotiating a clear route with the Swedes, you do know that the queen appointed Sir Walter Effingham as its head?"

"Of course. It is the talk of the court. For days, the

other ladies-in-waiting overflowed with stories that embellished the queen's savvy when it came to dealing with the Swedish ambassador."

"That may be true, Mary." Dudley's voice turned solemn. "Unfortunately, I received shocking news late last night."

I grew very still, and for a moment even Perseus ceased his hopelessly canine antics. "What sort of news?"

"Effingham was in fine health until two days ago. Now he is confined to his bed with a serious and mysterious illness."

"Who is the new expedition leader?" I asked, the name already rising up from the depths, laughing, proclaiming itself.

Dudley stared deep into my eyes. "Your cousin, Edmund Seymour."

Struggling to find my voice, I said, "The position carries with it great possibilities, does it not?"

"It is an opportunity such as very few receive in a lifetime."

"Please," I said. "Tell me what my cousin stands to gain."

"He will have the opportunity of becoming very rich and very powerful," he said, alert to any eavesdroppers.

"Russia is the gateway to an immense continent that includes Persia. As I told you a few weeks ago, we hope to establish a permanent trading route between England and the Far East."

"Why is the present such an opportune time?"

"For one thing, until fifty years ago we knew very little about this great continent. Newness always inspires the English imagination. Unlike France and Spain, with whom we have a long history, Russia is a country with which we've had very little dealing. Who knows if this Czar called Ivan is one to be trusted? I was more comfortable with Effingham as head, because I know him to be a trustworthy man."

Proceeding slowly, as if gauging every nuance of my response, he said, "I approach you now because I am not secure with Edmund Seymour at the head of such an expedition—"

"Edmund Seymour may be my cousin," I interrupted. "But that does not mean I in any way support his rise at court. In confidence, I tell you that I fear what might happen were he to become too powerful."

Dudley's face seemed to open. "Speak you in good faith?"

I hesitated. Could I really trust Lord Dudley? Perhaps,

despite his show of friendship, he was really an ally of my cousin's and wanted to ferret out any weakness so that he could destroy me. After all, more than once I had seen them deep in conversation. . . .

But it was also possible he spoke the truth. The strongest evidence in his favor was the story he had relayed in the carriage on our way back to Whitehall—*It is for my loyalty and friendship, and for nothing else, that our good queen has rewarded me.*

I had seen loyalty to the queen in Lord Dudley's eyes then.

A second time he said, "Speak you in good faith, Mary?"

I scrutinized Lord Dudley, struggling to read his character, but the great lord's face remained impenetrable. Lord Dudley was a courtier through and through.

"Well?" he asked again.

Plunging into the depths, I replied, "Yes, in absolute good faith."

Lord Dudley took my hand in his own, then kissed it. "You have just given me the best news I could possibly ask for. I need your help, and I feared you may be loyal to your cousin and therefore unwilling."

"My cousin has no reason to depend upon my loyalty," I said firmly.

Dudley's confidence increased. "Very good. You see, I am determined to block Seymour's appointment. Effingham is now in the hands of the finest doctors. He may get well."

"And if he doesn't?"

"If Effingham cannot be reinstated, then I would like the queen to find another man. Unfortunately, Edmund Seymour is one of Her Majesty's favorites. She has great plans for him." He eyed me significantly. "Many of her plans involve you."

"One entanglement I am determined to avoid is marriage," I said boldly. "Especially marriage to my cousin."

Dudley searched my face. "Mean you this, absolutely?"

"Absolutely," I replied.

"Then here's what I'd like you to do. Distract Seymour, keep him preoccupied so that I have time to do my work, and perhaps even convince him to delay the voyage."

"How am I to accomplish that?"

Dudley's voice did not waver. "You are now sixteen," he said, and his gaze traveled from my face to my neck and shoulders. "Use your woman's charms."

My rib cage tightened, becoming a band around my heart and lungs. My whole being revolted. "You want me to entice him?"

"Call it what you like," Dudley said bluntly. "I want you to keep his mind off my actions and give him reason to delay the voyage. He is quite obviously smitten with you and would therefore be most susceptible."

My resolve as well as my trust in Lord Dudley began to crumble, and I sought the comfort of a nearby chair.

Dudley's eyes bore into my own. He reached out a hand and tried to force me to my feet. "Mary—"

"No." I pushed his hand away. "Such work could be immensely dangerous to me personally," I said, searching Dudley's features for any sign of disloyalty.

"Please, Mary."

I folded my arms across my chest. "I won't do this."

"You must. Everything is at stake. If we can delay the voyage by at least a week, maybe ten days, I will have the proof I need to forever bar Edmund Seymour from the queen's graces. Perhaps she will even banish him from England."

"I'm sorry, sir," I said. "I want to believe you act in good faith. Yet you are asking a very great deal. By tempting my cousin I could lose my honor and my position here at court. If I am to undertake such a risk, I will require the greatest and most unflagging proof of your trustworthiness."

The great lord stared, and his voice almost broke.

"Isn't my tale of life in the Tower enough?"

"No," I said. "Not for such a request as this."

For a long time we remained together, caught in embattled silence.

I dared not look at Lord Dudley until at last he said, "I have it."

My eyes locked into his own. "What is it?"

"Not here." Dudley seized my hand. "Follow me."

Soon it was clear we were going to the lord's private rooms. I knew I could be exposing myself to some danger by going alone with him there—not just from Lord Dudley but from the gossipmongers at court, including Lord Teasewell, who spotted us as we passed. Still, I had no choice but to follow him.

I was far too nervous to notice much about the rooms themselves. Mostly, there was a lot of lustrous mahogany and ancestral paintings. Heavy curtains of burgundy velvet shielded the view through the window from sight.

Once we crossed into his sitting room, Lord Dudley closed the door behind us, then hurried over to his desk.

He rifled through the top drawer until he uncovered a yellowing piece of stationery. "Here," he said, and with trembling hands he gently pressed the paper upon me. "Here is all the proof you need."

Although the ink had faded, I was able to read:

December 1, 1557

My dearest Eyes,

*How I wish there were some way for me to make you my
lawful husband, but as we both know, such a relationship is
absolutely impossible, for I must make the governance of
our country my highest priority. Always remember you are
dearer to me than any man on earth, and yet I know myself
well enough to realize I would make the English people a
better queen than I would make any man, even you, a wife.
And Queen of England and Lady Dudley, well, both of these
identities I cannot possibly maintain. I will cherish your gift
always, and in turn I give you this gift of lapis lazuli, as well
as the gift of the innermost sanctuary of my heart.*

*With all of the love of the private woman, I remain your
Elizabeth
Still I must be a Virgin Queen.*

My fingertips seemed to turn to flame as I lay the paper
on the table and looked up at Lord Dudley. "This is Her
Majesty's hand."

"Yes." A single tear slipped from the corners of

Dudley's eyes, and for just a moment he looked like a chastened little boy whose deepest secret had just been exposed. "Now that I have shown you what I have never dared to show another living soul, do you believe me?"

Without hesitation I gave him my answer. "Yes."

He raised my hand to his lips. "Thank God. You see, Mary, I have nothing greater to give." Keeping hold of my hand, he said, "I need some fresh air."

We left his rooms and stepped out into the gardens.

While Lord Dudley composed himself, the revelation that Queen Elizabeth had loved him sank deep into my being. And yet, I told myself, she did not allow the rose to triumph over the purple of her aura. "In all things," Her Majesty always said, "a woman must think with her head, and not with her heart." My sovereign was living proof of these words.

With so much bubbling up within and around me, I tried to move on to the next part of the plan. Now that Dudley had told me of Seymour's ambitions, I needed to know if and how Vivienne Gascoigne was involved. Determined not to raise Dudley's suspicions, in a clear, emotionless voice I said, "Where does my ambitious cousin stand with Vivienne Gascoigne?"

Dudley's face turned solemn. "Why?"

"Please, just answer my question. Were there—at least, did the queen know of—any plans between Edmund and Vivienne?"

Dudley hesitated, but sensing my urgency he said, "Her Majesty had an inkling, but our good queen was not at all in favor of the match, and she made her decision very clear to your cousin, who is far too ambitious and shrewd to risk losing her favor."

"Why did the queen resist the match?"

"Such a union could threaten her own reign."

"How so? Neither has a claim to the throne."

"No, but their overreaching natures pose an indirect yet volatile threat. Elizabeth may favor Edmund Seymour out of true affection. Despite her princely nature, she has a woman's heart after all. But Vivienne." He shuddered. "Her Majesty keeps Vivienne at court in order to keep an eye on her."

"Yet Vivienne has left court," I reminded him, surprised at myself for ever believing the queen had been sentimental about Vivienne's superfluous finger.

"So it seems. The queen tells me she has gone to her family's estate on the matter of some private affair. Illness or some trouble with a pestilence in the orchards. A most remarkable request," Dudley added, "given that the

Gascoignes traditionally keep the estate locked up during the autumn and winter months."

"Why?" I asked, my heartbeat steadily increasing.

"The damp. On Her Majesty's only visit, our good queen caught cold there. As you know, Mary, Her Majesty has an absolute horror of illness of any kind."

"Yes," I replied, the tips of my ears tingling, for I felt very close to something. "What more can you tell me about her family's estate?"

"Only that I was there just once during Her Majesty's visit. With the exception of a general impression of an infinite number of poky rooms and long, drafty corridors filled with long-nosed portraits, the house itself I have forgotten. But the grounds"—his voice grew almost wistful—"the grounds were extraordinary, graced as they were by bright, late-blooming flowers."

I thought of Perseus's crown, and my mind raced forward. "Red and yellow flowers?"

Dudley thought a moment. "Yes." His eyes returned to my own. "Those were the precise colors."

"Does the house have turrets? Is it covered with ivy, and does it lie on wooded property?"

"Yes—why?"

"I'm afraid I cannot explain," I said, my body shaking.

"I know only that I must go there. How far away does the property lie?"

"A good half day's journey to the north." He laid a firm hand on my shoulder. "Surely you are speaking nonsense now. How do you expect Elizabeth to give you leave so soon after your return? Besides, you have made a commitment to help me."

"Lord Dudley," I pleaded, certain that Vivienne had entrapped Perseus's spirit somewhere on her property, "If you can manage a way to convince the queen to give me leave, on any grounds—on the grounds that my guardian is ill—I can promise you to make Edmund Seymour so in love with me that he will even forget his appointment as the head of the Russia expedition."

Although Lord Dudley did manage to convince Elizabeth to give me leave, he himself did not accompany me to the north. Not surprisingly, Elizabeth had urgent matters of her own and could not possibly spare the lord she still referred to as "My Eyes."

"But, Mary," Alice protested, when she found me packing in my rooms. "What is all of this about? There's a rumor afoot that your guardian is ill, and that Lord

Dudley is lending you the use of his carriage."

Reluctant to meet Alice's eye, I looked toward the window and said, "Yes, that's true."

"I'm terribly sorry about your guardian." Alice's lower lip trembled. "Is the illness very serious?"

"They do not know yet," I mumbled, hating my words as I spoke them.

"Perhaps I should accompany you. I have a bit of training when it comes to illness."

"Dear Alice," I said, laying a hand on her shoulder, and realizing again how much she cared for me, "I would love to have your company now, but I'm afraid I must go alone. My guardian, Lady Strange, prefers it that way."

Although Alice did not seem convinced, she said nothing further, just hugged me close and wished me a safe journey.

"I have secured the use of my carriage for your journey," Dudley told me quietly in the hall outside my rooms. "I do not know what you intend to gain. Nevertheless, do not doubt me when I say this: I trust you implicitly."

I curtseyed. "I am grateful for your trust. You have my trust also. Did you tell the queen that my guardian was ill?"

"Yes, and I said that she was asking for you. Truth be told, I played a trump card," he said almost guiltily. "Her

Majesty's father often denied people the right to see their loved ones in times of trouble. I knew she would not refuse such a request."

I felt both grateful to Dudley and also a little guilty, for we had deceived Elizabeth by drawing upon her own vulnerabilities, a trick no white magician should have to play. Yet I knew there was no other way. I had to find Perseus.

"We have come a long way since our carriage ride back to Whitehall, have we not?" Dudley asked.

"Yes, sir," I said with genuine satisfaction. "We have."

He extended his hand, and like two gentlemen entering into an agreement, we shook on it.

"One more thing . . ." He paused, nodding curtly to a maidservant as she bustled past, and waiting to be certain she was out of earshot before he handed me a beautiful but deadly-looking dagger with a mother-of-pearl handle, an encrustation of rubies, and a treacherously sharp blade. I ran my fingertip along the edge, knowing how easy it would be to press a little harder and split the delicate flesh. Dudley gazed intently into my eyes. "I want you to take this. You may need it."

I touched the handle, surprised by its coldness. "Why does the dagger seem so familiar?"

Handing me a piece of velvet with which to wrap the

blade, he said, "This is the dagger Henry the Eighth wears in the Holbein portrait."

I stowed the knife in my skirt pocket, wondering how such a thing had come into Lord Dudley's possession, and simultaneously aware that mother-of-pearl was the ocean stone of vengeance as well as fortitude.

CHAPTER TWENTY-SIX

J OLTED NORTH OVER BUMPY ROADS, I PLOTTED my strategy. Convinced that Perseus was hidden or trapped somewhere on the property, I trusted the dog at my side to lead me to that spirit. The borzoi might no longer have been enchanted, but he was still a brave dog.

We hit a particularly sharp bump, and the knife pressed into my hip bone.

Some seven hours later, the driver, one George Henderson, told me that we were nearing the Gascoigne estate.

"What are your instructions?" he asked.

"As Lord Dudley probably told you, this is a secret

errand," I said, alert to the gravity of my voice. "I do not wish my presence to be discovered."

"Understood." Henderson grinned, and in the process, he revealed a few missing teeth. "Would you like me to wait for you about a mile from the house?"

"That would be ideal," I replied. "Of course, you may have to wait some time, even through the night."

Henderson agreed to my plan, expressing neither surprise nor disapproval, a response that prompted me to wonder what sorts of events he had been privy to during his time in Lord Dudley's employ.

By the time the borzoi and I set foot on the grounds, the sun had already fallen, so I could only just make out the house. Yes, this was the place I had seen in my dreams. Here were the elaborate turrets, the vines of ivy, the dark woodlands, the lone stars. As Dudley believed and as I hoped—for I dared not contend with a household full of Gascoignes—the house seemed to have been closed up for the season, for only two lights glowed yellow in the upper-story windows.

For a long time we wandered along the woodland's periphery. By the light of the moon I scrutinized the stately walnut and oak trees and thick clusters of pine, wondering where the essence of Perseus might be hidden.

How many hours the borzoi and I spent wandering the obscured acreage in search of some sign, I know not. After a while, I lost all sense of time. My feet ached from scrambling over knotted tree roots, and my skirts were muddy, hems torn. To make matters worse, I had forgotten to pack a meal, and the growl of my stomach soon became as familiar as the ghostly howling of the wind through the trees.

By the time we arrived at an eerie precipice my legs trembled with fatigue. Thankfully, the borzoi reached it first, and so prevented me from falling over its edge. Immediately he began to bark.

"What is it?" I cried.

The disenchanted dog's barking only continued, so that I suddenly feared he would alert Vivienne to our presence on the estate.

At last I peered down. The precipice was in reality the lip of some sort of deep hole. I leaned over it and was instantly sick—the pit smelled of decaying flesh. Unable to look further, I drew back, then fled through the trees without any sense of destination. I only knew that I had to get as far away from that gruesome site as possible. And yet, as I fled, the branches of the trees seemed to become thousands of gnarled arms. A gale swept through, and the arms tried to catch me. I screamed and ran on.

I sought shelter in a clearing beneath a reassuring and very great oak tree. The borzoi lay down at my side, and before long, despite my knowledge of the gruesome pit, I drifted into sleep.

Mary—

I opened my eyes and looked around. "Who is it?" I cried. "Who's there?"

Again, I heard my name.

"Perseus!" I called out.

I felt a pair of arms around me, and it was as if those arms were pulling me into or at least through the tree at my back. These arms, however, were comforting. Unfrightened, I relaxed into the grip and felt myself growing lighter, thinner, almost transparent. The next thing I knew, I actually found myself inside the oak tree. Remarkably, the trunk was hollow, so that I could kneel (though not stand upright) in the round enclosure. I looked around and discovered the borzoi there, too. And beside me—or at least all around me—was Perseus, the spirit.

Just being in Perseus's presence again filled every part of me with a strengthening joy.

How is it that I know you are here, and yet I cannot see you?
I asked at last.

The spirit laughed. *I could not explain it, even if I wanted to.*

But are you all right? And what about your wound? Is it still there?
The questions came rushing out, for there was so much to learn, so much lost time to recover.

My body was injured, but it was my spirit Vivienne was after. Once she claimed that, all trace of physical injury vanished.

Please, I urged. *Tell me all you can.*

That night, Vivienne secreted me in a distant place on the castle grounds, Perseus began. *There she invoked more dark powers than is permissable for one black magician, even an immensely powerful one, to claim in a single night. Such an incantation cost Vivienne a great deal. My own suspicion is that the spell cost her any remaining control she once held over Edmund Seymour.*

You're moving so quickly, and there is so much I'm not sure about. Please slow down. Return to the point where I fainted.

Within the dim but sweet-smelling enclosure of the oak tree, Perseus did exactly that.

Once the queen's people carried you back to the palace, my attacker brought me to a hidden place you and I had never discovered in all our ramblings. There, I watched Vivienne step right out of Henry Clifford's body. One minute she presented his face to the world. In the next, she left his body behind and stood before me in

314

all her threatening fury, so that instantly I understood her purpose.

Shielded by darkness, she performed the actions necessary to render me unconscious—you and I shared that experience. While I was asleep she must have brought me here, for the next thing I knew I awoke to the smell of oak.

In addition to this fantastic tale, within the tree's seclusion Perseus fleshed out a more complete picture of the political intrigue at Whitehall. As I already surmised, Vivienne and Edmund had conspired together to oust Sir Walter Effingham from the position of expedition leader. Yet their treacherous allegiance ran much deeper. They had been sworn allies, until Vivienne discovered that Edmund had betrayed her by becoming interested in me.

Why Russia? I pressed. *What does my cousin hope to find there?*

A very potent form of magic contained in the Demonius Sapphire of which Lady Strange originally spoke. I don't know how, but somehow the gemstone has found its way to one of the caves deep in the Ural Mountains. A very rare sort of white fox guards it, but the white fox is not invincible. Were someone like Edmund Seymour to come into possession of the gem, he would be too powerful to defeat.

But what if a white magician were to lay hands on the Demonius? I asked.

No good. What you must understand, Mary, is that it's essential that no one, neither a good magician nor an evil one, possess the

Demonius, for such a thing would unhinge the earth's delicate balance.

My thoughts whirled. *You mean to say it's possible to have too much goodness in the world?*

Hard as it is to imagine—yes. At present, there is too much evil, hence your calling at court, hence our compact. Yet there must be some evil. Otherwise, good has nothing to define itself against. You see, Mary, dark and light must have each other to exist. Without that, time would end.

As history has proven, Perseus continued, *this is the world after the Fall. The gates of Eden have exploded, and we have been left darkling.*

Astonished by all that Perseus was saying—for how could there possibly be too much goodness in the world?—I tried to regain my bearings by returning to the circumstances confronting us. *If Edmund and Vivienne are no longer collaborating, why did she bring you here?*

Vivienne is determined to destroy you. To cripple you, she captured me.

If Vivienne wants to destroy me, it makes sense that she would separate us. What I don't understand is this: why does Edmund Seymour want me?

I knew we would come to this question, Perseus said. *I am now prepared to answer it.*

Were you unprepared before?

Not exactly. Yet my presence in the dog's body diffuses my strength. While I occupy a mortal creature I cannot bring all I know to the surface, and you are not yet mature enough to exist in the other realm.

I just stared, bewilderment and anxiety coursing through me.

But about Seymour, Perseus continued. *Cordelia has given you her history?*

Yes, and it's a monstrous one.

Perseus did not comment on this. Instead he said, *The spirit of the Edmund from her story lives on in the Edmund of your own. He is not the same person, but he belongs to the same evil. Do you understand?*

It is a fantastic thing to contemplate, but yes, I think I do. Still, is it possible for you to clarify the connection?

Certainly, Mary, the spirit said. (Had he possessed the borzoi's body, I felt certain he would have bowed.)

Upon Queen Mary's accession, the entire Seymour family lost all position and authority in England. Around this same time, Edmund Seymour renounced the moral codes of society.

So you're saying that it was only after his family's fall that my cousin pledged himself to no law except the law of individual might?

Precisely. The first Edmund was a bastard and therefore barred from inheriting titles, land, position; but your Edmund once knew these things intimately.

317

Until his family lost them, I said, reminded of what Lady Strange had said on my birthday—that there was an affinity between Cordelia and myself, one it would be up to me to discover.

Yes. All along we've known that Edmund Seymour craves power, known that he will stop at nothing to get it. The mistake the previous Edmund made was this: he did not try to claim Cordelia's spirit. Had he possessed her, he would have possessed the incarnation of goodness. Evil coupled with evil only goes so far. But if evil can control good— or vice versa—then that particular power is intensified.

Are you telling me that Edmund has only so much to gain by coupling with Vivienne, whereas an alliance with me, so long as he controls me, would strengthen his gifts?

Yes, although ownership of you, ownership of the good, is far more difficult. This is why he wants to go to Russia and find the Demonius Sapphire. Were he to possess that gem, he would be infallible.

Feeling bile rush to my stomach, I said, *We need to stop him.*

We do. There is just one problem. I am trapped in this tree.

The antidote Perseus proposed was more terrifying than anything I had previously attempted. To free the spirit I needed a lock of Vivienne's hair and a piece of her clothing. So, too, I needed the skin of the white serpent in her possession.

I knew the white serpent was not just a phantom in my dreams.

Not in the least, Perseus replied, *although trapping it may prove to be as difficult as holding onto a phantom in a dream.* It was then that I told Perseus about the deep pit and the sickening stench of rotting flesh.

Yes, Mary, there has been a recent murder here. I believe this estate has been the site of many such crimes.

But whose body is it? I pressed, recalling the sickening smell.

The body . . . Perseus hesitated.

Yes?

Though no longer recognizable, the body once housed the spirit of one Olivia Ormonde.

The name means nothing to me, I said.

Nor should it. She was a common girl, a dairymaid just a few months older than yourself. Poor Olivia shared a single tryst with Edmund Seymour—

—And for this she paid with her life?

Yes.

Did Vivienne kill her?

She did.

Jealousy? I fought off all memory of the hatred I always saw in Vivienne's eyes whenever she directed her gaze at me.

In part. More important, and of greater threat to the Lady Vivienne, was that Olivia, though of common birth, was a white magician.

What about the borzoi? I asked Perseus, dismissing poor Olivia, for I well knew I could not possibly pursue this subject further and still enter the murderess's house—and seek her out. *Shall I take him with me?*

In this single instance, Mary, it's wiser if you do not. Vivienne is a cunning creature. The borzoi, powerful and loyal though he is, may cause you to blunder.

I understand, I said, my stomach already tying itself up in knots. *I will set forth alone.*

CHAPTER TWENTY-SEVEN

How long it took me to reach the immediate environs of the house I know not, for my mind was spinning with everything that had happened, not to mention everything I had learned.

I thought of Cordelia, whose otherworldly goodness stood no chance on this earth, and simultaneously I was forced to remember my parents. Had not my good mother fallen in love with the corrupt, dangerous, slightly mad Thomas Seymour? Then there was the unknown Olivia Ormonde—a woman who shared my own calling. Her path crossed with my cousin's and Vivienne Gascoigne's, and now she lay rotting in some ignominious hole because she had loved, or at the very least because she had given herself to my evil cousin. *Yes, love had everything to do with foolishness, wrong partners, and sometimes even with death.*

Sheltered beneath the trees that surrounded the house, I took some comfort in what Lord Dudley had said about its desertion at this time of year, further encouraged by the two solitary lights I'd seen flickering earlier. Either the Gascoignes habitually wandered about in darkness (a thing I doubted, even in the blackest of black magicians). Or, as I so desperately hoped and needed to believe, Vivienne was here alone.

Shielded by tree shadow, I surveyed the surroundings. In the distance I heard panting. It did not take me long to make out six or seven dangerous-looking mastiffs patrolling the grounds. These dogs were as big as small horses but much stockier. Unlike the borzoi's strong, lean grace, their massive bodies were thick and muscular and menacing. How quickly a dog like that could tear into my flesh.

Trusting the mild breeze to prevent them from catching my scent, especially at this distance, I retreated farther into the trees and scanned my memory for some spell to get rid of them. What would both distract and give them pleasure? I asked myself, certain by the way they carried their haunches that all four were male.

A bitch, I realized.

Closing my eyes, I pictured an enticing illusion: a female mastiff so irresistible the pack would run after her at once.

To set the spell going I needed another creature: someone fleet who could outrun them, and for a little while at least, assume their form.

The spirits must have been with me just then, for a small dun-colored rabbit climbed out of her hollow and hopped over to me, then lingered, whiskers twitching. Having carefully memorized that early spell I'd botched years ago in the Canary Islands when I accidentally gave a hermit crab fins, I now performed it perfectly—"Cinnamon comes from a small sapling cut only when it's flush," I began, eyes closed, trying to picture the words as I spoke them. "But the golden grains of paradise are born from a glossy-leaved plant that bears fragrant, lavender blossoms when the sea is at high tide. Caraway, like mustard, is a seed. In order to increase one's store, the careful planter must only scatter the seeds to a mild, autumn wind. . . ."

Within seconds I had enabled the rabbit to speak to me.

"Are you offering your services?" I asked.

"I am." The rabbit went on to explain her own thirst for

retribution. "The beasts killed my brothers. I would like nothing better than to lead them into the pit on the far end of the property, then bury them alive."

At first I was astonished by the bloodthirstiness of this mild, chestnut-eyed creature, but then I recalled what I had read from countless books: cruelty could only beget more cruelty.

"Vengeance will be mine," the rabbit said.

"Not exactly," I explained, then told her that yes, she could lead the mastiffs to the pit, but she mustn't expect death to be their lot.

"You won't cover them with a pile of earth like the others?" she asked, her long ears alert to any note of threat.

"Others?" I asked, coming so close that I could see each twitch of her whiskered nose.

"The family who lives here. They have the habit of burying people alive. A few months ago, the daughter dragged the body of some young woman into that same pit. Odd thing, though," the rabbit considered, "this one she didn't bury."

"I am a white magician who must combat chaos and restore harmony," I interrupted, the foul stench returning. "Unlike the Gascoignes, I cannot bring death to others unless circumstances absolutely demand it."

The rabbit's ears sank. "Very well," she said, "at least I will have the chance to lead them to a smaller form of disaster. Surely you know that my kind rarely get such an opportunity."

"Very true," I replied, unable to not picture all the hunts I had witnessed. In every instance, the prey—whether stag, fox, or rabbit—was always the loser.

"Now, my friend, remember that the transformation will last only until dawn," I said very sternly. "By then you must lead the mastiffs to the pit and be well on your way."

The rabbit chuckled. "I won't need so much time. I'm the fleetest rabbit within miles. Otherwise"—she stretched out a long leg—"how could I have survived in a place like this?"

Assured that we understood each other, I stood over her, closed my eyes, and invoked the forebears of Lady Strange, trusting that they would be the necessary, vengeful forces to come to my aid.

When I opened my eyes, a thick, fierce-looking mastiff stood before me, her exceptionally long ears and fluffy tail alone attesting to her real essence.

"Good luck, my friend," I said, then watched her charge forth, with all of a rabbit's speed encumbered by two hundred pounds, as the other mastiffs immediately lumbered after her, howling and panting.

Only once they were out of earshot did I approach the house.

I turned the doorknob, and after a little jiggling, the door swung open and I stepped inside. Despite the dimness, I could make out the costly grandeur of a hallway that seemed to have been painted a red so deep it verged on brown. On top of a golden table just in front of me, fine porcelain vases shone like ghostly bodies. Unnerved by their presence, I tried not to think about Olivia Ormonde by focusing on the details of my plan.

Assuming that Vivienne slept on the second floor, I climbed the long staircase, grateful that the house, which looked to have only about one hundred rooms, was no palace. Surely I could find Vivienne before dawn. Besides, memory of the lights at the east end told me to proceed in that direction.

I crept through the halls, listening intently at each door. Here the solemn, often haughty faces of Vivienne's aquiline-nosed ancestors gazed down at me. Through the shadows I could almost make out their features, and the very idea of their painted eyes keeping track of my movements sent a stream of mercury coursing through me.

I must have passed a dozen rooms before I finally heard a noise.

As soundlessly as possible, I turned the knob and poked my head into the blackness.

Sure enough, from within came the sound of even breathing as well as a peculiar scratching. Was this Vivienne's room? Was this her breathing I heard? And why the scratching?

I crept deeper inside. The sound of breathing continued, but there was no sign of a person. Nor could I make out any furniture: no bed, no wardrobe, not even a stool or a broom.

At last the breathing seemed to be right beside me—or rather, directly below. I peered down, trying to make out some shape in the darkness, and my nostrils were flooded with a most awful stench, like urine. I lost my balance and found myself clutching only at air.

There I saw it. A very old, long-haired cat with fur the color of dirty snow slept on a ratty blanket surrounded by straw. Around the cat were coiled at least a hundred white mice. The smell came from the blanket and from the fetid bed of straw. The mice slept restlessly, here and there scratching at the floor in their sleep.

I sprang from the floor, then fled the room.

Why in the world would a colony of mice sleep with a cat?

With no time to pursue the question further, I drew the

knife from my pocket, then continued down the hallway, alert to any sound other than my own breathing and the frightened beating of my heart. I must have pressed my ear to the doors of a dozen more rooms before I heard anything else.

Again came the sound of breathing. More suspicious this time, I turned the doorknob, then stepped cautiously inside, moving gingerly on the balls of my feet so that not even the ancient floorboards creaked beneath me.

The breathing continued. Fighting off the urge to flee, I forced myself to go further, simultaneously tightening my grip on the knife.

A few feet from the bed, I found a pair of stockings. As long as the figure in the bed was Vivienne, I now had one third of what I needed.

I drew closer, and the figure beneath the blankets stirred. Even without a candle I could just make out Vivienne's face. Her eyes were closed. Around her neck, something white glowed.

I clenched the dagger more tightly, the iridescence of mother-of-pearl glinting between my fingers. Just as I was about to cut a lock of Vivienne's hair, the bloodred eyes of an enormous serpent opened, and it hissed a warning to its mistress.

"You!" Vivienne shrieked as she bolted upright. "How did you get in?"

I tried to flee, but before I could escape, Vivienne sank her nails into my skin. Hurling herself out of bed, she nearly fell on top of me. I could barely look at her just then, for her face was truly ghastly: eyes wild, features distorted so that I could see her bones beneath the sickly, semitransparent skin.

"You're not going anywhere, Mary Seymour," she snarled, squeezing my forearm so hard I thought she would break the skin.

I fought back with all of my strength, trying to shake myself free. I kicked at her bare legs with my sharp-toed shoes, but still she held on. Meanwhile, the serpent, who must have been six feet long, twined its cool, scaly body around my throat and began to squeeze.

I struggled for breath, only to see a ghostly army approach: *the white mice.* Hundreds of them, perhaps even thousands, their red eyes miniature torches.

"Now my little warriors," Vivienne told the mice, the serpent hissing its approval. "Seize her!"

The mice scrambled on top of me, their tiny whiskers brushing against my skin, their little eyes glowing as they explored my body, their feet so many thousand sharp needles. At least a dozen of them began to bite my ear-lobes, and a pack of others set about biting my nose and cheeks, even the delicate skin above my eyes.

The serpent tightened its hold.

I reached for my throat, grasped the serpent, and with all my strength, hurled it across the room. Then I began to scream, hoping that the piercing sound of my cries would frighten the mice away.

But my cries seemed only to intensify their unearthly hunger, and they continued to gnaw at my face and throat, at my arms and hands. Terrified that they would attack my eyes, I closed them. Then grasping the dagger, I began stabbing frantically at the creatures. Within minutes my body was soaked in their blood.

I opened my eyes to watch Vivienne lurch toward me and grab the dagger. Standing above me, she taunted me with its blade, letting it flicker just above my eyes, her extra finger now coiled like an infant snake. "How I would love to cut your throat right here," she said, laying the cold metal against my skin, her fetid breath irritating my raw flesh.

Just as I thought *I will die this way*, another creature descended on my shoulders. Sharp claws dug into my flesh, and I opened my eyes to meet the gaze of a huge owl whose own diamond-shaped pupils in their yellow orbs bore into me.

"Get rid of this vermin, Lightborn!" Vivienne laughed, and as my eyes met hers, I saw that Vivienne's eyes radiated the yellow-white of fire.

The fierce claws tightened their hold, and I felt myself lifted into the air as the last of the remaining mice lost their grasp and dropped screeching to the ground, red eyes burning even more vehemently as they fell into the open jaws of the white serpent's mouth. The great owl carried me out the window, and I felt myself grow dizzy. As I lost consciousness, the foul stench of the ditch containing the other woman's body seemed to wash over and through me.

CHAPTER TWENTY-EIGHT

I AWOKE TO DAMP AND THE SMELL OF mold. Opening my bruised eyelids, I scanned the room, understanding that Vivienne had locked me in the bowels of the house. Here there was only a single window just large enough for an injured girl to enter, but it was far too high for me to reach. My body hurt too much for me to stand and try the heavy door. Besides, I was sure it was locked.

My prison was an abject place, the stone walls lined with abandoned cobwebs full of at least one hundred dead flies and the decaying bodies of white moths. My stomach lurched, and I found myself seized by a series of dry heaves.

Not only had the mice left tiny but viciously sharp

bite marks all over my face and arms, but the owl's claws had left puncture wounds, and he had manhandled my shoulders so that my upper body resembled the body of one who has been whipped. My throat bore the marks of the white serpent's suffocating hold. Insofar as I knew, there was no magical cure for this.

Physical hurt, like emotional hurt, stayed until it healed.

Worse than my physical imprisonment was the fact that Vivienne, too, was in the midst of—or had already concocted—a spell, for she had clipped my fingernails. And she had cut off all my hair. The long, red-gold tresses were gone. I reached up and touched my shorn head, felt only spiky knobs where once I had known flowing locks.

Although I knew that magicians could gain power by claiming an opponent's hair, only the most venomous spell would require her to strip me of any sign of beauty and connection to my mother, for my auburn hair was exactly like Katherine Parr's.

My opal necklace, too, was gone, and with its loss, any physical trace of who I, Katherine Parr's daughter and the Virgin Queen's white magician, had been.

In that damp, awful place, the tears and the anger I had been holding back loosed themselves—tears and anger as old, perhaps, as the aching loss of my mother, who had given up her life just six days after my own began. "What kind of universe is this that allowed me to grow up without a mother?" I cried. "Why was I, an orphaned girl, given such a destiny?"

Instantly, the word recalled my first conversation with Lady Strange all those years ago; but just now it had lost all trace of the marvelous.

Desperate, I called on the raven a second time.

"Raven, raven, swifter than a shooting star, more deadly than a bolt of lightning, and more tenebrous than the most tenebrous night, I seek thee. . . ."

Through the open window, the bird flew.

The creature seemed to take no notice of my tattered, blood-stained state. Instead he perched nearby and measured me through indifferent yellow eyes that brought to mind Vivienne's eyes, while he waited for my response.

What sort of white magic is this, I asked myself, *that can be so indifferent to suffering?*

I had no writing paper or pen, so I tore a piece of fabric from my gown, then pressed my blood into the silk, trusting my guardian to know that I was in grave danger and needed her help.

I prayed the silent raven would be able to tell her where to find me.

How many hours passed, I do not know. But by the time hunger pierced my belly, the door to my prison opened and Vivienne entered, her features completely disfigured by the emotions that had established tyrannical authority within her. At that moment, her aura was an even sicklier shade of yellow, her eyes two focused points of cruelty. Around her neck, coiled like a macabre necklace, was the white serpent. Just looking at him brought nausea to my lips, and I remembered the creature's frigid, scaly clasp.

And beside Vivienne, looking absolutely downtrodden, was the borzoi.

"I've brought your companion." She laughed, and the serpent hissed its approval. "At least, I've brought his least valuable half. Where my mastiffs are, I know not, but I found this dumb animal waiting at the front door. He must have followed you here, followed you"—again the vile laugh—"straight into my lair.

"From the way you behaved, I'd say you found your spirit." Vivienne's eyes burned my skin. "You know, as I do, that he's not going anywhere. Your spirit is now a permanent resident of my estate."

"What will happen when the queen sends people

looking for me?" I said, groping for a way to buy time. "They'll find me here, and you'll be arrested."

"The queen will never think to search for you here," Vivienne replied. "She will have no reason to suspect me. Besides, in just a few days I will accompany Edmund to Russia. I do not intend to return to England unless I return as queen, and before I depart I intend to dispose of you."

I thought of the body in the pit, a white magician's body, and the picture set the rank room spinning. Vivienne intended to kill me—but how? She was about to leave, and I knew I couldn't let her do that. I had to find a way to keep her here. It was my only chance.

Thanks to Perseus, I knew that Vivienne's spell over him had cost her a good deal. It had certainly cost her much, if not all of her remaining power over Edmund. Remembering that Vivienne's hatred of me was motivated by jealousy, I recalled Cordelia's story of the two sisters who destroyed each other over their passion for one man. "Edmund Seymour loves me," I said boldly. "You may have been his ally once, but that is all over now. Sapphire or no sapphire, you know I speak the truth."

Vivienne's voice broke like a mirror, each shard cutting into me. "I could kill you now for speaking those words."

Despite the memory of Olivia Ormonde, I pressed on. "It's true. Do not delude yourself. He will never carry you to Russia. He will search for me, and when he discovers your crime, he will punish, maybe even kill you."

A haunted look came into Vivienne's eyes, and for a few minutes she said nothing, her already pale coloring becoming absolutely arctic.

I scanned the room for anything to aid me, eventually spotting a ragged coil of old rope not far from where she stood.

"How dare you boast of Edmund's love for you in my presence," she said at last. "Do you not see how easily I could slit your throat?"

The skin on the back of my neck turned cold. Still, I could not back down. There was no other way out of here.

"He knows I am here," I continued, concealing my shaking hands behind me. "You yourself have seen how he looks at me. You know he will come looking for me, and when he finds me locked in your cellar, his rage will know no bounds."

Vivienne's arms dropped to her sides. "I don't believe you."

"It's true."

The serpent hissed a warning to Vivienne, then coiled

itself more protectively around her throat. Disregarding its cautions, she stepped closer. Just then, my eyes flew to the rope. As Vivienne came toward me, I kicked my foot out, snagging the rope just before she reached it. When Vivienne did step forward, I tugged the rope so that she tripped and fell. The impact hurled the serpent against the dungeon wall.

Immediately the borzoi lunged, his huge body landing on Vivienne's chest.

"Good, Perseus," I shouted. "Keep her down!"

While Vivienne lay stunned, I grabbed the rope, cut it into sections with the mother-of-pearl dagger I found on her body—the dagger she had stolen from me. Then I bound her hands and feet. Next, I gagged her, leaving just enough space for her to breathe.

Struggling against my body's own weakness, I grabbed the huge white serpent. Clutching its throat with one hand and the dagger with the other, I thrust the blade into its scaly flesh. Its eyes became huge and malignantly red, until at last they closed, and its severed head dropped to the floor.

The last thing I did before making my escape was to cut a generous lock of Vivienne's hair and tear loose a piece of her clothing.

We found our way out of the house, then ran along the path that led to the woods. On and on we ran. With his long legs and his agile body, the borzoi was built for such movement, but I was not. Tired and hungry, I struggled to keep up despite the cramps piercing my insides, and the bruises and cuts along my body.

At last we reached the oak tree. There I stood, the body of the serpent, Vivienne's hair, and a swatch of her dress in my hands. I repeated the words of the incantation, my heart pounding an accompaniment.

This time, too, I fainted.

When I awoke, Perseus hovered above me.

I gazed into his eyes.

Success, he said, dog and spirit reunited at last.

I threw my arms around Perseus and held on tight. Despite the smarting in my shoulders and ribs, the throbbing head, the bruised throat, and the shorn hair, at that moment I seemed to drink an elixir of rose petals and sunshine. I had won, and Perseus was once again at my side.

Just before we reached Lord Dudley's carriage, a figure

stepped out of the shadows. Had Vivienne managed to escape? Was it her body looming through the darkness?

Frozen in place, and fearing mice and owls and cats, I watched the figure come toward me, trying to formulate some plan—

"Lady Strange," I cried, and rushed toward her.

Once my guardian stepped out of the cover of trees and into the moonlight, I saw the great change in her. Gray streaks wandered through her once pitch-black hair, the fineness of her skin was deeply lined, and she moved like an old woman—her back bowed, her bones creaking.

I hesitated for just a moment, but she motioned to me, and I hurried into her frail arms, relieved to breathe her beloved forest scent.

"I came as soon as I received the raven's warning," she said, holding me so close I could hear the beating of her heart. "The bloody clothing told me to use everything in my power to reach you."

All at once I knew. Lady Strange had given years of her life in order to channel the magic the raven required to come to my rescue at a speed otherwise impossible.

"You have Perseus back, but your hair . . ." Lady Strange moaned. "She cut off your hair, and—" Gently she touched my neck. "What happened here?"

"Yes, I know," I sobbed, clinging to her. "Vivienne's serpent tried to strangle me."

"Tell me, Mary," Lady Strange insisted. "What happened?"

On the grounds of the Gascoigne estate I told Lady Strange everything. With each revelation, her violet eyes seemed to open further, giving me a glimpse into the fathomless realm in which I did not yet exist.

"You have lived up to your calling," she said. "You are a true white magician, and in affirmation of your gifts Perseus has been restored to you. How I wish there were some incantation to restore your auburn locks, but I'm afraid you will have to be patient."

"And what about you . . . ?" My eyes scanned her wrinkled face, instantly reminded that I had been the fundamental cause of her aging, for I had called upon the raven's services two times, refusing, or at least unable, to consider the consequences.

"There's no time to discuss that now," Lady Strange said, and with each word her back curved a little more and the wrinkles deepened. "You are in need of a good rest if you are to recover your strength. When we part, request that your driver take you to an inn to heal for a few days."

"And then?" I said.

"And then Edmund Seymour needs to be prevented

341

from journeying to Russia," she said. "Do you know what you must do?"

"I must return to Whitehall and give Edmund Seymour every reason to believe that I will marry him, and so delay the expedition to Russia."

Lady Strange smiled, and the furrows around her eyes and lips deepened. "You are a smart, brave young woman, Mary," she said. "Still, he might suspect this turn in your behavior. You'll have to be convincing."

I trembled at the prospect of enchanting my enemy. "I know."

"Be very careful, Mary," she warned. "Seymour is powerful. Remember, you are susceptible to his power."

"No," I said, remembering my vow. "I am not."

Lady Strange stared deep into me, then took each of my hands in her own. "Please, my dear, do not be so quick to deny it. You may not have felt the full force of his attraction yet. Good is inevitably drawn to its opposite. Howsoever much the rational bars such affinities, it is the law of the antipodes."

"No," I said again.

"Think of your mother's example. After thirty-five years of prudent decisions she fell madly in love with your father, losing the good will of the king's children and the respect she had enjoyed as queen. She *was* vulnerable, Mary!"

"I am not like my mother in this way," I insisted. "Besides, I would never betray you."

"I would never believe you capable of betraying me," Lady Strange said. "Nevertheless, losing your heart is a serious matter, and a very human one. Take care."

Unwilling and unable to dwell on this subject further, I turned to the immediate problem: Vivienne Gascoigne. "I don't think my actions are enough to permanently stop her."

"Very well. Go to an inn and rest. Let me deal with Vivienne Gascoigne."

"You can't possibly. Think of Vivienne's owl and her army of mice. They're vicious." I held out my bitten arms.

"Those are nasty bites," Lady Strange said. "You'll need a compost of heal-all and witch hazel, not magic, to attend to them. Now go and find your driver, and let me deal with Vivienne."

"But—"

"Trust me, my dear. I can be dangerous, too."

Reaching into the deep pockets of my skirt, I produced the dagger.

Lady Strange's eyes turned the color of purple dawn. "Where did you get this?"

"Lord Dudley said it belonged to Henry the Eighth."

"This dagger once belonged to my father," Lady Strange said, a lightness like running water coming into her voice. "After his death it disappeared."

This, then, was the dagger with which Henry VIII had threatened to stab Lady Strange's father, a threat that proved unnecessary when the good man died of a broken heart. Again I heard the words he spoke to his daughter all those years ago. *When the time is ripe, you will avenge these crimes, not with any violence, but with the white magic that is your birthright.*

"Now I am able to return it to you," I said, placing the dagger in her hands.

"No. The dagger is yours now," she said, handing it back to me. "As you must know, my father would want you to have it."

For a moment, I just stared at the woman who had loved and cared for me throughout the last eight years. "I can't lose you," I cried.

"Don't you dare speak of losing me, Mary." Once more she pressed me close. "Remember, no matter that my body is temporarily out of sorts, I'm made of tougher mettle than even you might suspect."

CHAPTER TWENTY-NINE

I SPENT THE NEXT THREE DAYS RECOVERING AT a quiet inn. Before returning to Whitehall Palace, I instructed George Henderson, Lord Dudley's driver, to stop at a shop that sold makeup, with which I concealed my wounds. There, too, I found a wigmaker capable of matching my own red-gold hair—on a moment's notice. I should have known that the style of Katherine Parr had never really faded from fashion.

A few blocks from the wigmaker I found a dressmaker who gladly accepted my tattered silk gown as payment for a clean one of less expensive linen. Needless to say, for all of these efforts, each one a remarkable act of kindness and good fortune, yet not one of them truly "magical," I felt immensely grateful.

It was nearing sunset by the time we returned to Whitehall. No sooner had we swung onto the palace drive than my body fell to trembling. In the distance, I spied Edmund Seymour. Outfitted in riding gear, he and another gentleman seemed just about to set off for a ride. I drew back into the depths of the carriage.

But it was too late. He'd seen me.

Before I stepped down, he tethered his horse, then hurried my way, his long legs bringing him far too quickly toward me. I had no time to formulate a strategy.

"Good evening," I said.

He bowed, but his face seemed unusually melancholy. "Good evening. I did not expect to find you in Lord Dudley's carriage yet a second time. Why is he blessed with such favors? Dare I assume I have a rival for your affections?"

Choose your words carefully, Perseus warned.

"My guardian has been ill," I said politely. "I had to go to her. Lord Dudley offered me the use of his carriage, and I accepted."

"How I wish you had allowed me the pleasure of lending you my carriage," he said, fidgeting with his gloves.

When I did not answer, he said, "I trust your guardian is well recovered."

"Yes," I said.

Too much ice, Perseus said. *Remember, you need to entice him.*

Resisting the urge to disagree with Perseus, I forced coyness into my eyes and an unfamiliar, sultry languor into my voice. "You are going riding, sir. Might it be possible for me to accompany you sometime?"

Seymour's black eyes softened, although his voice remained wary. "You are not going to avoid me any longer, then, Lady Mary?"

"Have I been avoiding you, sir?" I said, longing for my opal necklace as each flirtatious note escaped my lips. "Until now there was another rival for your affections here at Whitehall."

Edmund raised my hand to his lips. "How can you say such a thing? Since your arrival, you must realize I have lost eyes for anyone but you."

I forced a grand smile. "Yet we have very little time, for you are to leave on the Russia expedition, and I will soon lose your company."

In the distance I could hear his companion calling to him, but he seemed entirely focused on me. "You will be sorry to lose my company?" he said, the usually smug expression crumbling, a dulcet tone like a morning breeze stealing into his voice. "Do you mean this, Mary?"

Good is inevitably drawn to its opposite.

"I do," I said, managing to speak the words with real conviction.

An indescribable sort of happiness swept across his face, and the hard lines smoothed away. "I never dreamed you would consider me in this light."

I was just about to rejoice in his successful capture when he stiffened and looked at me suspiciously. "How am I to believe such a change? Two days ago you recoiled from my advances. Now you welcome them."

"I cannot tell you this now, but seek me out when you are at liberty, and you will see how great a change there has been in me."

He stepped closer. "You are sincere?"

"Absolutely sincere," I replied, with all the seductive charm a woman like Anne Boleyn must once have possessed.

A warm glow suffused my cousin's skin. His features grew more youthful, and strangely, I thought of what Cordelia had said about the Edmund she had known. *"Had love come to him sooner, my own fate might have been averted. . . ."*

"I will await our coming meeting with the greatest of

anticipation," he said, then raised my hand to his lips a second time.

In spite of myself and my silver vow, Cordelia's words echoed anew, and I relished that mysterious kiss, then stood transfixed as he turned and walked away.

Beside me, Perseus had watched it all.

All that evening, the queen was sequestered in her privy chamber with her councilors, Lord Dudley and Edmund Seymour among them. In truth, I was grateful to be spared the queen's penetrating powers of observation, for I felt certain that she would remark upon the change in me. My wig was one disguise; the performance I needed to give was another.

For the moment I could avoid the queen, but Alice Cavendish I could not. Having learned of my return, she came directly to my rooms.

Although her eyes lingered for a few too many minutes on my face, she commented not on my hair but on the rosiness of my complexion. Nearsighted as she was, Alice mistook the mice bites, which I had covered with powder, for a healthy sort of blush. "You look well," she announced. "That's a great relief, for I've been terribly worried. You left so suddenly."

"I am sorry," I said sincerely. "As you know, my guardian took ill and I had to go to her immediately. I wasn't thinking properly, Alice." I took her hand in my own. "I didn't mean to be unkind."

"I know," Alice said, her voice more temperate now. "And your guardian? Has she recovered?"

"Lady Strange is feeling much better. Thank you."

At Alice's urgings, I went on to describe, in lavish detail, a pretend illness, all too aware of the actual, far more painful, circumstances in which I had left my beloved guardian.

"How stands the matter of the queen's marriage to France?" I asked her afterward, determined to direct Alice's attention away from me.

"It's all over." Alice's body relaxed as she spoke these words. "Her Majesty gave up all pretense when she learned of Russia's support of her Muscovy expedition."

Russia's support! "How did this come about?"

"Thanks to your cousin, Edmund Seymour," she said, her amber aura reassuring me that this was my same friend, dear Alice. "His skillful politicking with the Russians has further solidified his position with the queen."

I shot Perseus a sharp look.

This is a dangerous new development, Perseus agreed.

"I did not know that my cousin had any dealings with the Russians. How did he possibly manage this?"

Alice's face broke into a troublingly triumphant grin. "Apparently, Edmund Seymour secretly invited a Russian emissary to our court. He met with the visitor in private, and before long they struck a bargain. The Russians will do all they can to advance the voyage. So the queen no longer needs the French king for a suitor because she no longer fears intervention from the Spanish. Of course, Her Majesty refused the French king in the politest and most delicious manner possible.

"You should have seen the French ambassador's expression when our queen broke the news," she said, taking hold of my hand.

"But the Russian emissary?" I persisted. "Is he still at court?"

The playfulness in Alice's posture vanished, and she shook her head. "Unfortunately, most of us managed to get just the quickest glimpse of him. He was tallish and clever-looking, though I cared not for his coat made from rare white fox fur."

Was a white fox not the guardian of the Demonius Sapphire? My vision grew blurry, and I groped for a chair.

What had Edmund Seymour done to win Russia's approval? And what sort of deal had he made with this supposed emissary?

Just before retiring, I stepped outside, strolling among the flowers and drinking in the sweet night air, all the while trying to still my frantic brain. Although I was surrounded by the golden chrysanthemums and countless trellises of wisteria, the present beauty could not soothe me, as I thought again and again of Lady Strange, unable to forget how old she had grown.

You have to believe she is all right, Perseus said.

Yes, I know. Still, I'm peculiarly worried. After all, it was my fault. Perseus did not need to remind me of the words throbbing within me.

Every act of magic has its consequences.

It was then the hedges parted, and Edmund Seymour stepped forth from one of the shadowy paths.

"Do you still wish to meet me?" he called out. "Or has your earlier warmth cooled?"

Showering him with as radiant an expression as I could muster, I replied, "I am still eager to meet you."

He seized both of my hands, then pressed them to his

lips. "Your words delight me, Mary. In truth, I have not been able to stop thinking about you all night. With such beauty and intelligence as yours to absorb me, how could I keep my mind on the queen's matters?"

"I do not wish to distract you from your business," I replied, astonished by the change in him.

In my ear he whispered, "After my return from Russia, I wonder if you would consider spending all of your days and nights distracting me."

All of my days and nights? Was he speaking of marriage? A sticky feeling settled deep in me. I thought of my mother lying in bed a few days after my birth, the fever already sweeping through her, sealing her up in its fatal fire.

Relinquishing my hand, he drew back a little, then searched my eyes. "Have I said something to displease you?"

Mindful of the part I must play, I pushed this despairing image of my mother away. "No, nothing," I said. "I only wish we had more time together now. I only wish—"

Again he leaned close. "Yes?"

With calculated sweetness I raised a hand to his face, stroked the unexpected velvet of his skin. "I only wish you could delay sailing for a while."

This time he started. "Delay?"

"Yes." I sugared the word and made of my own eyes two

caressing pools, trying to ignore the fire surging through me. "Then we could spend a few more days together." My heart beat so hard I could barely hear myself think. "Wouldn't that be wonderful?"

I seemed to have forgotten that my hand was still pressed against his cheek. He grasped it and said, "Nothing would please me more."

I continued to gaze deeply into his eyes, dizzy now, my whole body racked with sensations I had vowed never to allow. "Then promise me something."

"Yes?" His smoky breath brushed against my cheek.

"Promise me that you will think about delaying the voyage for a few days," I said.

"Well—"

"Edmund," I said, making of his name a new intimacy between us. "Do not hesitate."

For a long time he said nothing, and the autumnal air felt thick with unseasonal warmth. Beside me, even Perseus seemed to stop breathing.

My cousin's eyes met my own, and had I not known him better, I would almost have believed I saw tears there. "Well?" I whispered, my breath catching in my throat.

"I will consider delaying the voyage," he said at last. "But only on one condition."

He stepped away from me, a new cautiousness in his manner. "For me to be convinced of your sincerity, I will need some sort of proof."

"And what evidence would suit you?" I said, dizzy with victory.

"One kiss."

My supposed power dissolved.

"Of course," he said, coming closer, "on this occasion, one which seals our compact, I ask that your loyal dog refrain from coming between us. You see, Mary, I would like to take you in my arms, and your dog always seems to defend you from me."

Unable to look at Perseus as he sank into the shadows, I feared that I would cry out, for I now understood the danger I must meet with solemn eyes and parted lips.

Edmund held me very close. As his lips pressed my own and his tongue found its way into my mouth, I tasted traces of tobacco, wine, and something far less identifiable and absolutely male—

No! My mind screamed. *This is wrong. You're a white magician. No form of magic, no deception should ask you to make love to a black magician.*

Yet in spite of the crystalline logic of my brain, my body and even my spirit had hungrily surged up to meet him. Certain the rose in my aura had made not just a reappearance, but a triumph over my silver, I kept my eyes squeezed shut and tried very hard not to think of the consequences.

CHAPTER THIRTY

TWO DAYS AFTER MY ARRIVAL, OVER TEA, Mary Hastings and a few of the other ladies-in-waiting raised the subject of Vivienne Gascoigne's continued absence.

"Her Majesty is thinking of punishing Vivienne severely," said Lady Arabella, whose long ears and buck teeth inevitably brought to mind the dun-colored rabbit with the taste for vengeance.

"Well then, at least justice will be served," said Mary Hastings, fiddling with the ribbons at her bodice.

"Justice," Alice scoffed, reaching for another scone. "Women like Vivienne always manage to find a way to avoid justice."

"It doesn't matter to me." Lavinia yawned. "Just so long as Vivienne keeps away. She's always so nasty. With her gone, I'll be able to assume her duties as well as my own with a lighter heart."

Listening to this chatter, Perseus and I understood the real truth behind Vivienne's absence. This was the sign that we'd been waiting for.

Lady Strange had been victorious.

Despite the resurfacing of treacherous rose in my aura, I continued to play my part, stunned by the way white magic, and specifically Lord Dudley's request, required me to weaken my power a little more each day, with each smile, each touch, each honeyed word I spoke to my cousin.

Although no white magician herself, the intelligent Alice clearly recognized the change in my behavior. Afraid that she would press me for the truth, or at the very least try to understand why I was cozying up to someone I swore I disliked, I now avoided the person I most trusted at court. Whenever I passed Alice in the hallway, or encountered her at mealtimes, I averted my gaze, pained both by the hurt I knew I would find in her eyes and by my own longing to confide in her; and aware

I was weakening myself by forcing myself to keep away from my closest female ally at court.

Even so, under my influence Edmund Seymour delayed the voyage for ten days. Each day I expected Lord Dudley to tell me that he had the proof he needed to dishonor my cousin and ban him from the expedition.

But each day, the incriminating evidence was not forthcoming.

Meanwhile, when I wasn't evading Alice's penetrating eyes, or answering her questions as curtly as possible—all the while struggling against confiding in her and asking for her help—I spent my free time in Edmund's company. At this point, the amulet was of no avail, for the charade wreaked complete havoc with my reason and emotions.

Required to feign passion for a man who was my sworn enemy, and lacking the strengthening virtues of my opal necklace, too often I found it difficult to keep my convictions separate from the womanly emotions that rose up to betray me. Taking my hand in his own, Edmund would bring the melodies of the spheres into his phrases, and even with Perseus at my side, I would have trouble remembering why I was not supposed to allow such talk.

Complicating matters further, the hours I spent in his company were stolen from my free time. Instead of using these precious hours to steel myself and strengthen my white magic through herbs and incantations, I was always with him.

In the late afternoons, once I had finished my responsibilities, I rode out at his side. We ranged over hills and across meadows thick with early October hollyhocks, goldenrod, and sweet Melissa. On occasion, I even allowed him to guide my horse over rocky terrain and across swift-flowing streams.

During that time, whenever the court gathered in one of the great halls for an evening concert, dance, or game of cards, we entered the room together. Confident of the queen's approval, Edmund now placed his hand on the small of my back. We walked so close to each other that my gown brushed against his legs. Sometimes he spoke to me of his love and our future.

And I listened.

On the morning of the seventh day of this performance, the queen's ladies-in-waiting undertook preparations for the court's departure for Greenwich Palace. The household had nearly depleted the supplies around Whitehall. More than seven hundred courtiers and servants quickly run through a region's milk, eggs, apples, lettuce, and meats. Of even greater urgency were the odors that now plagued Whitehall. The palace and stables would need to be cleaned.

In about a week the court would move on to Greenwich Palace along the Thames.

Busy with itemizing the gowns the queen would take with her, and unnerved by my private mission, I did not hear one of the maids come into the room. When I felt her hand on my back, I startled and cried out.

"I'm sorry to give you a fright, m'lady," she said. "But one of the great courtiers is looking for you."

Edmund Seymour, I thought.

I was about to ask the maid to tell the man that I required a few minutes alone, when Lord Dudley stepped into the room, his broad grin convincing me that I would at last be freed of my secret task.

Bowing deeply, he said, "I've been all over Whitehall searching for you. Would you take a few minutes to join me for a walk in the garden?"

"Yes," I replied, silently praying he would give me the news I so needed.

The women's eyes followed us, and I heard Lavinia say, "But I thought she was the darling of Edmund Seymour.

How is it that young Lady Mary now flirts with the other great lord, too?"

Dudley purred, "You have Seymour utterly captivated, and you have the queen's women fooled. *Bravo.*"

We reached the garden, and I drank in the scent of chrysanthemums, longing for the certain news that would free me from my task.

Instead, Lord Dudley told me he needed more time.

"But you've already had more than a week," I said, suddenly finding it difficult to breathe. "How is it you don't yet have the proof you need?"

"I'm sorry, but Seymour must suspect me, for he has erased any trace of foul play. He is determined to maintain the queen's good opinion, and he seems encouraged by your own favor. Perhaps," he suggested, "your cousin plans to reform."

"Do not toy with my mind," I pleaded, plucking a few dead heads off the faithful chrysanthemums. "I can keep this charade up for another two or three days, but I cannot continue forever. The work is exhausting—and confusing."

"I am sincerely grateful to you, Mary," he said, laying a hand on my arm. "I know you've done far more than I should have expected. Give me another day, two at the most. I'm sure to discover some concrete proof by then."

"I hope so." Then, in a low voice I whispered, "For time is running out."

On the ninth evening, the court gathered for a farewell dance. In the greatest of the great halls, a room lined with vast oriel windows, hundreds of tall beeswax candles blazed in every corner. Elaborate bouquets of speckled tiger lilies and white and yellow roses in silver vases adorned the lavish bounty of the tables. In the very center of the room on a platform covered with crimson velvet, a dozen musicians played a hypnotic sequence of madrigals. Meanwhile, the great lords and ladies danced.

The music wrapped me up in its lyrical embrace. "May I have this dance?" Edmund asked, his warm breath against my neck like the balmiest summer's breeze.

How could I possibly accept him? Dancing meant leaving the protective proximity of Perseus. And tonight I felt especially nervous. Recalling that recent, overwhelming episode in the garden, I was wise enough not to trust myself in his arms. Besides, how would I manage without the opal around my neck? How would I maintain my composure when Edmund's dark eyes seemed to drink the very strength of my spirit? How, when the touch of his body against my own left me dizzy and breathless and full of feelings I could not condone or forgive?

"Well?" he said, extending his hand, so that for the first time I noticed that his sapphire ring was missing. Why wasn't he wearing it?

"Come, Mary," he said a second time. "Let us dance."

I stared at him, for just a moment uncomprehending.

Dance, Perseus urged.

But the sapphire, I tried to tell Perseus. *It's gone.*

"You must come," Edmund urged. "The night awaits us. You must know I long to take you in my arms."

You must go, Perseus pressed.

What choice did I have?

The warmth from Edmund's hand passed into my own, and in spite of myself, the missing sapphire receded to the background. He took me in his arms, and we whirled around the ballroom. I tried to keep my thoughts about me; tried to keep my body rigid and my head tilted toward the stars.

But it was no use.

As my cousin guided me through the other dancers with such expert grace that I, too, moved like a gazelle, I felt myself becoming one with his rhythms. He extended his arm, and I leaned back into the night, filled with the subtle energy of his body. When he drew me close I let his hips linger against my own. Our legs, arms, backs, at times even our bellies, touched. After a while, with the music swallowing me whole and our bodies entwined as one, it became nearly impossible for me to tell where Edmund left off and I began.

Perspiration dotted both of our foreheads, at that moment reminding me of morning dew, and of diamonds. "You are an exquisite dancer," Edmund whispered, letting his tongue caress the whorled intricacy of my inner ear. "As with everything else you do, now too, you move like a queen—or a goddess."

Instead of hearing blasphemy in his words, I reveled in them, and for a time I actually did move like Venus just after she emerged from the ocean. I became all the women who had lost themselves to love: Persephone dining on the pungent red fruit of the pomegranate; Eurydice intoxicated by the playing of my lover's lute; Penelope reunited, at long last, with my Ulysses . . .

The voices trailed off into the distance as Edmund led me far from the swirl of the other dancers, far from the music and the seductive glow of candlelight. Just before we reached the door that led to the queen's gardens, the ambrosial air wrapped me up in its own embrace, and my gaze lit on a mirrored panel. I saw myself in my cousin's arms: my cheeks flushed, my shoulders bare, my eyes glossy with the thrill of the dance and my own womanly powers. Just then, nothing but our fine clothes separated us.

Perseus was nowhere in sight, and remarkably, as Edmund guided me into the starlight, his voice a loveletter from another world, I didn't mind my good spirit's absence in the least. To be truthful, with Edmund's arms around me, and the October wind soughing through the trees, I don't believe I thought at all.

CHAPTER THIRTY-ONE

THE FOLLOWING MORNING, I STOOD IN THE garden picking the last of the hollyhocks and the late-blooming purple veronica and goldenrod. Surrounded by their heady, honeyed fragrances, I allowed my thoughts to linger on the dance, the image of myself in Edmund's arms, the music embracing both of us, reoccurring again and again. Then I saw the two of us in the garden, my cousin's hands clasped around my waist, his lips against my own, our hips locked so that we stood belly to belly. (Queer that I would not have marked the significance of our similarity of height until now.) I even allowed myself to revel in the way his fingers touched my bare shoulders, the way his mouth caressed my neck.

I made absolutely sure that Perseus could not discern my thoughts, and my new secrecy shamed me, for I had never withheld anything from my trusted friend before.

The sun warmed the garden, and soon I heard footsteps on the gravel. In spite of myself, I half hoped the step belonged to my cousin. But when I looked up, it was Lord Dudley who stood before me.

"Good morning," he called. "I congratulate you on a part stunningly performed. I saw you dance with Seymour last night. I would never have dreamed you were acting. What a convincing temptress you make."

I could not bear to comment on this statement. "Have you found the evidence?" I said instead.

"Thanks to you," he said confidently, "we have gained the necessary time to make and practically conclude our investigation. On the morrow I shall have the proof I need."

Nearby, Perseus seemed to sigh with relief. Though he said nothing, he, too, understood that I was having trouble maintaining my clarity of mind and purpose.

I bit my lip. "Why another day?"

Dudley scrutinized my face. "Courage, Mary. You're doing fine work. The ship may sail tomorrow night, but Edmund Seymour won't be on it."

That afternoon I sat in the shade of one of the oldest oaks, thinking back to how much had changed since I freed Perseus from the tree on the Gascoigne propery, Lord Dudley's words replaying in my mind. *On the morrow, I shall have the proof I need.*

Tomorrow my cousin would know I had betrayed him.

I tried to take consolation in the fact that Edmund Seymour was evil. Had he not seduced Frances Howard on false pretenses? Was he not ambitious and greedy? Vivienne Gascoigne's former lover? A black magician and my enemy?

And yet, he delayed sailing to Russia to be with me. Might it not be possible for me to reform him?

Again I recalled the dance, heard the music, felt his hands on my shoulders, his lips on my neck—*no!*

Tired of dividing myself between reality and an increasingly enticing make-believe, I lay down, surrendering at last to exhaustion, and to a deep longing for the protective embrace of Lady Strange.

A voice called to me through the fog of my dreams.

"Over here," I called back drowsily.

A tall, slim figure dressed entirely in violet stepped forth from the tree shadow.

"Lady Strange—"

My wish had been granted. Although wrinkles still marked the corners of her eyes and mouth, she walked upright and with resilience.

We rushed into each others arms.

"What are you doing here?" I asked.

"I bring news of the highest importance. I dared not trust a messenger." The strength in Lady Strange's voice and the glow in her complexion proved that some measure of her lost youth had been restored.

"When Perseus and I learned of Vivienne's detainment, we were absolutely sure you must have been victorious."

"A natural assumption. And yet, unbelievable as my news will surely sound, my success in this matter was greatly aided by your cousin, Edmund Seymour."

A deep shiver coursed through me. "Impossible."

"Improbable, my dear," Lady Strange said. "But not impossible. I dare not tell you all that happened, for it might confuse you, and yet—"

"—But you must tell me."

"Very well," she said, linking her arm through my own as we walked among the trees. "Still, you must be patient.

You have come a long way, my dear. Nevertheless, you have yet to master this virtue."

I nodded, no trace of patience anywhere evident in my fluttering hands, my nervous heart.

"After you left me, I returned to the Gascoigne house," she said. "Within its walls, I managed to cast a spell on Vivienne. Had the spell been effective, she would have been prevented from leaving her family's property. And she would have lost all memories of her dealings with you.

"To my great misfortune, my spell-making proved faulty as I was short two essential ingredients. Hence the effect soon wore off, and as a result, Vivienne recalled everything, then hunted me down on the grounds of her estate."

Recalling my own gruesome encounter with Vivienne, I shuddered. "And then?"

"And then she forced me back to the house and imprisoned me in the same gloomy place where she had hoped to leave you." Lady Strange rolled up her sleeves and revealed the torn flesh of her arms. "The wicked creature even set her vicious army of white mice upon me."

"What did you do?" I asked, expecting some miraculous action that Lady Strange alone could perform.

"Do, my dear?" Her features became solemn, and her shoulders drooped, and for a moment she once again seemed old. "What more could I do? I despaired. I confess, I even began to prepare myself for death."

"Oh, Lady Strange," I whispered, unable to imagine a world, no matter how good or evil, without the woman who had so loved and inspired me.

"Two, perhaps three days later—I wish I could be more exact, but in that grim place I lost all sense of time—I heard the most piercing series of screams. Like the shrieks from a cat fight. Before meaning could register, the door to my prison opened and your cousin stood on the threshold."

I scanned her features for any trace of deception. Was this really Lady Strange?

"Yes, Mary," she said, speaking with a reassuring clarity that so exactly recalled our first meeting in the drafty hall at Grimsthorpe all those years ago that I could have no doubt.

"Fantastic as it sounds, your cousin released me from the shackles Vivienne had clamped around my wrists and ankles. Then, kneeling beside me, Edmund Seymour himself administered a very rare, very costly antidote. Where he got such an elixir, I know not, though I know its price to be as great as that of the raven, for it contains the powder of a sapphire."

I thought of the missing ring—

"I drank it down and so regained a small part of my former strength and a portion of my lost youth."

"And Vivienne?" I asked, my heart pounding, my head awhirl.

"When I asked him about Vivienne, he said, 'She will not trouble you again. She has joined the forest that encircles her property.'"

"Extraordinary," I cried. "Why, he must have trapped Vivienne in a tree!"

Lady Strange's violet eyes took on an otherworldly glow. "There has been some change in him, Mary. I do not know how to account for it, nor do I know what will be the outcome. And yet it is so. Were it not for your cousin I would not be sitting here with you now. . . ."

"Lady Strange," I began, then proceeded to tell her about my cousin's missing sapphire and the remarkable change in his behavior toward me.

"If he used his own sapphire to concoct the antidote, then the change in him has indeed been an amazing one," my guardian said. "For such a sacrifice will have cost him dearly."

Lady Strange did not stay for very long. She would not go into great detail, just told me that she needed to rest, then alluded to the hours after her release, hours she'd spent giving poor Olivia Ormonde a proper burial.

"But what am I to do about my cousin?" I asked her just before we parted.

"Have faith," my guardian said. "Have faith, my darling Mary, and you will find what you need."

"But where?" I pleaded.

"Look within yourself," she said gently.

CHAPTER THIRTY-TWO

The following morning I awoke to the knowledge that on this day my cousin would surely be arrested. Somehow I could not entirely believe in this possibility, nor could I disbelieve it. When I was with him, I allowed myself to float on cerulean waves in a far away sea. As the days passed, those peculiar waters had become increasingly real.

Edmund Seymour saved my guardian's life.

Trust yourself, Mary, a voice within myself said.

Such was my state of mind when, immediately after breakfast, Alice brought me the astonishing news that the queen had released me from my chores. Although the other ladies-in-waiting had to continue preparations for removal to Greenwich, I was completely at liberty.

"But why?" I asked. "Why this exception when there is so much to be done?"

"I cannot give you a definite answer," Alice replied coolly, running her fingertips through Perseus's sleek coat. "Still, I have my suspicions."

"And they are?" I asked, fighting the urge to apologize to Alice for my recent behavior.

"Do you really want to know, Mary?" Alice said, speaking with such chilly frankness that I knew how much I had hurt her.

"Yes, Alice," I said, and reached for her hand. "I know I have been distant these last few days."

"Distant!" Alice said. "That word does not do justice to your recent coldness to me. Why, you could have been in India or on the moon for all the minutes you have had for me."

"I'm sorry. Please forgive me." Then, sensing that Alice was on the verge of asking me for an explanation, I said, "I cannot tell you the reason now. I ask you only to trust me. In time you will understand."

"Very well," Alice said. Her spectacles slipped down her nose a little as she smiled.

She went on to tell me why she believed I had been excused from the work of the other ladies-in-waiting.

Apparently, she'd seen Edmund Seymour in close conversation with the queen. "I found them closeted together in her breakfast chamber earlier. Afterward, your cousin sought me out, then asked me to deliver this message."

I unfolded the note, trying to be polite as I shielded its contents from Alice's curious eye.

Darling, meet me at the stables as soon as you can. Important news. I cannot wait to be with you. Do not delay, for I have a possession which you wish to have restored to you. Longing for you, I remain

Yours, Edmund

I stared blankly into space, seeing nothing, registering nothing, until at last the words of one of my mother's letters, written to my father, came flooding back.

My Lord, whereas you desire to know how you might gratify my goodness, I can require nothing more than I have, which is your heart. . . .

For the first time, my mother's words began to make sense.

Perseus watched me with his depthless eyes. I did not need to look to see rose peering through my silver aura.

You must not meet him alone this morning, Perseus said.

I must, I said, *and I will.*

By the time I reached the stables, Edmund was ready and waiting. Having saddled both of our horses, he stood just outside the stable door, on the lookout for my arrival. "At last!" he called out. "I don't want to lose a minute of this day with you."

Taking hold of my hand, he raised it to his lips, then led me over to one of the queen's finest horses, Arcadia, a sleek white filly.

"What about the brown mare?" I asked, still dizzy from his touch. "Am I not to ride her today?"

"This is a special day, and it needs to be marked appropriately." His energy, his certainty dazzled me. "Today you have Her Majesty's permission to ride Arcadia. Besides, we will ride quite far, and only Arcadia can handle such a distance."

"But my clothes," I said, staring down at the cumbersome skirts. "Dressed as I am, I cannot possibly manage such a ride on such a horse."

"I thought of that, too."

To my amazement, from a corner of the stable he produced a man's riding uniform. Yet the colors and the fabric—a creamy, ivory velvet trimmed with a reddish gold exactly the shade of my hair—were absolutely feminine.

Without another word, my cousin stepped into the shadows, and I changed my costume without being seen.

"You are a vision," he said, once I had finished and called to him to return. "I could stand here all day and simply drink you in."

"But we must ride," I reminded him, disquieted by the blush I knew suffused my cheeks. "Besides, you have gone to so much trouble. We shouldn't waste the afternoon."

"You're right," he said, bending to kiss my cheeks, my forehead, and then my lips.

I allowed him to help me into the saddle, my heart lifting as I noticed the place on his hand where the sapphire ring had been. *He saved my guardian's life.*

Edmund gave his horse the command, I spurred Arcadia into motion, and we were off. He rode Saturn, easily Arcadia's match.

Liberated from my woman's clothes, I had no trouble keeping up with him. We rode swiftly over the wildflower-filled meadows surrounding Whitehall, then far out into the countryside, where autumn's red-and-orange touch was at full play in the oak trees and elms. As we journeyed farther from the palace, and farther away from the protective presence of Perseus, I felt myself drifting more completely into the surreal dream of this impossible union.

Edmund Seymour and myself.

In that most fantastic source of magic—the imagination—I became Lady Seymour, just as my mother had, some seventeen years before. I saw myself reforming the black magician into a devoted husband. Trapping and channeling his black magic as he hoped to trap and channel my white.

At last he slowed our horses to a trot. "The animals need a rest."

"And so do I," I confessed, feeling the horse's heaving flanks beneath me.

He pointed to a particularly shady spot beneath a great willow. "Shall we stop there? I see a stream."

"That would be lovely," I replied, picturing myself dangling my feet in the cool water, Edmund beside me, the wise old tree providing us with privacy and shelter.

We dismounted, and he gently led the animals to the water so they could drink. When he reached for my hand, I did not even think to resist. I simply yielded, then allowed him to lead me to the water's edge.

"What say you to giving up the grandeur of court for a while and resting here with me?" he asked.

His smile prompted my own, and I replied, "I would like that."

We sat down beside the water's edge. The willow tree's movement in the breeze became the exotic yet soothing sound of a faraway country. Relaxed and tired from the ride, the peaceful setting opened up the space for a new kind of ease between us. For the very first time we spoke of our childhoods. After detailing my lonesome years as the Duchess of Suffolk's ward, with Jack as my only companion, I told him a camouflaged version of my loving life with Lady Strange.

He told me stories about growing up as the Duke of Somerset's son after his father's execution, his own words verifying all that Perseus had told me on the grounds of the Gascoigne estate.

"When Queen Mary came to the throne, she showed my family no kindness or compassion," my cousin began, his voice somber and unforgiving. "Despite the fact that John Dudley had ordered the execution of my father under the falsest of charges, we remained the tainted children of her half brother's Protestant adviser. I well knew she resented my entire family deeply. We were the Protestant kin to Jane Seymour, and the unhappy queen could never forgive my father's sister for bringing Henry the Eighth a male child and heir. It was Jane's son who forever displaced Mary's tenuous place in her father's heart, and more important"—our eyes met—"in the succession.

"Following her coronation, Queen Mary humiliated us, stripping our family name of as many titles and accoutrements as she could. Our life became perversely hard," he continued, betraying no self-pity. "Eventually, my mother died of shame—"

"—And a broken heart?" I added.

"I don't know about that," Edmund said. "My mother was not an especially good-natured woman nor was she an affectionate one. Prestige and position were the most important things in the world to her. Without them she was lost. Still"—his features gentled—"you are very kind to think so highly of her."

Inclining my head, I remained silent on this point, urging Edmund to resume his own childhood history instead.

"My parents left behind nine children, of whom I was the oldest male. It became my duty to provide. Yet I'm not like you, Mary," he said, touching my cheek. "Milk and honey do not flow through my veins. Society's laws failed my family, and with that betrayal I turned my back on the law. I wanted power and influence. Perhaps, too, I wanted to avenge my father's death."

"So you fell into the black arts—" The words just tumbled out of me.

An uncanny smile, like a stream of light in a cave, crept across Edmund Seymour's lips. With one hand he reached up and stroked my face. With the other he reached into his pocket and drew out the opal necklace. For just a moment it hung there between us, neither one of us saying a word.

"I believe this is yours," he said at last.

Solemnly, I bowed my head and allowed him to clasp the necklace around my throat, his touch and the stone both scintillating against my skin.

Impulsively I grasped the hand that had always displayed a sapphire and pointed to the place where the ring had been. "You sacrificed your own power to save my guardian."

"See how you have affected me." He laughed softly, hauntingly—a laugh that almost gave me pain, though I knew not why—and the willow tree shivered. "We have violated the order of things in coming together like this," he said. "We fight on opposite sides."

I looked down at my hands. How I wished, just then, that I could restore to him his sapphire. Black magician or not, at that moment, with the October wind rustling the leaves, I did not want his strength weakened.

We sat beside the water for a long time, and I allowed my head to rest against his shoulder. I knew my thinking had become distorted. I even thought of Olivia Ormonde—that horrible open grave—and yet I felt powerless to resist.

I did not want to resist. . . .

But what about the others who were counting on me? Perseus's betrayed look continued to plague me. If Cordelia learned of this encounter, would she not feel absolutely abandoned? Underlying everything, I knew my guardian had invested her best energy in my training. And then there were those faithful words of her father . . .

How well I understood that Edmund Seymour could not be allowed to voyage to Russia. Were he to possess the Demonius Sapphire, wouldn't he overthrow my queen's authority, and so make a pathetic failure of my role as her white magician, guardian of her good reign? Besides, if Edmund Seymour possessed the most powerful gemstone in the world, he would possess me.

No.

I could not allow myself to drift any further on this current. The relationship was all wrong. Good cannot change evil, I told myself.

And yet, had Edmund Seymour not shown me some

sign of goodness? In caring for me, perhaps, had he not made a step in my direction? And was that not a victory, howsoever small, for white magic?

Or was my love for him a sign of evil within *me*? Was I, like my mother, drawn to the lurid energy of the Seymours?

Think of what your mother's love for your father cost her, I told myself.

And yet I was the fruit of that union—the child of light and darkness.

The wind picked up, lifting thousands of leaves from the branches of the surrounding trees. Trembling, I watched their hypnotic fall to earth.

"I'm afraid," I whispered, convinced I could taste the first frost in the air.

He held me close. "Of what, my darling?"

"Of my feelings—for you."

Our eyes met; we seemed to understand each other perfectly.

"I'm reminded of my parents," I said, aware of his beating heart—and my own.

Edmund Seymour stroked my hand, then pressed it to his lips.

"My father was no good," I said, the truths of my childhood bottled up inside me. "He was mercenary, selfish . . ."

He laughed, but it was a quiet laugh, like the lullaby of April rain.

Have faith, Mary.

I seemed to hear my guardian's voice in the wind.

"Has it never occurred to you that your father truly loved your mother?" Edmund said, holding me closer. "Perhaps it was not only ambition and the grasping after power that propelled Thomas Seymour into Katherine Parr's life."

I said nothing. This was a reading I had never allowed.

"Well?"

"Up until this moment, I believed my father cared only for the elevation such a marriage would bring."

"And now, Mary?" he said, his voice a caress. "Has your opinion begun to change? Now can you begin to see your parents' history in a different light?"

I closed my eyes, and the words of one of my father's letters reverberated through me.

From the body of him whose heart you have. My father had always signed his letters to my mother with this passionate declaration.

Edmund turned me toward him, and I looked into his face, struck by the glimmer of another face, a boy's face, within or behind his own, waiting to come out.

"What if your father loved your mother with the very best part of himself?" Edmund asked, his eyes wide and bright, his face open and clear. "What if your mother's love for your father was not intoxication but something ennobling and pure?"

My heart beat fast, and the blood rushed to my face, my hands, my feet. Every part of me seemed about to burst.

Very carefully he removed my false hair, then stroked the new growth. Had he known all along?

"What if the loss of such a love was the cause of Thomas Seymour's loss of reason?" Edmund said, looking at me with what could only be love. "What if her death loosed the negative elements in his character?"

I grasped his hand, pressed his fingertips to my lips. "Once," I told him, "my mother wrote, 'Truly love maketh men like angels. And of the most furious, unbridled, carnal men, love maketh meek lambs.'"

"Did she write these words to your father?"

"Yes—"

We held each other closer, and just even the trees, the wind, and the leaves seemed to share our uncanny new joy.

"Your mother's love curbed your father's ambition, his grasping, his intrigue," my cousin continued. "Without that love he was lost." His words and tone created an intimacy between us. "Was this not the reason why he hatched those rude and desperate plots?"

Edmund's words ultimately brought back a picture I had barred from my imagination. But this time, the image, no matter how forbidding and sad, did not terrify me. For the first time, I allowed myself to see my father kneeling on the chopping block on Tower Hill. For the first time, I heard him cry out to his few remaining friends to avenge his miserable death, as the headsman sharpened his axe. Then I watched the axe fall—

Have I been false to my father's memory all of these years? I asked myself.

I looked into my cousin's eyes, and for the first time ever I saw his aura. I can only believe that at this singular moment of truthfulness between us, he wanted, actually allowed, me to see it.

Without Lady Strange's revelation, without this conversation, I would never have been able to believe that Edmund Seymour's aura was silver like my own. Of course that silver was deeply marred, obscured by the impurities of iron, the result of many years of crime and self-indulgence. Was it possible that through the arts of alchemy I could remove the iron so that his silver once again shone brightly?

He leaned closer, and I knew that my own silvery glow was being clouded over by rose, romantic rose. No longer able, no longer wanting to resist, I willed the world to narrow to the space we two occupied.

Edmund kissed my lips and each of my eyes, then told me the queen had given her consent to our marriage. He slipped an emerald ring onto my finger. "You are worthy of any jewel," he said, buoying me up with his words. "I chose the emerald because it is the gem of prophecy and unclouded vision. With you, Mary, I see clearly for the first time."

I stared at the ring, realizing that with this remarkable gift, each and every color in my opal gemstone had come together: rubies, pearls, amethysts, and emeralds—except one.

The sapphire. This gem continued to elude me. *Or is Edmund Seymour my sapphire?*

He took me in his arms and kissed me again and again, holding me so close I could no longer tell his heartbeat from my own. Even the boundary of skin seemed to disappear.

To this day, I still believe that as Edmund held me to him, the iron in his silver diminished slightly, overcome at last by that incriminating, transformative trace of rose.

CHAPTER THIRTY-THREE

In an open meadow on the way back to Whitehall, we spied a circle of men, Sir Christopher Hatton and Lord Dudley among them.

"What do you make of this, my soon-to-be-lawful wife?" Edmund asked in a voice that seemed more curious than suspicious.

"We must fly this place," I replied, then spurred his horse and my own into an immediate gallop.

Ten seconds, maybe twelve, was our only advantage. Yet even as we fled, I heard the torrential thunder of the horses behind us, as well as the cries of the men.

On we raced, digging our heels into our horses' flanks as we urged them to run faster, harder.

I was about to lose everything, and still I felt as if I were soaring. My daring horse jumped a creek, then bolted up a hillside as Edmund and Saturn led the way. Fleeing, my memory returned to those final moments—just a short while ago—when I lay beside my cousin, his arms enfolding me, both of us listening to the almost human sound of the wind in the trees, the rush of the stream, and our own voices.

Despite our skill as riders and our horses' speed and agility, we had little chance of eluding the queen's guards. Only the most potent form of magic could have saved us, and such magic needs preparation and time, neither of which we had.

The riders caught up with us within a space of minutes.

Sir Christopher Hatton ordered the guards to encircle us. He himself seized Saturn's reins and ordered Edmund to dismount. Meanwhile, the men startled at my costume.

"Is it a boy or a woman?" one of the guards muttered, and I realized I had forgotten to replace my wig.

Uncaring, I sat tall in the saddle and raised my chin high.

"We found your gown in Her Majesty's stables," Lord Dudley told me. "We—"

"What is the meaning of this outrage?" my cousin interrupted, as his aura, clearly visible, blazed black iron and silver.

Lord Dudley replied, "We have a warrant from the queen for your arrest."

My cousin laughed. "Absurd!"

"No." Dudley spoke coldly and calmly. "The warrant is real."

In that moment I hated him and the alliance we had made.

"Sir Edmund Seymour," he continued, his voice menacing yet formal, "Her Majesty, the Queen of England, charges you with stealing monies from her treasuries. She charges you with bribing the so-called Russian emissary whom you brought to court. We have it on oath that you promised him a share of the Russia expedition's profits if he supported your appointment. Worse yet, you have unsanctioned designs of your own in Russia. This same emissary, apprehended at Dover, confessed that you are after some rare jewel. You well know that private ventures have no place in Her Majesty's expedition. Finally, the Queen of England charges you with the heinous crime of attempted murder. You poisoned Sir Walter Effingham in order to secure the expedition's commanding appointment for yourself."

Sir Christopher Hatton said, "We have orders to escort you to the Tower of London, immediately, to stand trial."

Lord Dudley's eyes met my own, and he did not have to say a word. Our entire history, our alliance, all of this was visible in the gaze that passed between us.

And my cousin saw it all.

In an instant, Edmund Seymour's aura vanished; he looked at me through the eyes of a cornered wolf, who is most feral when most vulnerable. In a low but clear voice he said, "I loved you, Mary. In spite of my own nature, I loved you."

"And I loved you, too." At that moment I did not care who heard my declaration. In a strong voice, I said, "Edmund, I love you now."

Sir Christopher Hatton ordered three of his strongest and most heavily armed men to dismount. Unable to avert my gaze, unable to move, I watched these two men press Edmund Seymour between them, feeling almost as if I were watching my father's arrest some fifteen years earlier.

The guards bound Edmund's hands together with treacherous steel cuffs. Throughout the ordeal my cousin stood motionless, his eyes unseeing, or at least far away.

Then the guards forced him to climb back into the saddle.

Throughout, Edmund avoided my gaze.

Seconds, minutes, perhaps half an hour later, Hatton gave another command, and the small group rode off with their prisoner, raising a gale of dust as the horses burst into motion once more.

As for me, once my tears began there was no stopping them. Whether they were the pearls of heaven or not, I cannot say. I know only that they seemed to have no end. I cried for myself and for Edmund. But bound up in my tears was a river shed for my mother and for my father, Thomas Seymour. The tears streamed down my cheeks and into my mouth, and I sat there on the queen's prize filly, Arcadia, wondering at the perverse irony of the name.

How far from a civilized paradise was I at that moment, watching my cousin's figure growing smaller and smaller, knowing this was the last time I would see him.

This black magician.

This man that I loved.

EPILOGUE

As I walk through the queen's garden, my mind wanders back to that fateful day just two months ago, when Edmund and I sat beside that clear stream and told each other our histories.

As I confided at the start of my story, when I was just a small child, barely old enough to understand my mother's fate, I vowed never ever to fall in love.

Perhaps, as the spirit of Perseus suggested, I was fated to love my cousin, as my mother was meant to love my father, for light cannot exist without darkness—why the Demonius Sapphire can never belong to a white magician. Good and evil are strange but necessary companions in this life, although the advantage must always be on the side of the good. Or else chaos reigns.

As every act of magic has its price, so does every instance of love.

Still, despite the way rose crept into my aura at Whitehall, I have not renounced my vows regarding love and marriage. Yet I cannot deny that these vows have softened because of my relationship with my cousin.

Even Alice Cavendish, who holds steadfast to her commitment to learning, has altered her views. Just before Christmas she told me of her plans to marry Charles Cobham, a new scholar in Elizabeth's court, one renowned in the fields of both literature and oceanic science. When she told me of the engagement, which our queen has sanctioned, Alice proudly confided, "Dear Charles does not love me for beauty or for wealth. He loves me for my mind." Most fittingly, Alice's fiancé, who is even more nearsighted than she is, possesses a special interest in coral, the most resilient of rocks.

In her marriage, Alice will most certainly prove the scholar Vives wrong. He may have said romantic love clouds a woman's ability to think, but it is my belief Alice will be the one to show love can actually solidify a woman's powers of reason.

"*Video, et taceo,*" Perseus has become fond of saying: *I see all and say nothing.*

Had anyone else said such words, I would have thought they were boasting. But in Perseus's case, I believe these grand words to be true. Every day Perseus proves himself infinitely wise, not to mention gracious. Why, on the very day of Edmund Seymour's arrest, once I returned home alone, Perseus said absolutely nothing even though he already knew all that had happened. Since then, he and I never quarreled. Instead we have become as two within one.

Now, wherever I go, Perseus always accompanies me, so that if he decides to sleep late or feels a bit under the weather and I go out without him, everyone I meet asks, "Where's Perseus? Not unwell, I hope."

"Not at all," I reply. "Perseus is sure to live forever."

Perseus, who remained absolutely steadfast when the rose in my silver lured me toward my cousin.

And it was that attraction that revealed to me so much about my own parents' history.

My lord, my mother wrote to my father all those many years ago, *I can require nothing more than I have, your heart: and your good will during this life. . . .*

Without any doubt, I, the child of their union, know this now.

"You are a grown woman, Mary," Lady Strange told me just before she voyaged once more to the Canary Islands to recover her health. "Of even greater significance, you have proven yourself an accomplished white magician in your own right."

Such praise from the woman who rescued me from Grimsthorpe, loving and caring for me like her own daughter throughout so many years, went straight to my heart, reminding me once again of the importance of my vocation.

Insofar as I know, the Demonius Sapphire is still out there. Somewhere. My greatest hope is that no magician, white or black, will ever find it. In this life it is enough to find the precious stones of Eden's fractured gates on a few important—and in most cases, responsible—fingers.

As my cousin promised Lady Strange on the day he freed her from that dank prison on the Gascoigne estate, Vivienne has not reappeared to trouble any of us again. Still, it unnerves me just a little to think of her scheming away, even if her malice is confined to the space of a tree.

Of course, I could not neglect to tell you what happened to my dear cousin.

On the night of his arrest he was taken directly to the Tower of London under a heavily armed guard. Although he was supposed to stand trial for several accounts of treason, the trial never took place. Instead, on the morning after his arrest, the guards came to check on him, but found his prison cell empty.

Truly Edmund Seymour was the most powerful black magician in England.

Now, during the hours before dawn, at the times appropriate to my cycle, I secure myself in my room at Greenwich Palace and continue to meet with Cordelia. Yet she never speaks of Edmund Seymour, and instinctively I know not to ask her where he has gone. And I confess it gives me a sort of pleasure to think that somewhere in the vast world, my cousin is still out there.

Be careful what you wish for.

Startled, I turn to Perseus, only to find my noble friend sleeping in a pool of moonlight.

As I gaze up at the stars, a sudden curl of smoke silvers the night, and the burnt-leaf smell of tobacco fills the air.

AUTHOR'S NOTE

Have you ever wanted to rewrite someone's life story? That's exactly how I felt when I read about Katherine Parr's death from puerperal fever six short days after she gave birth to her only child, Mary Seymour. How cruel that this woman who had cared for other men's children all of her life, and so wanted a child of her own, should lose that child so tragically. I couldn't accept the end of this story because a part of me identified with Katherine Parr. She was a person I would have liked to call my friend. She was smart and good and managed to stay alive during a very dangerous time. How could I not admire that?

But my desire to rewrite history wasn't just about Katherine Parr. I felt especially sorry for her infant daughter, Mary Seymour, who never even had the chance to grow up. According to Susan E. James, Katherine Parr's biographer, the former queen's "'so pretty daughter' almost certainly died sometime around her second birthday," for little Mary Seymour disappeared entirely from history at that time.

For months I continued to think about Katherine Parr and her daughter and raged at the unfairness of life. Until I realized a fiction writer's biggest advantage is her ability to re-imagine history, and I did exactly that. Instead of

Mary Seymour disappearing from history, the novel allows her to grow into a young woman of whom her mother would have been exceptionally proud. And yet, in envisioning Mary Seymour's life, I did not want to limit her choices. Typically, a sixteenth century girl grew up and got married. Not that I have anything against marriage, but I wanted something more for Katherine Parr's spunky, auburn-haired daughter. I wanted to give her opportunities and powers that her well-educated mother—who had been a wife four times over—did not have.

In casting about for possibilities, I quickly settled on magic as the most enticing because magicians don't have to play by the same rules as everybody else. Because Mary is on the side of the good, her powers enable her to use enchantment to uphold the laws her calling requires her to honor. Of course, it isn't always as serious as all that, which is one of the reasons why Mary's chief helpmate is a borzoi dog named Perseus.

Mary's spells have a whimsical, earthy quality to them, for they almost always involve objects from the natural world: bird's nests, cat's whiskers, molasses. I love the outdoors, just as Mary does, and I've always found the most magic in my environment. Listening to geese migrating high above my head, I'm awed by the distances they travel, by the very fact that they instinctively know where they're going. The first crocuses that return each year, often before the snow has melted, are equally amazing to me. I grounded Mary's white magic in the extraordinary aspect of the ordinary in the hopes of encouraging readers to see that magic is all around us if we know how to look for it.

ACKNOWLEDGMENTS

Despite what they say, writing is not a solitary enterprise. *The Red Queen's Daughter* could not have been written without the support of many people who, as that Renaissance poet Ben Jonson almost said, "Took my book in hand, read it well, and helped us both to better understand the story and its characters."

Abiding thanks to my stellar editor, Alessandra Balzer, who shepherded Mary Seymour and her story through the final stages and so brought this novel into being. Thanks, too, to Margaret Cardillo and to all of the faithful readers at Hyperion; to the head of school and library marketing, Angus Killick, for his humor and devotion to ferrying this book to its audience; and to art director, Anne Diebel, whose gorgeous cover brought Mary Seymour visually to life.

To my agent, Sara Crowe, I am forever indebted for believing in this novel and enabling Mary to find her way to Hyperion.

Friends and family proved as valuable as the many cups of hot tea that sustained me throughout the days and nights of writing and rewriting. I am particularly grateful to Claire Carpenter, Eileen Bonds, Margaret and Lorenz Lutherer, Kirsten Sundberg Lunstrum, and Julie Nelson

Couch. My sister, Christine Kolosov Pitt, enabled me to find the goodness within Edmund Seymour and never doubted this story for a minute. My father, George Kolosov, proved to be the book's first copyeditor and so demonstrated that he could have had a second career in publishing. My mother, Helene Kolosov, has always believed in me and continues to be a faithful reader. And although she is no longer here, I am grateful to my grandmother, Helen Kolosovas, who kindled in me the desire to find and tell stories. My husband, William Wenthe, read the book aloud to us both one particularly wintry December and always proved ready and willing to plunge into the Elizabethan era, no matter the weather or the hour. And how could I forget my own loyal dog, not Edmund but Edward, a Welsh corgi who has always been the Kent to my King Lear, as well as the Falstaff.